IN CASE OF WAR BREAK GLASS

Bob Davy

Freestyle Aviation Books

1st Edition published in the UK in 2008-07-09 by Freestyle Aviation Books.

13 digit ISBN 978-0-9544814-1-4

Printed and bound in UK and USA by Lightningsource Inc.

Freestyle Aviation Books

18 Woodhurst Road, Maidenhead, SL6 8TF, England

Email: ACCassidy@aol.com

Web: www.freestyleaviation.co.uk

Foreword

Did you ever want to know what it was like to fly a Hurricane or a Spitfire? *Properly* know, two thirds of a century ago during World War II - to fight with one strapped to your back, head-to-head with another fighter or bomber, the crew trying to kill you before you killed him or them? What would be going through your mind?

Could you pull the trigger - the moment of truth - could you kill someone? Often the pilots you would be trying to kill would be the same age as you, with the same interests and aspirations as you would have had as a pilot.

Inevitably, in battle they'd be as scared as you were.

Ironically, some of the survivors from opposing sides met up after the war and became lifetime friends.

If you survived your first flight against the enemy, could you fly again: have another go, and another? Could you ever get used to it? What would you do when you landed, knowing that you had to do it again the next day, maybe four times the next day?

What would you do in your time off? I know what I would do.

There's no doubt in my mind that the few hundred allied pilots who fought before, during and after the Battle of Britain turned the tide of the war. They stopped Germany invading us, made America realise that we had a vague chance of winning if they helped us, and just as importantly changed people's attitudes towards what had been seen as Germany's unconquerable force.

The Few showed the world that we could all fight back - in the modern vernacular, they changed our hearts and minds. Our modern world, the largely free world, in its present shape, owes much of its form and existence to The Few.

This story starts in the spring of 1940, with new pilots joining a Hurricane squadron in the weeks before the Battle of Britain. And one particular pilot, at home in one place and time, sitting on the line between courage and cowardice - a line that every man I've ever met, and the majority of the women, wonder which side they sit.

The Squadron I describe consisted of part-time, Royal Auxiliary Air Force pilots: many were wealthy men who learned to fly during the peace and then became full-time pilots in full-time squadrons when war broke out. The *Six hundred...* squadrons.

The primary characters in this story are fictional. That's what my lawyer told me to say. The battle sequences are either factual, or based on combat reports, actual accounts and personal diaries. The correspondence to the main character from his brother is original. The language is a bit strong on occasion, which is what it was like. There's a small dictionary at the back to help you with the acronyms, abbreviations etc when I would have stretched a sentence by explaining them in context – I've added quite a few that didn't appear in the book, because I found them entertaining.

Sometimes the aerial fights, survival stories and the pilot's personal lives might seem exaggerated. They're not - they didn't need to be.

Acknowledgements and thanks.

For their support, enthusiasm & individual help with research;

William & Jack Davy.

The Lord Ed Manners.

Captain Nigel Rhind.

Nick Seaton.

Alex Smith.

Keith Wilson.

Lawrence Hawthorn

Adrian, Alex, Bruce, Dave, Gary, Greg, Jock, John, Mark, Nige, Simon, and Steve.

Anthony Hodgson: for letting me fly your Spitfire.

Captain Jim Musty: for letting me drive your 1932 Alvis Firefly.

John Tinsley: for original research, and for letting me ride 'Mary,' your Matchless motorbike, and your 1942 Norton.

The ATA ladies I met in June 2008 at White Waltham who sorted me out with intricate details of WWII, and ATA practises.

The late Paul Portelli & the crew of LK-Q: for inspiration.

Rhody Sims: for the cover design and photography.

Len Boxwell: for teaching me to fly.

For The Few, J.B Healey and Robin Olds.

1

Flight Lieutenant Harper looked up through the small windshield, his face framed, blank, expressionless, his eyes wide open, unblinking, his jaw slightly open. It was a black night, but the chromed windshield frame caught the reflection of a golden light, which illuminated the dark features of Harper's young face.

Harper tried to get his bearings. He had been unconscious for less than 30 seconds - now he didn't know who he was, where he was, or what the hell he was doing. There was no noise, just the golden light.

Everything, still blank: time ticking away. Harper's panic started to rise. Then, pain - his right hand instinctively came up to meet the blood trickling down the right side of his forehead. Next, the smell of petrol and charring leather. More pain: broken ribs? And that golden light: growing, roaring.

FIRE? Harper's *fight or flight* survival mechanism burst into life. Instinctively he pulled himself away from restraint, kicked open the door to the right of his thigh, dived out of the cockpit and onto the grass. He stumbled forward, straightening up as he accelerated. Behind him the flames were spreading, ironically better illuminating the field of fire - the wreckage where he had crashed. Yes, that was it, he had crashed. Harper slowed slightly, turned and ran backwards as he surveyed the impact site, his open flying jacket flapping out of rhythm as his steps shortened. The scene was inexplicably, strangely thrilling - Harper noticed that he had to suppress a laugh. More realisation; he had crashed his sports car – an MG, not his Hurricane - and there had been a passenger.

"OH SHIT!!!" shouted Harper as he ran back towards the flames. He sprinted around the burning wreck, as close as he could get without getting burned, shielding his face from the heat with one hand. The remains of the car were becoming completely engulfed. Surely she couldn't have been inside? The horror of a burning corpse flashed through his mind, the new surge in adrenaline bringing more focus. But his sports car was a tiny MG with no roof - surely there was no way she was in it? He ran along the wreckage trail and up towards where the car had come through the hedge, the bend that he had crashed out of just behind it. There, at the base of the hedge Harper spotted a pair of upturned legs, a ripped skirt barely covering them. Stooping down, Harper grabbed the girl by the ankles and carefully pulled her clear - she was moaning slightly but she looked unharmed. As he pulled, her dress rode up further, revealing the tops of her stockings - Harper tried not to look. Then he kneeled beside her and gently tapped her face on each side.

"Linda!"

Linda was coming round but carried on moaning. Harper reached inside his Irvine flying jacket pocket with his right hand and felt for his hip flask - it was still there, minus the stopper. He pulled it out, some of the contents pouring over his right leg. He cursed again quietly as he allowed some of the whisky to run through his fingers, then put them gently on her lips. Suddenly Linda coughed and opened her eyes.

"Uh? What?" she said, coughing again.

"We crashed - you ok?" Linda was conscious.

"You… stupid… idiot!" she hissed. More annoyed than injured, she sat up too quickly, then held her head with both hands and sighed for a moment. A moment of composure and, finding her handbag still hanging from her right arm, she swung blindly, instinctively, at the left side of Harper's head. The soft beige leather made a satisfying slap as it met, flat-to-flat with Harper's left temple, spraying a few drops of blood on the other side like that of a defeated boxer. Linda looked over to the blazing wreck and slowly moved her head from side to side.

"You've only had it... three months?" she whispered as she properly came to, watching the flames. It was true. Not many RAF pilots even had a car, let alone a sports model. But like a few other pilots in the Royal Auxiliary Air Force, Flt Lt Tom Harper had been lucky with his parents. He had named the bend that he had just crashed through: Harper's Arse End. He'd been round it more times than he remembered, each time - depending on conditions - adding a little to the entry speed. This time he had entered the bend at 50mph, which was approximately 5mph too fast for the car and 10mph too fast for Harper in his condition at the time. He had been awake since dawn that day waiting eagerly and without rest for his first squadron scramble. All day. When darkness fell he had called in at The Ship for a couple of whiskies with Linda, and had just been trying to get her back to the nurses' home before the curfew.

"Jesus" said Harper, as he first heard the sound of the bells of an approaching police car.

2

At 7am the following morning Harper was back at the dispersal area in full flying kit, washed, shaved and ready with his Hurricane, just like the day before, and the day before that. He was sitting outside in the cold, in a deck chair, with a large mug of industrial-strength tea - there were three sugars in it. Last night the police had given the couple a lift home, after they helped him beat out the remains of the fire. And after he had satisfactorily explained the strong smell of whisky – he told them how he had poured it down his trousers rather than the traditional form of consumption. The police had very kindly dropped Linda off at the nurses' home and Harper off at the gate house, which was less than a hundred yards from the officer's mess, the still-open bar, and eight squadron pilots who bought him quite a lot more drinks whilst he told them what happened at Harper's Arse End.

Harper kept his eyes closed and tried to sleep. But he couldn't. A succession of his friends - the few who hadn't been out last night - asked a series of questions; why did he have a bandage on the side of his head (surely there hadn't been any action yesterday, only training flights,) where was his car (they hadn't seen it in the car park this morning,) and was it true that Linda had dumped him (yes it was.)

"Very sorry to hear about your prang" said Gazzer, a mildly irritating but very amusing *new boy* like Harper. "Do you know what's the difference between a car accident involving a hedgehog, and a car accident involving a Frenchman?"

"No."

"There'd be skid marks in front of the hedgehog!" Harper groaned and kept his eyes closed. He wondered what all the fuss was about. He had already crashed a couple of cars. And he had crashed his first vehicle, a lawn mower, when he was 10 years old on the family estate – Harper had been trying to see how steep a bank the lawn mower could traverse, when it suddenly toppled over and rolled down a hill. He had been thrown clear. The lawn mower was repaired and Harper suffered the cost deducted incrementally from his allowance for the next year.

His mishaps weren't as a result of a 'lack of mechanical sympathy' on the part of Tom Harper - he was actually very good with machines, particularly flying machines. He had scored 'above-average' in his RAF technical training, he had scored 'excellent', top of his class, during the flight training. And he was a superb shot, having been hunting since he was 10 years old, ironically because his grandfather gave him an old 12-bore shotgun to cheer him up after losing his pocket money. It wasn't just any old gun, but a 1908 Purdey. Pheasants, pigeons and, occasionally, teal or grouse had appeared on the table ever since, until Harper left the family estate, commissioned as a full-time RAF officer at the outbreak of war. Harper was 28 years old, getting on a bit for a fighter pilot. His younger brother was learning to fly too, aged 18. It was now late spring, 1940 and he had just been posted to his first operational squadron at a fighter base in Essex.

After the gossip got round the dispersal hut, Harper's chums finally left him alone. He slept for an hour, walked once round the perimeter track for a bit of exercise, and then slept in the hut next to the fire for another 2 hours. 2 hours was enough time for Harper to start dreaming, his brain having been deprived of REM sleep the night before and so looking for any opportunity to rest. The only way for the brain to rest is to dream.

The sound of the scramble bell incorporated itself into Harper's latent imagination. It became the sound of a fire bell, the sound of the fire engine chasing him as he ran, burning, through a field, after crashing his Spitfire. Except that he didn't fly a Spitfire. And he hadn't crashed a plane - only a few cars. And a lawn mower.

"SCRAMBLE!" Harper was up and out of the deck chair, that same stooping-then-straightening acceleration, the result of a rugby-based education at a public school for Eton rejects. He completed the 200 yards to his Hurricane in 30 seconds in full kit, just behind Jones, his rigger, despite Jones' 10 second start. Harper was a bloody good runner, even with a hangover. He landed his right foot into the extended stirrup step at the wing root, jumped up on the left wing and then supported his weight on the canopy frame with his arms as he swung himself into the cockpit, hurriedly but precisely clicking into his parachute. Jones helped him with the Sutton harness straps, which would keep him in the aeroplane. Radio lead connected, oxygen on, engine primed, switches on, thumbs up, a thumb up from the fitter, and he hit the starter button on the left of the control panel, plus the booster button next to it. The 1030 horsepower Merlin engine turned three blades of its propeller and then roared into life in a cloud of grey smoke. Jones ran round and pulled out the trolley battery connection without permission. It didn't matter. The aircraft generator was already on line and Harper was now running through the after-start checks as the fitter pulled out the wheel chocks. Harper's rising adrenaline level had already negated his hangover - he wouldn't feel it again until long after he landed.

There have always been people who could cope under pressure, and people who couldn't. That first engagement, the *moment of truth*, squeezing the trigger with the enemy in the gun sight for the first time - the most negative ways to deal with it seemed to Harper to be the most powerful; fear of cowardice, fear of letting his side down, letting his friends down. Then, there would be the second engagement, if he survived the first one. Some said that it would be worse, because he'd know what was coming.

Harper had been in quite a few scrapes in a short life, but never before in such a clear cut, all-out dangerous event such as this one. He realised that it required a very different form of courage to deal with something that occurred in life unexpectedly versus the drawn-out, pre-meditated act to put oneself in a field of fire which he was now embarking upon. Flt Lt Harper wondered if he would cope. Or *how* he would cope. His knees were literally knocking as he waited for his turn to take off.

The previous Hurricane was airborne as Harper turned onto the preferred length of field for take off and then smoothly opened the throttle with his left hand. If he did it too quickly he wouldn't be able to counteract the torque from the propeller before the rudder gained effectiveness - this was his main lateral control on the ground once the tail lifted. So he moved the throttle slowly, counting 'one thousand, two thousand, three thousand' before he had it all the way forward. The aircraft was at maximum weight, full of fuel, its eight.303 machine guns fully loaded, but the acceleration was still impressive after the Harvard, Harper's first military trainer after a few hours in a little Tiger Moth biplane. The Harvard had a similar weight to the Hurricane but approximately half the horsepower. Harper pushed the joystick slightly forward with his right hand, his right foot pushing on the rudder pedal to keep the aircraft straight, the movements lessening as the rudder became progressively more effective in the slipstream. Without any control inputs the Hurricane would have exited the runway to the left, a moment or two before becoming the world's most expensive 'rotorvator' in the field beyond. At 30mph or so the tail wheel left the ground, the aircraft now *wheeling* on its main gear. Harper checked the joystick to the neutral position and held the attitude until the whole aircraft left the ground at 75mph. He selected the landing gear hydraulic lever to *up* to raise the main wheels. The tail wheel stayed fixed down.

Harper looked for the rest of Red section - there were four aircraft ahead and to the right, another three still taking off behind him. One Hurricane had stayed on the ground, Pollock, its pilot, having collapsed with stomach pains - or nerves. Harper pulled the power back slightly and rolled into a right-hand climbing turn, being careful to visually check the area he was about to fly into beforehand. There was a lot of traffic around down here, hopefully all of it friendly – another squadron had also been scrambled from Rochester airfield just a few miles away and visual contact had not yet been made between the two.

Harper was a very instinctive pilot - the Chief Flying Instructor had written 'at home in the air' in his training file. He was now climbing at 2000 feet per minute and 150mph in a high performance aircraft and yet he had still had time – capacity - to assess how he was feeling before the potential of first contact with the enemy.

"I... am ... so... fucking... scared," said Harper to himself. And yet, he was performing as if calm. Harper had come to terms with an early death on many occasions, during the infinitesimal period between incident and accident, when adrenaline seemed to slow time itself; maybe allowing a way out, maybe allowing a quick contemplation at the end of one's life. This event didn't feel so massively different, just considerably more drawn out. Not like running off a bend and waiting for the impact - this time the incident was getting airborne. The accident might be what happened next.

The altimeter needle in Harper's Hurricane wound up through 5,000ft. The squadron had formed up in two groups of three and one of two, the missing aircraft in the last group conspicuous by its absence. Harper was second in the second group, with Gazzer Tyler in front and 23 year old, Flying Officer Ginger How on his right. Harper was busy scanning ahead and around for possible enemy contacts, interspersed with checking the aircraft systems, fuel quantity, glycol coolant temperature, oil temperature and pressure. Pilots called it a check of *Ts and Ps.* Then Harper first spotted the curving vapour contrails of a previous engagement above and ahead in the dark blue sky. So, the Luftwaffe actually did exist - it wasn't a dream after all.

Harper went into automatic - what pilots refer to when going through a much-rehearsed drill or procedure. He switched his reflector gun sight on and armed the guns by turning the ring around the gun button on his joystick from 'safe' to 'fire'. Then, keeping his right hand on the stick and checking that the sky was clear ahead, he pushed the button with his thumb. The eight, red protective patches on the leading edges of the wings vaporised, replaced by eight yellow jets of flame. A satisfying shudder returned through the airframe, the aircraft's nose pitching down slightly in recoil. Half a second was enough for the check - conservation was king with ammunition. If he held his thumb down the magazines would be empty after 15 Seconds.

Harper was still acting calmly - except that his knees were knocking again. As his left hand came off the throttle to adjust a strap he noticed that it was shaking too. He told himself that this was due to the cold. After all, the outside air temperature was now -10 degrees centigrade and falling, by roughly 2 degrees for every 1000ft he climbed. The temperature in the cockpit was much higher, due to the coolant pipe running along the floor to the radiator. It kept the cockpit relatively warm. Too warm in the summer. Harper had been momentarily distracted - suddenly he noticed his flight leader calling on the radio.

"Tally Ho Reds! Three Me 110s at 10 o'clock low!" Harper instinctively looked left and down. He couldn't see the enemy but, if his battle-hardened leader could, then it was good enough. He watched Red leader roll into a left turn with his two wingmen, then his own leader and followed, careful of the other wingman as he rolled and pulled on the stick to pass well clear. The two groups of three fighters stretched out into two lines, each aircraft roughly 100 yards behind the next. The other two Hurricanes stayed well back but on the same intercepting course.

There! Three spots just below the horizon, flying straight and level and left to right in front of him. 2000 yards and closing - Red leader banked slightly right – he was going for the front aircraft. Gazzer instinctively went for the rear. They didn't appear to have seen the attacking Hurricanes yet. The section closed in until the fighters' markings were clearly visible. The black and white crosses on their wings and fuselages made them the most terrifying objects that Harper had ever seen. The white in the crosses seemed to glow in the daylight. And yet Harper was feeling remorse – this was too cold-blooded. Surely the enemy had to fire first?

"BOLLOCKS!" Harper shouted to himself. His country was at war. And this was defence. He rolled right, progressively released the back-pressure on the stick to unwind the G-force, closed in to 400 yards behind the Messerschmitt 110 and hit the firing button. The visible tracer shells danced away in an almost-straight line - he was aiming high and right. And he was too far away. He continued to close in, aimed lower and left and hit the button again at 250 yards. DIRECT HIT!! Puffs of smoke appeared on the fighter's left wing and engine, large pieces of debris whizzing back past Harper's cockpit. The twin-engine fighter rolled and pulled hard to the right. Harper followed, a quick glance over his shoulders to check that his wingmen were still there – so easy to get sucked in fighting an aircraft in front of you only to be shot down by someone behind.

Suddenly there was a muffled 'WHUMP!' from somewhere in front. Harper's aircraft shuddered slightly. Christ, he'd been hit! The stench of steaming glycol hit his nose and he instinctively looked at the temperature gauge. Nothing moving... but then… yes, it was climbing. The engine was going to quit.

Another "BOLLOCKS!!" from Harper. A moment of indecision - events getting away from him - and then his concentration came back. He pressed on with the attack, aiming well out in front of the banking fighter, and hit the firing button again. The tracer hosed out in front of Harper's Hurricane in a long curve, falling well behind the fighter, even though he felt that he had aimed so far forward. Harper pulled the stick back harder now, up to 5G, the oxygen mask sagging down on his face.

"COME...ON!!" he shouted, trying to pull a little bit more G, get the lead a little bit more, and get his nose more ahead of the Messerschmitt before the next burst. The turn and bank tightened. Another burst - the bullets curved down behind the tail again. Another 100 feet forward and he'd have him. This was a classic dogfight, just like he'd done in training. But now the fighter was pulling away. Harper's engine really was quitting.

"SHIT!" said Harper. Ever so reluctantly, he radioed Red leader, rolled the Hurricane onto its back and pulled on the stick. As the aircraft reached a vertical dive he checked the stick forward to neutral and let the speed climb to Vne, maximum speed, before pulling the throttle back half way and pulling on the stick again. On a 45 degree down line the speed stabilised on the wrong side of Vne - Velocity never exceed - in the thin, high altitude air as he left the field of fire as rapidly as he dare.

3

Jones, Harper's fitter heard an aircraft calling on the tannoy, the loud speaker mounted outside of the dispersal hut. Red 5? That was his aeroplane! He crossed himself with one finger and raised his eyes simultaneously. Jones had a pride of his aeroplane, and a healthy disregard for the new pilot. He left the doorway of the Anderson shelter – the air raid siren had gone off - and jogged purposefully towards where he thought Harper would be parking. Jones stopped where the generator trolley was placed, kneeled beside it, and sheepishly rolled a cigarette – it was forbidden in the shelter, but anywhere else *airside* as well. In the distance he began to hear the sound of a Merlin engine. He looked up over the top of the trolley and spotted a distant Hurricane making a steeper than normal approach. And trailing smoke.

"He's bloody broken it," said Jones to himself.

"PUT THAT CIGARETTE OUT JONES!" shouted a military policeman from the mouth of the shelter. "I'LL PUT YOU ON A CHARGE!" Jones turned a shade of red as he dropped and stamped on the butt, his eyes never leaving the sight of what was now obviously his/Harper's Hurricane making a glide approach. On a normal approach a small amount of engine power would be used during the final stages. With the wheels and flaps down and throttle closed, a Hurricane would glide like a manhole cover. If the pilot suspected his engine might give up he would do a steep approach so that he could still get to the field if it stopped. That's what Harper was doing. He crossed the airfield perimeter at 150ft and 85mph, 100ft higher and 10mph faster than normal, pulled the stick back harder than normal to arrest the greater descent rate, and kicked the aircraft straight with the right rudder pedal as it started to depart left. The Hurricane straightened and touched down on the two main wheels simultaneously, the tail wheel still in the air. Harper checked the stick forward slightly to stop the aircraft flying again and then started to apply wheel brakes with the lever on the stick, simultaneously pulling the stick back to stop the aircraft nosing over onto its propeller. This was a very skilled landing for a new pilot and many people not in the shelter watched the aircraft's progress as it ran across the landing strip, chased by two fire engines and an ambulance.

With the outcome assured, Harper switched off the magnetos and battery in the cockpit, the engine immediately seizing solid as it stopped firing. He used the last of the speed to coast off the side off the runway, coming to a halt in a cloud of steam and oil.

The Hurricane was towed back to its stand by a fire engine, Harper still aboard to man the brakes. As it came to rest Jones ran up and started undoing the side cowls to the engine. Steam poured out of every gap and opening, laced with the heady smell of hot engine oil.

"Got shot up on my second burst at a '110" said Harper "Bloody hit him too - it would have been my first kill." Suddenly he grimaced, his ribs had brushed the side of the cockpit as he climbed out.

"You injured sir?" asked the fireman.

"No… slipped in the bath." His ribs were cracked, not broken but he would still have been grounded if the station doctor knew about it. Changing the subject, Harper called down to Jones as he climbed out of the cockpit and onto the wing.

"Where was I hit Jonesy?"

"You weren't hit."

"What?"

"Weren't hit! The coolant jacket on the left bank fractured." The Merlin was a V12 engine with two banks of six cylinders on each side. "The engine's fucked though." Harper didn't know what to do with himself - he experienced a dose of relief and frustration at the same time.

"Whose bloody fault is it?" he mumbled to himself as he climbed down from the wing, his ribs hurting again. Corporal Jones ignored the quiet question for a while, carrying on unbolting the coolant jacket. And then, as Harper departed the scene;

"I'd have a chat with Mr Rolls and Royce if I was you."

Harper couldn't be bothered with a slagging off of the fitter. He was just glad to be back on the ground without being shot at, killed, injured, pissing in or soiling his flying clothes in combat. Many pilots faired worse. Then something told Harper to put his hand to the front of his trousers – he realised that he had indeed pissed himself. He felt disgraceful.

"Mr Royce will be a bit difficult, seeing as he's dead," said Harper, covering up the damp patch with his Mae West and hurrying away before anyone noticed. "Anyway its beer o'clock. I'm going down the bloody pub" - via the mess to shower and change. Harper knew full well that he wasn't supposed to go, and that he was supposed to be debriefed by Intel (the intelligence officer) about his attack on the '110. But he went anyway.

4

Harper was at The Ship and on his third whisky when his friends walked in. The pub was between opening hours but pilots and other service personnel could always get a drink if the barman was on the premises. And whisky was in short supply but Harper had his own arrangement. In other words, he was paying a lot of money for it.

"You'll get pissed drinking that neat, old boy," said Ginger How. He was 6ft 3in, unusually tall for a fighter pilot. Harper was 5ft 10in.

"Well done Ginger."

"Not used to it eh? Too strong for me."

"I always drink whisky"

"Closest thing I'd get to it is *horse's neck*."

That's a waste of a good malt'. You'd be better off putting water in it than ginger and lemon."

"Have to tell you, you might have missed a patrol this afternoon. Except they cancelled it a couple of minutes after it was issued.

"Oh really? How did they do that?"

"They fired red flares. A few of the boys took off anyway, until they realised they were on their own. C/O will be having a word with you for buggering off." Harper tried not to give a damn, even though he did. "Anyway, I tried Harper's Arse End last night in my MG (a slightly later model than Harper's). 55mph, and only a bit sideways on the exit. I reckon you must have been drunk when you pranged, sorry if I sound contemptible."

"Oh really? Of course I wasn't you silly sod - sorry if I sound contemptuous."

"No one's called me that for a while old boy."

"I wasn't drunk – I had a couple of ales in the pub and was on my way home. And I have every right to be getting drunk now, considering I've just shot at my first hun."

"True. Well, I got awarded a kill today. Bit of luck - its left engine had stopped. I just picked it off. I actually started to feel a little bit sorry for them but then they all jumped out. Three crew on those you know."

"Half a kill."

"Say again?"

"Half a kill. If it was the left side it was the one I attacked before my engine quit. Where were *you* looking?"

"At you of course."

"Oh yes of course, sorry."

"Well you'll have to take it up with Intel - or the C/O when he gives you a bollocking."

"I don't give a damn about scores. I just want to get as many of the bastards as I can before they get me" said Harper. Subconsciously he was kicking himself for not reporting to Intel. What if that was the only action he'd ever be in? It might all be over tomorrow? Harper told himself to shut up and not be ridiculous.

"Excuse me?" Harper had a tap on the shoulder. He turned round to see a very pretty redhead, about 21 years old and 5 feet tall. She was in nurses' uniform, as was her ginger friend, now talking to Ginger.

"Sorry to bother you but we've just posted from London… And we don't know anyone here… and… I've always wanted to meet some of you fighter pilots. Sorry if that sounds forward but I just wanted to say thank you. We've been watching you up there. You can see the smoke trails when the clouds aren't there. My name's Lucy by the way."

"Well I wasn't a real one until I knocked a few bits off of something today" replied Harper. "But I suppose I'm real enough now. I'm Tom." He twisted round as he rose from the barstool and then sat down again, wheezing and sucking in breath. "...And its not smoke, its water vapour from the exhaust systems. It condenses at high altitude to form a sort of man-made cloud." Not even the drink could cancel the pain from his chest.

"Were you injured?" asked Lucy, genuinely concerned.

"I might have cracked a couple of ribs. I cracked up in my car last night."

"Show me?" asked the nurse. Harper guided her hand inside his uniform jacket and onto the side of his chest where he had bandaged them up with wide sticking plaster. The nurse gently ran her hands backwards and forwards over the area - Harper held fast, trying not to wince as the pain came and went. Then he caught a whiff of her perfume, the pain lost as he quickly developed an overwhelming urge to lunge forward and kiss her. The barman watched the scene unfold whilst slowly moving his head from side to side, wondering if 30yrs old was too old for signing up to be a fighter pilot. It was.

"I don't think you've broken any but you could easily have cracked them," said Lucy, her hand now right around the back of Harper's chest, her mouth only inches away from his. "There's also a layer of cartilage between each one and if it gets torn the pain is just like you get from broken ones." Intuitively Harper narrowed the gap between his lips and hers, paused for a moment, and went for the kill. A loud 'SLAP!' rang out as the nurse brought her hand across his face. Lucy stomped out, leaving the two pilots and the ginger nurse behind her. Harper and the barman looked at each other for a moment, started to laugh and then continued to drink their whisky, whilst Ginger argued a case for the other girl not to follow.

5

Harper was summoned to Tiger's office at first light.

"…And you can't come and go as you please! It's not a fucking flying club! Dismissed!" Harper marched out the office and past Gazzer, who was trying not to laugh. Harper decided that the best thing to do after a bollocking would be to make himself a nice cup of tea – just what his mother would say - but it wasn't to be.

"Red section! SCRAMBLE!" shouted Intel. Harper ran the 200 yards to his Hurricane only slightly slower than the day before. Jones was ready on the battery trolley as Harper jumped up with his right foot on the extendable stirrup, left foot on the wing, and swung himself into the cockpit. A snapshot glance at Jones for $1/10^{th}$ of a second as he climbed in and he clocked the fatigue on the fitter's face, induced by a sleepless night replacing the ruined Merlin. Harper's mind wandered for just that instant in time, thinking what a strange combination of a man was Jones: a great pair of hands and attitude to the job on someone with such a well-pronounced chip. In the next instant Harper was on to the job in hand – and the immense fear came flooding back.

The brand new engine burst into life after only two blades. It ran roughly for a few seconds and then settled down to a steady, rumbling crackle, the exhaust fumes stinging Harper's eyes and hitting the back of his throat. There was also another smell. Faint traces of inhibiting oil burning on the exhaust stubs - the engine had been stored in a crate since its manufacture, doused liberally with oil to stop the onset of rust and corrosion. Occasionally, little puffs of grey smoke came out of the gaps in the engine cowlings, slightly disconcerting for a pilot when the greatest fear in combat was burning to death. Eventually the smoke stopped. The Merlin's cocktail of sound and smell was incredibly emotive, because Harper had already learned to associate it with deadly action. And he also felt ever so slightly more worried than the day before, even though he had already been bloodied. Then again... he hadn't been shot at the day before, just the victim of a leak. So that wasn't being properly 'bloodied' after all, was it?

"Oh do shut up!" Harper told himself as he taxied away from the dispersal area and out towards the runway. He was 'Red 3' of a section of three Hurricanes.

"Reds. It's a rhubarb" radioed Tiger, Red section leader. 'Rhubarb' was RAF slang for a patrol looking for lone targets of opportunity, same as the previous day. Ginger was in the other Hurricane. That was good - in the air he was in his element. As Harper wheeled and bumped over to the take off point he ran through the before take off checks, then checked full and free movement on the flying controls. The main control stick articulated roughly half way up its length from side to side for roll control - this freed up space around the pilot's legs. It moved fore and aft at its base for pitch - up and down control. If the stick was held hard back whilst the aircraft was flying, it would perform a loop, providing the aircraft had enough airspeed at the entry. The rudder pedals controlled the aircraft on the ground and assisted roll control in the air.

Fighter pilots tended to be short and stockily built - for a fighter pilot a low *centre of gravity* was advantageous for resisting high and prolonged G forces experienced in combat. A lack of G tolerance could be the difference between life and death. It was even advantageous if the pilot had higher-than-normal blood pressure. The Hurricane was much slower but could turn tighter than a Messerschmitt 109, the most-feared German adversary in 1940, and so maybe get onto its tail in order to start shooting at it. But it was no use turning tighter for longer than the enemy if the pilot lost consciousness under the effects of G force. He might wake up as he was being shot down. If he woke up at all.

All three Hurricanes took off successfully, cutting through a thin layer of cloud between 800ft and 1200ft, and into blue sky. The radar controller vectored the fighters to the south east, out across the coast.

Over the water the cloud had dispersed and Red leader led them back down to 200ft above the waves, their camouflage blending in with the grey dark sea. The controller called in multiple plots on her radar set, relaying this to fighter command and then onto Red section. Suddenly Ginger called out on the radio.

"Target 12 o'clock! 1 mile!"

"Bandit 12 O'clock high! TALLY-HO!" replied Tiger. The bomber was clearly visible, tracking at 90 degrees from the Section, from right to left, 500ft above the sea. The bomber crew hadn't noticed them yet – no evasive action. Tiger rolled right and then left to come up on their tail, the two other Hurricanes in line astern, Ginger first, then Harper.

Tiger started firing, the tracer going high and wide, The bomber pitched up, then down, the result of the surprised pilot, the rear gunner immediately opening up with deadly accuracy - but the spray of machine gun fire went back past Tiger and straight into Ginger's cockpit. The Hurricane pitched up for a moment and then dived vertically into the sea, disappearing in an enormous explosion of fire and water, several hundred feet high.

"WHAT? BLOODY WHAT?" Harper tried to understand what had just happened, desperately trying to focus. Now Tiger was pulling up to the right, the arcing tracer hosing up to follow him.

"Red three... ATTACKING!" radioed Harper so that he didn't inadvertently shoot Tiger if he came back in for another go.

Harper lined up behind the He111, its grey/green camouflage clearly visible now – stark, black and white crosses on the wings, black swastikas on its tail. Its rear gunner had been stunned by his success but now he started firing again. And it was aimed at Harper.

"CHRIST!" Harper shouted to himself. He pulled back and right on the stick, the Hurricane lurching up and over on its right wing tip. Then he reversed the controls, stick left and slightly forward, the fighter now bunting left and down to run in 500 yards right of its original course. The carburettor momentarily starved the engine of fuel and it coughed for a moment, the negative G lifting all the dust from the cockpit floor, plus a tumbling cigarette butt.

"Bloody Jones!" hissed Harper. He centralised the controls and then re-directed his aim onto the rapidly closing bomber. The tracer from it was whizzing just a few feet over his head as he hit the gun button on his control stick, his eight Browning machine guns peppering the top side of the Heinkel's fuselage. The Heinkel's rear gun stopped firing, the gunner dead with a single shot to the head, the co-pilot stitched across his back, slumped in his harness. Harper told himself to release the gun button but he... just... couldn't. The bomber rolled and pitched, trying to evade fire. They flew together in wide sweeping turns, in across the coast, frost-covered hills replacing the sea, the bomber now down to just 50ft above ground. Harper realised that he couldn't hear or feel his machine guns firing. He was out of ammunition. Revulsion and bitter resentment came across him. He wanted to ram this bastard - but it would be pointless. The Heinkel's right engine had erupted in flames. The bomber was slowing up, the wheels and flaps coming down in quick succession. Harper pulled high, wide and clear, now that he knew what the outcome would be. The bomber crossed a series of farm fields in a shallow left turn, decelerating as it did so and lining up into wind. Harper traded speed for height and continued round in a climbing left turn as he watched the aeroplane put down hard into a ploughed field, screwing round in a left skid as it lost its main gear, then hitting a tree with its right wing and jack-knifing to the right. It stopped in a sea of smoke, flames, steam and mud.

6

"I don't bloody smoke" said Harper as he climbed down off the wing, holding a cigarette butt in his hand and grimacing with the pain of brushing his ribs against the cockpit canopy as he had climbed out.

"Yes you do!" Said Jones as he met Harper at the trailing edge of the wing. You hurt boss, sorry, sir?"

"No. I'm not. Don't smoke in my bloody aeroplane Jones. Have you seen Tiger?"

"Yes sir. He's here – he got hit in his radio but he's down safely. Where's Ginger, I mean Flt Lt How?"

"He bought it" replied Harper, his eyes filling with tears, turning his head away so that Jones wouldn't see. Yesterday pissing in his trousers, now crying – Harper wondered what was happening to himself. Inadvertently he turned towards Tiger's Hurricane as he rubbed his eyes– Tiger was walking purposefully across towards him. Harper noticed that he was limping.

"Did you see him go down?" asked Tiger as he drew close.

"He bought it - not a chance." Tiger pondered for a moment.

"Did you get the bastard?"

"Yes sir."

"I took a couple of hits in the cockpit; electrics and radio. I came back for another go but I couldn't find either of you." Tiger noticed that Harper was looking down at his left leg. There was a small tear in Tiger's uniform trousers just below the knee - the opening was blackened and smeared with blood. He stooped and pulled up the leg of his trousers to reveal a dark, bloody depression on the right side of his calf. A piece of the bullet that took out his radio had ricocheted and was now embedded in his flesh. Tiger hadn't felt a thing until now.

"Fuck it," he said, starting to go light-headed. "I'm sorry Harper but I need you to go up again. Get airborne, angels 10, head south and wait for orders." Harper helped the now sagging Tiger towards the back of a nearby ambulance and ran back to his Hurricane.

A quick turnaround, to rearm and refuel. The engine cowlings were up and Jones was inside checking for oil and coolant leaks on the new Merlin, the exhaust system still clicking and pinging as it cooled from the previous sortie. Fuel was being pumped from the bowser, topping up to 33 gallons in the right wing tank, 28 in the fuselage tank, and 33 more in the left. Another fitter was changing the oxygen bottle in the cockpit, two more on the wings feeding belts of .303 ammunition into the eight machine gun magazines. Hurricanes' guns were set to concentrate their fire on a point from 300 yards down to 150 yards ahead of the aircraft, depending on pilot preference. Harper had the 250-yard, default setting because at this stage he didn't know any better. His aircraft had been towed to the range the previous week, when Harper arrived on the squadron, its tail lifted up to get it level, the guns fired, and fired again until they aimed according to where the reflector gun sight in the cockpit indicated that they should. Other squadrons used periscopes inserted into the gun barrels but nothing replaced the accuracy of real-time firing if available. Jones closed the engine cowls one by one and then went round to the left wing, up on the stirrup, up to the leading edge and then round to the front wind shield to clean it.

As Harper waited for the fitters another wave of revulsion and grief, coursed its way through his body. He imagined what the remains of Ginger's Hurricane looked like on the seabed. The remains of Ginger - maybe he was still at the controls - or in a hundred pieces, more like. Harper steeled himself and got ready to climb back in. The battery trolley was already connected to take the strain off the internal battery during engine start. One by one the mechanics cleared the scene, leaving Jones alone to pull out the cable from the battery trolley after engine start. Jones nodded silently and Harper climbed back into the Hurricane.

Harper paused, desperately trying to concentrate on the sortie ahead. This would be a 'hot start'. It was important not to over-prime the engine with petrol: otherwise it might suffer a carburettor fire. The engine hesitated, then fired, after six blades – not bad for a 'hotty.' Jones pulled out the battery cable, still without permission, and Harper taxied out across the grass without delay. At the holding point for the runway he opened up the engine, checked that each of his two magnetos could run the engine independently, checked that the propeller went from *fine* to *coarse* and back again (the same effect as going from a low gear to a high gear in a car; *fine* for take off and landing, *coarse* for high speed flight) and that the engine ran with the throttle all the way closed so that he would be able to land without the engine cutting. Then he lined up on the runway and slowly opened the throttle. His full concentration was coming back.

Count 'one thousand, two thousand, three thousand', full throttle, controls firming up, lots of right rudder. 40mph, 50mph. Tail up with the stick, catch the swing with the rudder. 60mph, 70mph. Stick back a little and... airborne. Harper squeezed the brakes with the lever on the control stick to stop the main wheels spinning, and then raised them with the hydraulic lever on the right side of the cockpit. It looked like the gear stick in a car, slotting into an 'H-shaped' gate. Moving the lever between '2nd' and 1st' via a safety latch raised the wheels, from '4th' to 3rd' raised the flaps, and vice versa - it was easy to get it wrong and operate one when he wanted the other. Harper had been told to go 'buster'- that meant full throttle all the way, so he kept the throttle where it was. Instead he traded height for speed, allowing the Air Speed Indicator needle to wind up rapidly through 250mph before starting to pull back on the stick to gain altitude. He was getting to know this aeroplane. It rolled best at 250 mph – about 90 degrees per second, still sluggish compared to a '109 or a Spitfire but more than a match for the other German aircraft. Too much slower than this and there wasn't enough air going over the wing for optimum roll, too much faster and the aerodynamic forces built up so much that it was a two-handed job to make the aircraft manoeuvre at its best. Out ahead, Harper could see a couple of thin layers of stratus cloud at low altitude – perfect cover for a lone bomber on a hunting mission. The sector controller asked Harper to turn left onto 145 degrees, south-east, level off at Angels 5 - 5000ft - and search for a target which was appearing on the radar intermittently, probably due to the low altitude. Harper checked oil and coolant temperature, and the fuel contents - he was using nearly a gallon every thirty seconds at this power setting. Above him the sun shone brightly through thin layers of cloud, then less bright, obscured by thicker cloud, and bright again. He could sense his speed in relation to the cloud layer - it was beautiful. The ASI needle nudged 300mph. He couldn't always get the sensation of speed - only when near to the cloud, near to the ground, or near another aircraft.

THERE! Straight ahead. And head on! The Heinkel 111 flashed past him in the opposite direction, 100 yards to his right. The closing speed was over 500mph. Harper instinctively tensed his stomach muscles and the calves in his legs, as he rolled right and pulled on the stick as hard as possible, the blood draining from his head despite it. He 'blacked out'- lost vision - for a few seconds but not his consciousness: *situation normal* for a fighter pilot. The Hurricane could pull up to 7.5 Gs but most pilots lost their vision after 5. With most of the 180' turn complete, he relaxed the back pressure on the stick and regained his sight. But the bomber had disappeared. Harper rolled out heading north west and checked around the sun by blocking the light from it with a raised thumb. The bomber was gone.

"This is red 5. I had contact but I lost him."

"Red 5 standby. No radar contact."

Harper looked at the tops of the clouds rolling by beneath him – sometimes aircraft would leave telltale grooves in them due to the disturbance of the air. But he couldn't see anything now.

"Red 5 radar contact. Target in your 12 o'clock, 1 mile, closing slightly." They were both going in the same direction, the Hurricane behind the bomber and slowly catching – but he still couldn't see the bloody thing. It must be hiding in the clouds below.

"Red 5 come left 20 degrees – target manoeuvring."

"Got that. Left 20, Red 5." The situation stayed that way for a long minute.

"Red 10 you're almost on top of him." Harper looked down into the murk. He still couldn't see anything. Oh, yes he could!! A dark shape in the cloud, a machine gun flashing in bright contrast to the grey cloud beneath it, a bright curve of starkly contrasting tracer hosing up towards him. Harper pulled up sharply, counted to three and then bunted forwards again. Again it had disappeared.

"Red 5 contact?" asked the controller.

"Red 10 roger... I mean, Red 5 negative. The bastard's in the cloud again."

"Ok... Red 5 come right 40 degrees. Target manoeuvring in your 2 O'clock, and closing."

"Red 5 right 40." This was really frightening. The machine gun hadn't been effective but it was very, very disconcerting being fired at by something he couldn't see.

"Red 5 standby. We lost contact."

"Stuff it!" exclaimed Harper. He checked over his shoulder - not easy in a Hurricane - and then the round the sun again, blocking with his thumb. He wasn't going to be bounced by a fighter while he was concentrating on this bloody bomber. Another check of temperatures and pressures – t's and p's - and fuel, down to half tanks on the mains'.

"Red 5. No contact. Patrol and pancake." That meant return to base. Harper flew for another thirty minutes with the throttle brought back to conserve fuel, and then reluctantly turned towards the airfield. He was bitterly disappointed - his blood had been up. Now he was thinking about his friend again.

7

Harper was having another drink with his flying mates in the local - the generally accepted way to say goodbye to a friend, without actually saying it. Tiger was there too - looking at him gently leaning against the wall by the fireplace, no one could have guessed that he had just had half a bullet dug out of his leg.

"There were more than two hundred holes in that crate when the lads found it. Good shooting Harper" said Tiger. "I'll leave it until tomorrow to discipline you about misuse of the radio."

"Thanks boss. Sorry boss." A combined "well done" from his comrades. A raising of glasses.

Lucy walked through the door of the pub, her white nurses' uniform only slightly disguised with a grey, unbuttoned overcoat. She immediately spotted Harper among the mass of blue by the fire - luckily the barman saw Lucy before he did. Frantic silent waving, tears and cigarettes in the car park, ten minutes to get composure. And then she walked in again.

"Well look who it is" said Lucy, as she approached the group; smiling and bold, secretly sad and intimidated. A bunch of young and hopeful faces smiled back, one by one fading slightly as they noticed the centre of her focus.

"Good to see you!" said Harper, suddenly looking furtively over her shoulder for the friend, and quickly back again to Lucy.

"On your own?"

"Yes this is on the way home. Only one extra bus. If I'd known the whole squadron was here I would have invited some of my friends too." As usual, Flt Lt Gazzer Tyler was the first to reply.

"We're... having a special celebration. But I'm sure we can all be here tomorrow night, and the one after that if your friends are coming!" A group 'here, here!' and another raising of glasses.

"I'll see what I can do!" replied Lucy. The smiling faces returned, a few more pleasantries exchanged before Harper led her to a less intimidating corner. Gazzer piped up again once the couple was out of earshot.

"Can't imagine they'll all be as pretty as that one."

"Don't worry" replied Flt Lt Rhino Rhinde. "We'll just have to make sure we've got our beer goggles on before they get here."

"Well done on your first kill, I mean victory, today Tom" said Lucy in earnest, raising her glass.

"I didn't realise that the word got round?"

"The barman told me. I think he's a fan of yours."

"He's a tip top chap, that one. Not sure about the adulation thing though. Hold on... did he tell you anything else?"

"Yes."

"Well, I suppose he saved me a bit of work then."

"Sorry Tom."

"Thanks, we're all sorry..." horrible thoughts, quickly suppressed. "...That's the way it's going to be from now on." Harper drew towards her to whisper. Lucy drew back. A frown and a waggle of a finger from Harper and she closed in again to listen.

"It was the moment of truth for me today" he whispered. "They were shooting at mummy's little boy up there. But I kept going. I missed another one and I was bereft. After Ginger I don't have a problem with it. I mean I do – I was scared shitless – but I could function."

"Were the enemy killed, do you know?"

"Two of them were. The C/O asked if I wanted to visit the one who got out and I said no – if I did I would have wanted to take a gun."

"He killed your friend. Or he was part of it." Harper knew he didn't mean it about the gun – but he had shut down any emotional connection with their fate. They were probably the same age as him; loved flying, as he did. They might all have been friends in a different life. Now he wanted to try and stop himself from dwelling on thoughts like these.

"Evidently we're going to put a memorial on the gravestones. Wonder what they'll do for us when we get shot down over Germany?"

"The war might not go on much longer" replied Lucy. "There's going to be a big push soon. One of my patients - somebody important - told me." Suddenly Harper leaned forward to kiss her. And this time she let him.

8

Flt Lt Thomas Arnold Harper was standing to attention in Tiger's room in the dispersal hut. All the other pilots were in the hut too, because it was too cold to be outside. The walls were very thin between rooms - one breezeblock width or hardboard studding. Consequently they couldn't help but hear the one-way conversation next door, even if they didn't want to.

"....so DON'T SWEAR ON THE BLOODY RADIO!" shouted Tiger. There was muffled laughter from the other side of the wall.

"Yes sir."

"DISMISSED!"

"Thank you sir." Harper turned on his heels to the left so that Tiger wouldn't notice the empty coffee mug he had in his non-saluting hand, buried halfway into the sleeve of his flying jacket.

"And Harper?"

"Yes sir?"

"Start taking me seriously."

"Yes sir." The officer marched out of the room. Tiger pondered about Harper and his place in the squadron. He was a good flier and he had been brave yesterday, especially having to go up again after Ginger - not everyone had coped. He was already getting respect from his peers, very confident for a new one. He was also good - looking and extremely well off. Perhaps he had it too easy? There were no doubts about his strengths - he had many of the characteristics of a really good fighter pilot.

"I blame the bloody parents," said Tiger to himself as he settled down to go through more of the previous day's combat reports.

Harper walked back into the main room to be met with smiles and suppressed laughs. Gazzer was at the head of the pack. A balding, slightly overweight Geordie, he looked a little older than his years. He made up for that with an oversized personality and an ability to extract laughs from almost any situation.

"Tom, there's a deliveryman waiting for you outside," said Gazzer. "Hurry up man, he's been waiting for you to finish your chat with Boss."

"Deliveryman? Ah yes…" Harper remembered that his father had sent him a letter promising to arrange a replacement for the car. Harper walked outside the hut. There was no new car, but a man who he didn't know was standing next to a BMW R71 – a German army motorbike.

"Flight Lieutenant Harper?"

"Yes."

"I got instructions to deliver this to you. Sign here please" he said, handing over a large document and a pen.

"What the heck is it?" said Harper. Gazzer had already put the word round and the boys were spilling out of the hut.

"What were you expecting Tom? A Rolls Royce?" said Gazzer, laughing loudest. As much as he tried, Harper couldn't hide his disappointment. But at least it had novelty value.

"Look here old boy" said Gazzer, leaning under the fuel tank and pulling out a letter. Harper reached for it but Gazzer wouldn't give it back, jogging round the bike to evade capture whilst opening it at the same time.

"It's from… your Uncle Percy." A note of recognition spread across Harper's face. He called off the pursuit as Gazzer continued reading.

"Says here... he bought it off of a trawler skipper who... took it off a French chap... as payment to ship him across to England in the trawler." Uncle Percy was the eccentric older brother of Harper's father, currently working on *naval matters* at Portsmouth. "The Frog stole it... at night from a border position... took the sidecar off and painted it, and then drove to Cherbourg on it!" Harper leaned down underneath the frame and scratched it with the door key from his crashed car. The brushed-on black paint peeled away easily to reveal a smooth, bluish grey camouflage. "He says its probably the only one in England and when your father told him about your prang he thought you'd like to borrow it for a while!"

"It could only happen to you Harper," said Abbo Abbot, a 30 year old, dark-haired, white Rhodesian. "I've driven one of these at home." He jumped on, checked the bike was in neutral, with his right hand on the stick gear change sprouting out of the gear box, turned on the little fuel tap under the left side of the tank, then leaned down and pushed a button on top of each of the carburettors - one on each side - until fuel dribbled out and wetted their aluminium lids. Then Abbo stood on the kick-start. It started first time, with a small cloud of oily grey smoke coming out of the twin exhausts and emitting a small but satisfactory roar as Abbo gunned the throttle, a caricature of the fighters. Then Abbo selected first gear and immediately stalled it. With the jeers of the squadron boys - led by Gazzer - almost deafening him he reselected neutral, kick-started it again, climbed off and held it steady whilst Harper got on.

"Shut up Geordie – you've got a crop failure on top there man. Gears are one down, three up. And mind the brakes – they're rubbish." Harper, selected first, let out the clutch and pulled away perfectly, then drove up and down along the dispersal area, increasingly fast, accompanied by the catcalls of his friends in mock German accents. He decided he liked the bike after all, resolving to go the whole hog and get it back to its original paint. Then the scramble bell rang.

9

The patrol initially followed the same pattern as the previous days – yet another 'rhubarb,' looking for lone targets of opportunity, or small numbers of them, guided by the 'Chain Home' radar controllers and then maybe 'Chain Home Low', an independent guidance system for close-in manoeuvring.

But now the weather had broken - a cold, unstable air mass had moved in. Six Hurricanes were flying in a beautiful blue sky, with towering white cumulus clouds thousands of feet high emphasising airspeed and altitude. Tiger was Red 1, Abbo Red 2, and Rhino as Red 3. Harper had been moved up to Red 4, the lead aircraft in the second group of three, with Gazzer as Red 5, and Johnny as Red 6. The formation pattern of each three aircraft was a Vic, with Harper ahead and one aircraft each side aft abeam Harper's wings. Away from the clouds the air was completely smooth, the formating Hurricanes just gently inching fore and aft, up and down, left and right with the smallest of control and throttle inputs to hold station.

Chain Home was back in business.

"Red section. Multiple targets at 12 O clock, 10 miles. Climb to angels 15."

"Red section roger. Climb angels, 15" - the unmistakable, clipped, Home Counties accent of Tiger. Harper strained forwards to see, inching his Hurricane's throttle up to compensate for the thinner air. Every thousand feet or so he had to do it again. Now the formation was becoming more ragged, both Gazzer and John inevitably starting to look for the targets as well as trying to hold station - Harper anticipated it.

"Red section, attack formation two" said Tiger, The four wingmen instantly moved farther out and back - a better position to attack, or counter one if they were surprised first. Thumb up - a quick check around the sun - and then Harper strained forward again. Still nothing.

As usual, Tiger saw them first - not the targets but another squadron, six Spitfires moving in at 3 O'clock and closing. Another call from the controller;

"Red and Blue. Multiple targets 1 O'clock, 5 miles. Come right 10 degrees."

"Red section, right 10" replied Tiger, a mute "Blue section, right 10" from the Spitfire section leader as Tiger initiated the move. '2 and '3 followed, spreading out even more, then '4, '5 and '6 in trail. Nothing for a minute - an eternity - then;

"Bandits 12 O'clock! Tally-ho!" Tiger was in control. Harper had been busy turning, looking, checking. And now, looking forward again he saw them - ten growing specs, level. No, not specs, tiny aircraft running left to right. And turning. And no, not tiny - they were fighters! Messerschmitt 109s!

"Bloody hell!" said Harper to himself as he adjusted his course slightly left again to get in on their tail. He noticed that the Spitfires were accelerating away at buster - full power - everyone had gone to it, the Spits' performance advantage immediately showing itself. Harper could feel the slow, creeping terror building from within. Must keep control.

"Hold fast," Harper repeated to himself – a Royal Navy phrase, Uncle Percy's influence. Miraculously, importantly, although the Hurricanes weren't *up-sun*, the '109s hadn't noticed them yet. And a new dynamic – of course, the Spitfires would engage first. What did this mean for the Reds - a change of strategy? Tiger piped up.

"Red section. Tally. Targets as they bear!" That meant engage the enemy whenever, whatever came first. As the six Spitfires and six Hurricanes closed in - 1000 yards to go - Harper crossed himself with his shaking left hand and then put it back on the throttle. The right hand was on the stick, thumb on the gun button. A quick squirt – all working. Then he checked the sun again with his thumb and…

"CHRIST!" Two fighters coming straight down. "REDS! HUNS IN THE SUN! BREAK! BREAK!" shouted Harper, pulling his nose up directly towards the nearest one. Harper's formation broke up, his wingmen disorientated for a moment before peeling away to fight their own battles. He couldn't hold this crazy upward angle for long but the '109 was closing at massive speed. The speck suddenly loomed large. Harper hit the gun button, the tracer going straight - no curving, no deflection - the '109 dead ahead and right in his sights, closing incredibly fast. And now firing back - Harper could see the muzzle flashes from its wings, and then more flashes from the canons in the top of its nose cowling. More from the wings, then more from the nose - in that instant in time, Harper asked himself why. At the last possible moment he started pushing out to miss it - an instant later the fighter screamed over his head, so close that Harper's whole aircraft shook from its bow wave. Was it hit? Was he hit? No time to know - the engine coughed and lost power. Harper rolled the Hurricane onto its back and started pulling. The engine coughed and barked into life as the positive G pushed fuel through the carburettors and into the engine again. Airspeed? 200mph and climbing fast as he started going vertically downhill. A vague recollection of a Spitfire to his far left, also vertical, guns blazing. Another look over his shoulder - another '109, 300 yards behind him, tracer now going past Harper's cockpit. "SHIT! SHIT! SHIT!" shouted Harper, instinctively trying to hunch down and make himself smaller as he pulled hard on the stick. Five successive 'whumps!' in the tail, then the metallic 'CLANG!' of a bullet right behind his head. HE'D BEEN HIT! And now he had lost his vision because of the G, but he couldn't unload the stick to see behind him - because that would let the '109 stay on his tail. Flying blind! The aircraft was now at 45 degrees nose down – Harper finally unloaded the stick and threw a glance over his shoulder. More tracer – IT WAS STILL THERE! He pulled as hard as he could, then moving the stick to the right as well, the Hurricane corkscrewing through the sky twice, finally pointing vertically down, way past Vne, maximum speed. Stick to neutral. His eyesight returned again - no more tracer. A hurried glance over both shoulders – no more '109. Harper pulled the throttle back and eased out of the dive as gently as he could, the altimeter needle spinning wildly. But he could pull out before hitting the ground – he had enough room. As he did so he realised he was panting, sweating and shaking from head to toe. Still nothing behind, nothing in the sun - nothing anywhere! Just a few vapour trails far, far above. Harper put the throttle all the way forward again and checked the altimeter - 800ft. He had lost over 14,000ft trying to shake off the '109. With the speed coming back down through 300mph he moved the stick and rudder pedals a little to check the flying surfaces, the Hurricane bobbing and weaving as he did so – everything ok, apparently. Harper checked his fuel - half on the main tanks. He contemplated returning to 15,000ft. But the radio was quiet, and what if he had been damaged? After all, he had definitely been hit. Harper decided to 'pancake' back to base, still panting, and shaking like a leaf.

10

"Fucking hell sir" exclaimed Jones. The fitter was looking at a distinct groove in the armour behind the Hurricane's seat. "Luck of the bleeding Irish."

"I went a bit over Vne - can you check the tail Jonesy?" Harper climbed down from the cockpit, trying, and failing, to act nonchalantly. His hands were still shaking like mad.

"Don't want you to bust this one sir" replied Jones, trying not to notice the shaking, and concentrating instead on the line of bullet holes along the right side of the fuselage. "This is a good crate – I've seen Wednesday planes, believe me."

"Who's back?"

"You're first." Harper was consumed by guilt. Seeing it, Jones was quick to add; "…not to worry, lots of them calling in on the radio. Sounds like you all did ok." Harper immediately climbed back up onto the wing and looked into the cockpit. The evidence was there for all to see – a cut in the wires behind the radio, an exit hole in the cockpit wall. Tiger last time, and now Harper.

"I was listening out, really! I didn't think there were any more engagements. I got shot at, I… fuck it."

"It's alright - it really is" interrupted Jones - officers shouldn't be, but it was appreciated. Harper calmed down a little, and waited impatiently for the rest of the squadron to return. And they did, all of them, over the next 20 minutes. Rhino was the last, badly shot up, his Hurricane trailing smoke as it crossed the airfield boundary at 85mph. That was too fast. The Hurricane landed heavily on its main wheels, its tail end dropping, its tail wheel hitting the ground and putting the aircraft at an increased angle of attack to the airflow. And producing more lift – more than the aircraft weighed. The Hurricane bounced back into the air and flew for another 100 yards, finally slowing up and then falling to the ground in a *three pointer* - all wheels together - bouncing and rolling off to the left of the landing area. Harper could see that it looked wrong - he started running towards where he thought the aircraft would stop. The canopy was already open - as he got closer he could see Rhino slumped forwards at the controls.

"YOU OK!" Harper shouted, more an exclamation than a question, as he ran the final few yards to the smoking, steaming aircraft. Rhino managed a little wave but didn't move back from his slumped position. Harper jumped the 4ft up onto the wing without using the stirrup and steadied himself by grabbing the canopy rail. The engine had stopped, the smoke dispersing. It wasn't on fire. Harper looked into the cockpit. There was a fine mist of blood on the right side of the canopy. His gaze went down and across Rhino's right arm. He was clutching it firmly with his left hand - the right sleeve of the flying jacket was torn through.

"I don't want to move it. Hurts like hell."

"Anywhere else?"

"No. Think my wedding tackle's ok." Harper looked at him in amazement - only Rhino could crack a joke with a bullet wound.

"Christ, that was a one-handed hoosh (fast landing). They'll be putting you onto Spitfires next" said Harper, quietly concerned what would be found when the jacket was off. The ambulance crew arrived, helped Rhino out of the Hurricane, peeled back his flying jacket, and the uniform jacket underneath it. The arm wasn't broken but there was a deep lateral flesh wound across the triceps - his blue shirtsleeve was now magenta.

"It's a deep graze. Must have been a bullet," said the doctor to Rhino as he bandaged the arm. "If it had been a canon shell it would have taken your arm off."

"Oh thanks for that!" said Rhino, nevertheless relieved, and to Harper; "I saw you go for the top cover. Well done you."

"Don't know about that - I've cracked up my machine. Did you see what happened to the one I went for?"

"No, I peeled right and one of the finger four bounced me." German fighters flew in loose formations of four, spread out wide and at slightly different heights. It was a better tactic.

"Me too. I've got some hits. Lost my radio – like Tiger. Anybody get a kill?"

"Gazzer did I think."

"Bloody bang on!" replied Harper, thinking of his closest friend, as he climbed into the ambulance with Rhino to hitch a lift back to the dispersal. This time he would definitely be going to the intelligence officer, but first he wanted to know about his Hurricane.

"You've given it a bit of a hammering," said Jones, as Harper leaned down and peered into the rear fuselage. The fabric skin had already been sliced and peeled back. "The joints look wrong here (pointing) – and these tubes are out of true." The Hurricane had a skeleton of square tubes braced with wires and covered with doped, shrunk fabric, plywood or aluminium sheeting. It was old-fashioned, the same design as the biplane fighters that the Hawker Hurricane was derived from - and very unlike a Spitfire. "I think the tail will have to go into a jig. It's not what we can fix here."

"What about those?" said Harper, referring to the bullet holes.

"They just need patching. And there are a couple of patchable tube holes, apart from the one that hit the radio. And this one." Jones produced a handkerchief from his overall and unfolded it to reveal a splayed, flattened bullet. Jones had found it embedded in a tube behind the cockpit. Harper took it and rolled it around in his hand.

"Can I keep it?"

"You can make a fucking necklace out of it if you want sir."

11

At the end of the afternoon Tiger called a debrief in the dispersal hut. Sqn. Ldr. Greg Ball, the intelligence officer stood next to him – he had been a fighter pilot in World War I. Most of the squadron pilots were in attendance.

"Good ops. But finger four formation caught us out a bit. I got wet and tried to fire on one at 400 yards. Then at 200 yards and a 2-second burst took him down. I recommend you all get your guns realigned to 200 yards, and make sure the armourers put 50 tracer at the end of your magazines to remind you when you're running out. I spent a long time fighting another one - lots of wasted bursts too far away again - finally got on his tail and then found out I was on empty. But its your call at the end of the day. One more thing, I've taken to flying with a bit of rudder trim in. That way if someone gets on your tail without you knowing, chances are that the first shells will run wide of you, because you're not going where you're pointing. "What happened to you" gesturing to Harper.

"I got in a burst against one of the top cover, boss. Didn't get him, but he didn't get me either. Another one was onto me when I rolled out. He took out my radio - wondered why it all went quiet..." A quick glance of recognition between Harper and Tiger.

"You did actually."

"Sorry?" asked Harper, looking around - someone had spoken from the back of the room. It was Johnny; 23 years old, small, quiet, and very punchy, bordering on jumpy.

"You did get him. He never pulled out."

"Well, well! Two in two days" said Tiger, nodding to Greg Ball. "Anyone else?"

"I got one boss," said Gazzer. "The one on Harps' tail. He must have shot down his mate – too busy trying to get Harps that he didn't notice me closing in. I couldn't shoot at him to start with because I didn't want to get Tom. But then they pulled out of vertical - I hosed him before we all lined up again. Some of the tail came off and he went straight down."

"Good work Tyler. And that's one for all of you - don't take your eyes off the bloody ball. Keep the scan going, no matter what. Any more?"

'Abbo' Abbots chipped in; "You touched on it just then, but, I'm thinking more and more that their finger four works better than our Vics. They must spend less time formating and more time doing the important stuff. We're rearranging deckchairs on the Titanic." A few murmurs of approval from the other pilots.

"I agree. The fact is they are more experienced than we are, they had plenty of time to learn new tactics in Spain. Our book was written in the Great War, isn't that right Greg?"

"Probably the Boer War." The first flight of a powered aeroplane was 1903. The Boer War ended in 1902.

"There's a lot of talk about it at Group (headquarters) at the moment. Pairs or multiples of pairs, instead of in Vics of threes. I'm not the only one saying it. Until then we're under orders." Harper raised his hand. Then, with a nod from Tiger; "when I was head to head with the top cover he kept swapping from wing guns to nose cannon and back again. I don't know what that was about."

"Its because they use the tracer in their machine guns to sight their target, then use the canon. I wish we had bloody canon." More murmurs of agreement from the pilots, louder from the experienced ones. "I do have something for you though. It looks like we will be getting *de Wilde* rounds - incendiaries. Group are going to approve it from what I hear. They go straight into our Brownings (machine guns) with no modifications. They do a lot more damage than straight rounds and can ignite the fuel tanks." Messerschmitt 109s had a rubber membrane between the aluminium skins which formed the fuel tank walls. The rubber resealed the tank when a bullet entered. "There's a report about four Spitfires trying to knock down a single bomber last week. They used 17,000 rounds between them and it still flew home." Lots of laughs from the boys – there was intense rivalry between Hurricane and Spitfire squadrons. "Standard ops tomorrow. We're back up to 18 ships again. Rhino's non-op for a few days. It's getting lighter so I think an early beer to toast Gazzer, Harper and Rhino. But in bed by 10 all of you! Hands off cocks, on socks at 0600 tomorrow, breakfast 0630, dispersal at 0700." There were lots of 'here here's' for Rhino - now being looked after by nurses and secret hip flasks in hospital - and back slaps for Gazzer and Harper as the pilots filed out of the dispersal hut.

"Not you Harper" said Tiger.

"Sorry sir?"

"You'll do a ferry flight to our CRO for repairs. Your fitter told me its ok for a ferry. But no aerobatics, got it?"

"Oh right… absolutely!"

"That's great" said Gazzer as they left the dispersal hut, out of earshot of the boss. "It means I get to go down the pub and chat up your bride!"

"Ask after her for me will you?"

"Yeah right!" Gazzer never gave in to anyone. "Don't forget to draw a line on the map."

"Bugger off fatty. Why are you so fat anyway?"

"Because every time I boff one of your girlfriends she gives me a biscuit."

It was true – about the map - Harper would have to draw a line on a chart to navigate by. Not something that he'd done much since leaving flight school. It was also too good to be true - Harper had to fly his Hurricane to a Civilian Repair Organisation unit to get the tail fixed, at a base near Norwich. One of his best friends lived near the airfield in a beautiful country house - Harper had been at school with him.

"Bloody marvellous" he said to himself as he legged it across to the telephone in the mess to call his friend.

Twenty minutes later, Harper was getting airborne for the second time that day, and feeling good about going flying without having to fight. Before take off he had got Jones to re arm the guns just in case he needed them, and top up the fuel to full tanks. Immediately after take off he made sure that his IFF transmitter (Identification Friend or Foe) was switched on so that he wouldn't be mistaken for an enemy raider - the radio was still U/S and he had no way to be able to identify himself, or call off an attack. As he cleared the circuit he started his stopwatch and turned north to follow the coast for a few miles, heading out across the Blackwater estuary. On Harper's chart was a straight line, with small marks along the line 20 miles apart. He had planned the trip at 200mph and the marks represented where he would be every 6 minutes. Once Harper had confirmed his heading with what he had calculated on the chart, he folded it and put it down the side of his seat to concentrate on flying the aeroplane.

It was late in the day, a beautiful afternoon. The sun was behind and left of the aircraft, so no glare and no squinting required. The countryside was spread out in front of him, perfectly illuminated. A stunning sight. He crossed back across the coast at Mersea Island – he could see the remains of the causeway the Romans built between it and the mainland, which flooded on spring tides. Then he dropped down to 500ft and pulled the stick back, checked it to neutral and held it hard over, the aircraft doing a beautiful victory roll across the island. For Harper, a victory roll didn't count as aerobatics.

After 5 minutes he picked the map up again and checked his position. Timing was spot on – as the last minute counted up on his watch Harper could see the river Stour running left to right and passing underneath him. His line should have taken him directly over East Bergholt but he was 2 miles to the right. So 2 degrees to the right and ¼ of total distance covered. 2 divided by ¼ equals 8, so he turned left 8 degrees using the compass mounted on the floor between his feet. Then, map folded away again, he concentrated on flying the Hurricane and enjoying himself. Fuel burn was just over a gallon a minute –

plenty to complete the journey and have some reserves for a diversion if required.

After 5 more minutes he picked up the map again. This time he could see that he was converging nicely with the straight bit of railway line between Stowmarket and Diss. Harper counted the villages along the line; 1st, 2nd, 3rd, 4th along it - track and time spot on, map away again. Just before 18 minutes elapsed time he crossed the A11, South West of Norwich and... he... couldn't... help himself but to peel off hard left for a buzz of his friend's estate. He selected full throttle, dropped down to less than 100ft, turned hard right across the lake, flew up the slope of the garden and rolled upside down over the beautiful 18th century house at the end of it. As he did so, from far behind him there was a loud 'crack.'

"CHRIST!" said Harper as he pulled out of the dive at the end of the victory roll, doing it so gradually that he ended up just 10 ft from the ground, passing between two lines of trees at the edge of the estate where it bordered onto a road. As he did so he crossed in front of a milk lorry, which braked, slid into a broadside to avoid him, and shed its load. Harper didn't see it – he was too busy easing his aircraft back up to a safe height and across to the CRO without losing his tail.

12

"Nice fly-by!" shouted Daniel, the owner of the estate, across to Harper as he cycled the last few feet up to the main entrance of the beautiful 18th century hall. Harper climbed off the bike and Dan rushed forward to give him a brotherly hug, Harper wincing with the pain in his ribs but not letting on. They walked up through the main entrance, through the grand hall and straight into the dining room, to have a bite to eat. "I liked the pull out at the end of it. Or lack of it actually! I thought you'd gone in for a moment. Did you have any twigs in the wheels when you got to the airfield?"

"Its not a Tiger Moth!" replied Harper. "We don't fly around with the wheels down." Tom and Dan had learned to fly together after leaving school. Dan would have joined the Royal Auxiliary Air Force like Harper, but instead he had been persuaded to run the family estate. Many wealthy amateur pilots joined the RAAF as part-timers in the '30s. Not many of them had guessed, when Harper joined in 1935, that one day they'd be flying fighters in a full-blown war.

"Had a very upset milkman at the house not long after you went by – you spilled his milk."

"Eh?" Harper had cycled past the devastation on the way in, and hadn't added up two and two. "Oh bugger, sorry. Any comeback?"

"He asked me if I knew who the pilot was - managed to get round it. But I had to pay for two churns of milk and four crates of empties."

"Really sorry old boy."

"It was worth every penny, believe me. I didn't shed a single tear…"

"Stobbit, I'll piss myself."

"What's the Hurricane like to fly? As difficult as it looks?"

"Oh really tough. Doubt you'd be up to it." Harper tried not to laugh. Dan looked up, a little hurt look on his face which changed into a broad smile when he saw Harper's. "Do about 5 hours in it and you'll probably be good enough to fly a Tiger Moth". Both the Hurricane and Spitfire were easier to fly in many ways than the trainers pilots learned on first; the Tiger Moth and, for fighter pilots, the Harvard after it. Dan had his own 'Moth, which he shared with his father. It was parked in a hangar on the edge of the estate.

"Well I did wonder. Bloody shame it's only got one seat."

"If they build a two-seater I'll be straight up here with it." Dan topped up Harper's wine. They ate duck, freshly shot on the lake at dawn that morning. Harper was ravenous. He hadn't eaten since breakfast – a bacon butty rustled up by Gazzer in the dispersal hut at first light. "I've got something to tell you actually."

"You look serious old boy – not like you!"

"I shot down a fighter today - a Messerschmitt 109. And I got a fighter-bomber yesterday – the fucking bastard shot my friend down. One minute he was out there on my wing. Next he went straight down into the sea. I had no remorse bagging the bastard. No more than you did shooting these ducks" as he prodded his dinner with his knife. "And not today, neither."

"Christ Tom! Well done, seriously well done." The two clinked glasses – no mirth, just mutual respect. "I've got something to say too actually."

"Yes?"

"Well… after school, when you joined up, I wondered how you'd get on with it frankly. All that bull shit, and all your mucking around, you know. I just wondered how you would go down with the Air Force? All of my friends too, when they joined the 'Auxiliary. But now I think you fit the job. Its like someone threw a switch. Just try and stay alive will you for Christ's sake! So here's a cheers, lets finish our dinner and get one of my chaps to give us a lift down the pub. Not flying tomorrow are you?"

"I doubt it" replied Harper, thinking about the looks on the faces of the engineers at the CRO when they had examined his tail plane.

After dinner, Dan lent Harper some clothes to change into – it was the first time in over a year that he had been out of uniform, and he craved the novelty of anonymity. They travelled into the local village of Windham in style, in the back of Dan's father's 1928 Rolls Royce Phantom - maybe not so anonymous after all, but an acceptable disguise. As Harper enjoyed the ride the irony wasn't lost on him that the car manufacturer also built the engine in his Hurricane. And yet the power plants in the two machines couldn't be more different. The Phantom's engine – a 7.7 litre, 120 hp, *straight 6* - ran as smoothly as it was possible for a piston engine to do - when the car was parked Harper had trouble noticing whether it was running or not. Whereas the 27litre, 1030 hp, V12 in his Hurricane was a highly stressed power unit at the edge of technology - flying behind one was like sitting inside a metal dustbin being whacked on the outside with cricket bats. The huge supercharger, as big as a dustbin lid itself, was by far the noisiest component, a whirling clash of pistons and gears only just in the background. The Phantom's engine would be good for 30 years. A Merlin would run for just 400 hours or so before it needed a complete rebuild - if the aircraft survived that long.

The Rolls' coasted into the quiet town and dropped the friends off at a 13th century wood-built pub, which butted up neatly and ironically to the back end of a church. The two walked into its tiny public bar, making a good show of sobriety, despite the occasional swerve, as they steered themselves into the snug by the fire.

"Good evening. Two ales please" asked Harper to the barman "…and two whatever's for those lovely ladies" pointing to two girls chatting animatedly to each other, sitting at the other end of the room. They stopped talking for a moment, one smiled and the other blushed. "How sweet" said Harper, thinking how much easier life would have been if he was wearing his uniform again. "Do you ladies live here?"

"We do now" replied the smiley one, the bolder of the two. "We've not been here long. We've both come up from London to work at a

Civil Repair Organisation. Don't suppose you know what that is do you?"

13

Harper woke up with a start. That bloody nightmare again. A burning Spitfire, him running through a field completely on fire, a fire engine screaming along the road next to the field, trying to get to him. A stupid dream in the cold light of day, but that didn't stop the horror it evoked when it recurred.

Harper pondered about his life for a moment – he was lying on his back, in a huge bed, situated in a south-facing bedroom on the top floor of the hall. The sun was just coming up, the sound of small birds and swishing trees coming through the open sash window, the occasional honk of geese down on the lake, and a small murmur from the girl under the sheets. Harper had a sudden flashback of the night before. A party of four squeezed into the back of the Rolls', two bicycles lashed to the back, a brief, mad little shindig by the fire, and now this. Except that Jane hadn't let him 'go all the way' last night: that was it, she had decided that they were both too drunk to make the right decision. Harper gently raised the sheets. She was sleeping on her front, to his left, her head on her hands and turned right, away from him, a mane of chestnut hair fanning out behind her head. Her bra was nowhere to be seen, but she still had her knickers. She had a fabulous body – slim and well-toned, no doubt something to do with having to wield machine tools as a day job. Harper gently rolled over towards her and started kissing the back of her neck. A sigh came back, a signal of approval. Harper brought his right hand across and stroked the small of her back, working his way up towards her neck, then down, past the point of first contact and across her knickers - they were soft, white cotton. Harper smiled and then suppressed a laugh with a gentle cough – he had just amused himself as to how apt it was for a fighter pilot to be mounting an attack from the rear. His hand carried on down onto her beautiful, long smooth legs, as far as he could reach whilst still being able to continue kissing her neck. Now his hand came slowly back up between her legs, past the backs of her knees and inside her thighs, until swiftly grasped by her right hand. Down in flames again.

"I have to get to work!" said Jane, springing out of bed, one arm strategically covering her breasts as she went for the door to the bathroom. "Don't worry" Harper called after her. "You won't have to bike it - we'll get a lift together with Dan. And I want to see how my aeroplane is coming along."

The group travelled in the Rolls the few miles across to the CRO. Dan drove, sitting in the open cockpit of the car with Jane's friend. Jane and Harper were in the enclosed cabin, hand in hand, an occasional wave from Jane out of the window, in a regal way, when they passed someone on the road. Dan had to drop them off at the main gate - for security reasons he wasn't allowed onto the airfield. They all made their farewells; the girls would be visiting Dan at the hall again soon for tea, Harper would be writing to Dan and Jane. Dan gave Harper another hug (ribs again) and a large bag with a dozen duck in it, kissed both girls on the cheek, and blasted off in the Phantom trailing a cloud of dust. The girls walked across to a large, tin-clad, single-story factory unit. Harper said goodbye to the girls in a formal way – his uniform was gaining attention again – and reported to the guardroom. The security man checked his 'ID' and sent him in the direction of what looked like the result of a large plane crash on the other side of the airfield, maybe the crash of a whole squadron. As Harper walked towards the debris he heard the rumble of a lorry behind him and turned to see a big, green "Queen Mary" lorry moving slowly across the field, a 'low loader' with another crashed aircraft on the trailer. With crosses on it.

"What in hell?" said Harper, completely unprepared for such a sight. Then he noticed that crosses and swastikas were everywhere - he hadn't noticed the day before when he arrived, distracted by his self-imposed dilemma. The CRO was recycling panels, fixings and fasteners from crashed German aircraft to repair British ones, melting down the aluminium to send off to the aircraft manufacturers. A small man with a long, light brown working jacket approached. He had a pencil sticking out from behind his ear and carried a clipboard under his arm.

"You coming to pick up the '1b sir?"

"I wish." The man was referring to a Spitfire.

"But you're the ATA pilot?" The ATA was the Air Transport Auxiliary, the delivery unit responsible for ferrying RAF aircraft. It was crewed with pilots from all nationalities, over 30% of them female.

"No, I brought my own kite up yesterday. I'm with a *Six Oh*. Mine's a Hurry?"

"I got you. Buggered tail. You might be a bit early, but I know that had a priority, you being operational. Hear you've been a bit busy in Essex recently."

"Busier by the minute." The two walked round the side of the largest pile of debris, alongside a hangar and on to a flight line of Spitfires, Hurricanes, and Shorts Sterling bombers.

"No, you're ok. That's yours second from the end. The lads must have done a night shift."

"Well good on them! Look, I know it's a bit of a cheek, but would you mind if I got a swastika?"

"If its fabric you can have it. We can't recycle the canvas. Everything else though." Harper ran back to the wrecks and brought out his pocket knife, cutting the swastika out of the tailplane of the tail section of an unknown German aircraft. The rest of the aircraft was missing - Harper wondered if it had already been recycled, or never recovered. Maybe the remains of the crew were still inside it at the bottom of the sea - he noticed that there was sand and dried seaweed inside the tail section. Harper rolled up the fabric and stuffed it inside his flying jacket. The boys would be ecstatic.

14

Harper's Hurricane was performing beautifully, perfectly balanced and trimmed to fly 'hands off' at cruise speed. It was better than new – the aeroplane had always flown slightly left wing low before. Harper couldn't resist the temptation to fly a few aerobatics on the way back, including another victory roll over Mersea, pre-booked and perfectly timed to impress his father as he cycled along the beach on the south coast of the island, near their holiday home.

Harper arrived at dispersal at 1100, the only airworthy Hurricane on the airfield, and waited for the rest of the squadron to return. They did, one by one, over the next half an hour. Harper waited proudly by the wood burner in the centre of the dispersal hut, his swastika unfurled and draped across a blackboard at the back of the room. Abbo was first in, then Johnny, two new guys, Gazzer, Tiger of course, and Rhino, helping out behind the scenes, despite an arm plastered from shoulder to wrist.

"How's it going chaps?!" asked Harper, noticing as he spoke that the two new boys, both Pilot Officers, were silently crying.

"Fancy a cigarette old boy?" asked Gazzer, nodding towards the doorway. "Absolutely, why not " replied Harper, turning on his heels and walking outside.

"Bastards got us good" whispered Gazzer as they got through the doorway, then dragging on his cigarette. "Bloody finger four - two in the sun again - shot down their mate (gesturing over his shoulder to the two new pilots). He only got here this morning. Twenty fucking nothing."

"I'm sorry," said Harper, swallowing the emotion.

"Anyway, where have you been, what you been up to?" asked Gazzer. Harper took the offer of a change of tack, and told him briefly about his trip, but not about Jane. "Bit of action this end old boy. Big bloody scrap in The Ship last night. Linda met Lucy!"

"How?"

"Well, It was sort of Abbo's fault. But, don't blame him old boy - he's innocent of all wrong doing… because it's my fault in a way."

"Actually old chap, this sounds like a load of bollocks."

"Well, Lucy popped in on her way home, accidentally on purpose again, if you know what I mean. Didn't know you weren't there and we couldn't tell her anything - security stuff - except that you were OK of course. Then Abbo went and bought her a drink so she stayed on. Then I went outside for a ciggy and who was walking down the lane but Linda! So she just had to come in for a drink and I introduced her to Lucy. And turns out that Linda thought she was still going out with you, sort of."

"No she's bloody not. It was her call and I'll stick to it."

"Well you'd better tell her that old boy. But now I don't think anyone's going out with you."

"They are actually. I met a lovely girl in Norfolk."

"Don't know how you do it!" Gazzer started to laugh. Harper joined in. "I like the swastika! Where did you get it?" Harper's trophy would have been hung over a fireplace, but the dispersal hut didn't have one, just a log-burning stove in the centre of the room – its black chimney pipe going straight up through a hole in the roof - with a few school chairs placed round it. The pilots had added some old armchairs and a settee in one corner, and in another corner were two iron beds. A black, Bakelite telephone sat on a table next to the main door so that the pilots outside could hear it. The walls were adorned with official charts and instructional posters; a map of the south east of England with operational airfields and squadrons, posters with profiles of enemy aircraft. And friendly ones too. The pilots had scrounged pots, kettles and crockery from home, knives, forks and spoons from the mess, and there were always two cardboard boxes filled with eggs, bacon, bread, jam, butter (black market), tea, milk and sugar next to the wood burner. Incredibly the station commander had complained to Tiger about the pilots missing/ignoring published meal times. Breakfast didn't even start until 7am, dining hall doors being locked to discourage early arrivals. The station commander needn't have bothered – with the days getting longer the boys were already at dispersal by 6am. Tiger sent a memo back telling the station commander that he would attempt to contact the Germans, and tell them to co ordinate their air raids with the published meal times. Luckily the kitchen staff had taken pity on the pilots and every day another two boxes of rations arrived in front of the door at first light.

Despite best intentions and ad hoc decoration, in any other setting the hut would have been a dreary place, but instead it had an incredible atmosphere - crackling with tension, gut-wrenching emotion and sometimes, incredible hilarity - occasionally all of these in the space of a few minutes. Gazzer decided to nail the swastika into the space above the main door.

"Nice to see you back Harper." Said Tiger as he marched in through the doorway just as Gazzer had climbed down from a chair in front of it, hammer in hand. Tiger threw his flying gloves into the open doorway of his office. "What did you think of the CRO?"

"Incredible place sir" replied Harper, gesturing to the swastika.

"AHA! Bloody marvellous!" roared Tiger.

15

"Same circus, different tent!" shouted Abbo to Harper as they ran at full pelt together to their Hurricanes, both parked the farthest away from the dispersal hut – it was still before lunch but the squadron had been scrambled again. "Twice in a bloody morning! Gazzer should have the farthest place, he's the fattest!"

"Too right!" replied Harper, panting, false-laughing as he bounded up the left hand side of his aircraft - a good ploy of Abbo's to crack one off and break the tension, but everyone was just as scared as last time, one of the surviving new pilots bordering on catatonic. Jones had been caught by surprise and was busy stamping on a cigarette butt at the same time as pretending to do something to the starboard tyre of the Hurricane. Then he jumped round and helped Harper. The aircraft still smelled of dope, a cellulose coating which had been painted onto the replacement fabric to shrink it down across the fuselage and flying controls - when the engine cranked and started the other familiar smells replaced it as they hit the back of Harper's throat.

The Hurricanes flew in three Vics, climbing and turning to 9000ft, heading east, vectored by the controller. Harper could see Canvey Island, then Southend with its pier, way down beneath him as the formation levelled off and bustered at full power for their interception, tracking along the south coast of Essex and out into the Channel. Despite his various prangs, Harper's mechanical sympathy couldn't help but make him concerned about using the engine at full power like this. And yet he knew that RAF bombers used the same Merlins, times two or four, running at full power for several hours at a time.

"Red section. Twenty plus bandits. 12 O'clock. 5 miles."

"Roger. 12 O'clock and 5!"

"Twenty plus?" questioned Harper to himself, his voice lost in the noise inside his Hurricane's cockpit. As much as he tried he couldn't imagine seeing twenty enemy aircraft in front of him. How could they possibly engage an enemy with a ratio of more than two-to-one against?"

"Reds tally! 12 O'clock low!"

There! Twenty or so Stukas - small dive-bombers – flying in loose formations. They were out looking for shipping. And they looked slow, vulnerable. Despite the fact that above them were at least four Messerschmitt 109s, travelling faster and weaving to stay back. The Hurricanes were already at full bore, and now they picked up even more speed as they descended, well over 300mph as the Stuka formations started to break up, the '109s turning to meet the Hurricanes head on.

"Guns, damn it!" said Harper, remembering that he forgot to arm and test. He unwound the arming ring and squirted a few rounds in the direction of the enemy, followed by his wingmen, which meant they had forgotten as well. Surprisingly one of the '109s started firing back, even though they were still a mile off. Harper decided two things in that instant; the pilot in that aircraft must be 'green', and Harper would try his hardest to shoot him down. Red section had strung out in three lines, with Harper the leader of the second three again. He rolled in a little right bank, his trajectory easing his Vic gently away and to the right of the other six aircraft. Nevertheless, ten aircraft were now hurtling into the same piece of sky. They crossed almost simultaneously and all pulled hard into various turns. Tiger's Vic had all been firing for the last couple of seconds on the way in, but Harper couldn't see if he had hit anything. In fact he couldn't see anything at all, his vision cancelled by the G force for a moment until he unloaded out of his steep turn. Harper looked around frantically. The '109s were gone but below were the Stukas. Harper chose the nearest one, diving away vertically. He followed it down, quickly caught up to it and throttled back to idle so that he didn't shoot past. Then he opened fire with a two-second burst, being careful to aim slightly high to counter the nose-down recoil. He missed anyway, re-aimed, then fired again. The bullets went home - The Stuka immediately started to disintegrate and burst into flames. Harper broke off the attack and pushed the throttle all the way forwards again, simultaneously pulling hard out of the dive and climbing back up. Maybe to see if he could get another one. Or find that '109. His speed wound down through 200mph as he traded speed for height – he felt vulnerable flying this slowly in this theatre, but there was nothing else for it if he wanted to get back into the fight. Harper checked the sun and his tail every few seconds, his head constantly turning, the skin on his neck getting progressively more sore as it chaffed against the collar of his flying jacket, the pain unnoticed. Ahead and above he spotted a turning fight – two Hurricanes on the tail of a '109: trailing smoke, straightening up, then more smoke, flames, canopy off, pilot away, no parachute, still no parachute.

"Lost your brolly," said Harper as he watched the black dot fall away to earth - he was utterly impassive. Another check on his tail, another thumb in the sun - why wasn't he feeling shit-scared? He wondered how the new ones were getting on? Were they dead yet? He hoped not, and then forgot about it.

No more bandits. Way below Harper could see a layer of cloud only a few hundred feet thick. He reasoned that was where most of Stukas must have dived. He was right. One had even gone for the option of diving all the way through and underneath the cloud layer - except that it was a fog bank. The remains of the aircraft were now at the bottom of the sea.

Harper wanted to feel euphoric about his kill, but instead he felt cheated. He already knew - because he had been told - that Stukas were easy pickings for a Hurricane. At least the cloud kept the shipping safe - the Stukas could only attack if they could see it.

Where were those bloody '109s? Harper suddenly realised something significant. For the first time, they weren't chasing after him. He was chasing them.

16

On return to dispersal the pilots had been asked to attend the mess by 8 o'clock sharp in full dress uniform. For drinks, followed by dinner at 8.30. Harper used the opportunity to introduce himself to the new boys. They both appeared more in control than earlier, though they looked detached from the main gaggle of pilots, the noise of conversation and laughter building steadily with the consumption of wine and beer.

"I'm Harper. Or Harps. And you two?"

"We're both called Smith sir" replied the smaller one; pale skin and red hair. The taller one - taller than Harper - had dark, Celtic features and shared Harper's black hair. They were both very young - under 21 for sure.

"You must have different initials, nicknames?"

"I'm Andrew." The Ginger one.

"And I'm T – Terence sir."

"Well that's easy then. Until further notice you shall be known as Smith A and Smith T. And this is Tyler F.B - which stands for Fat Bastard."

"Your neck's rather red old boy" replied Gazzer, laughing. "What you been up to - ringing it?"

"It's a bit sore actually. Probably because I look round a lot more than you. No bullet holes in your tail today I take it." Harper's ribs were sore too – he couldn't decide what hurt the most.

"You need a silk scarf – it's not just for show, man." Most fighter pilots wore silk scarves to protect their necks, a tradition started in the 1st World War. In addition some of the richer Auxiliary pilots had their uniform jackets lined with silk. 601' at Biggin Hill had gone one further. Their pilots had jackets lined with red silk - one of the reasons why they were known as the millionaire squadron.

"Why *are* we here exactly," asked Harper?

"Well, you'll have to ask Johnny. You know what he's like, but he got one of the '109s today." The four raised their glasses. "When he got back he phoned the Bobbies where the plane went down – estuary near Southend - to see what happened to the pilot. And got him on the line at the station. And John invited him for dinner! Ok'd it with Tiger first of course - that's why we're here old boy."

Johnny arrived at 8.15pm, when he knew they would all be in attendance – better to get the introductions over with all at once. He walked in with the German officer close to his right, both of them very slightly drunk.

"I'd like to introduce you all to Oberloitnant Gunther Schmidt" said Johnny, quietly but assertively. "I'm sure you will welcome him into our mess. And no he doesn't have a gun – because I've got it." Muffled laughter building, along with that of the Oberloitnant himself – he spoke very good English. An armed military policeman stayed back at the entrance to the hall – the barman had been briefed to supply him with regular drinks. One by one the pilots walked forward and shook the Oberloitnant's hand firmly. The two Polish pilots had decided to stay away. Tiger was most vociferous in his welcome.

"Sir, our honour to have you. I trust you like game – we have the most excellent roast duck this evening, brought down from a rather grand estate by Harper here. However I cannot reveal its location as I wonder that it might otherwise appear on the Fuhrer's invasion plans." Uproarious laughter joined in by Gunther himself. The Squadron had a great dinner, the guest of the evening proving to be an exceptional raconteur. The pilots avoided sensitive topics, sticking to stories about aeroplanes, women, drink and food. Eighteen bottles of red wine were drunk with the duck, boiled carrots, beans and potatoes. And then the toasts were started with brandy, brought in from private stashes. Rationing – despite the black market – meant no proper cheese or deserts. After the usual formalities it was the turn of the guest of honour to speak.

"Gentlemen, I thank you for so hearty a welcome, and not expected, however very much appreciated. I now have the duty and honour of the offer of a song or a joke. Please bear in your minds that European senses of humour are widely different, especially in the present climate." A general stirring of laughter.

"I'll do a joke if you sing a song" shouted Gazzer.

"My honour" replied the prisoner. Gazzer motioned to Tiger – a nod of approval. The Oberloitnant sat down and Gazzer stood up.

"A German couple had a perfect child. He walked at 6 months, obeyed at 12 months, could read and write at 2 years. But he didn't speak. The German parents worried. So they threw a big party for him at 3 years; clowns, a circus, ponies and a big cake - still not a word from the child. At 4 years, they held a quiet party. And everything *was* quiet until desert. The child looked up and said 'this apple strudel is very sour.' The parents exclaimed; 'you can speak!?' And the child replied; "yes, but until now everything has been satisfactory." The growing shouts of laughter echoed out of the mess hall, the German officer with tears in his eyes as he stood up again. Finally the room was quiet enough for the German to reply.

"And now, the only song I know. Gentlemen, after me if you please, or shoot me;

> *The flag flies high on the masthead.*
>
> *We'll sing for the freedom of the Reich.*
>
> *No longer will we tremble… at England's military might.*
>
> *So give to me your hand Fraulein.*
>
> *Your lily white hand Fraulein.*
>
> *For tonight we march against England.*
>
> *England… England's island shores, island shores, island shores. Seig Heil!*

"Seig Heil!" shouted the squadron pilots. Now they had the verse.

"And if I fall in battle and sink to the bottom of the sea – splish splosh!"

"Splish splosh! Splish splosh!" sang the pilots.

"Remember this my darling... my blood was spilled for thee.

So give to me your hand Fraulein.

Your lily white hand Fraulein.

For tonight we march against England.

England... England's island shores, island shores, island shores.
Seig Heil!

"SEIG HEIL! SEIG HEIL!" shouted the pilots, in unison, the laughter accompanying it raucous and friendly. So lucky that the Polish pilots had declined the invitation.

17

"I really can't believe it. Bloody cheek" said Rhino, still bandaged up, warming himself by the stove at dispersal. First light again, earlier by the day.

"What's that?" replied Johnny, resting his head in his hands, seated in one of the big armchairs. And thinking that if he warmed himself up too much, he would throw himself up as well.

"The kraut said that all the fighter boys tell their Intel's and C/Os that they got shot down by Spitfires. Really, bloody ridiculous."

"Bloody Spitfire snobbery" said Jones as he stuffed his face as close to the stove as he dare to get a light for his roll up. The shabby hut was nevertheless considered an extension of the officer's mess and he shouldn't really be in there.

"That's the one Jonesy," said Harper in an attempt to brush over, and ushering him out of the hut with a mug of tea before anyone could kick off.

"Jones is right," said Abbo. "We're doing a lot more metal than the Spits. We get the bombers and the Stukas, plus the fighters. They go get the fighters and the glory

"All I want is a fair fight. Fighter on fighter" said Smith A, completely out of the blue.

"If you end up with a fair fight then you've set it up wrong" replied Abbo. He was correct. The highest-scoring aces had no time for fair fights - they would kill at 50 yards from behind if given the chance, previously unnoticed. If they missed they would often dive away to escape rather than get into a turning fight. The idea of chivalry was anathema to them. Something from the first war - not this one.

"I feel sorry for Gunther – holed up in a shitty little wooden hut in Dunstable, for months maybe" said Johnny.

"A bit like this then" replied Smith A. Everyone looked up in astonishment, Abbo, Gazzer, Harper, John and Rhino exchanging looks of surprise and grudging approval at the assertiveness of the new boy. Harper wondered if perhaps he might survive after all.

"Can I have a word Harper?" Tom looked up to see Tiger beckoning at the door of his office. Trouble? He wasn't aware of what it might be this time. Harper walked in sheepishly, Tiger shutting the door quietly behind him.

"I need a job done. It's a new one to you maybe, even though you're getting on a bit - don't suppose you've been to many funerals in your time. Parents still alive?" It sounded something like a perverse quiz.

"Not sure, what - sorry, what is it sir?"

"I would like you to be squadron representative at Howell's funeral. Any objection?"

"No. Except who is he?"

"Exactly. That's why I want *you* to go. Except you mean who *was* he. Joined with the Smiths yesterday. And got shot down yesterday."

"OK, got it. Not an issue sir." Actually Harper hadn't been to a funeral before. The concept was dreadful - even though he didn't know the corpse.

"How did they…? I mean what happened to him?"

"Got bounced by two '109s. His fuel tank was hit, probably. Exploded in the air. Went in off the coast at Hastings."

"I heard all about the crack up, just didn't catch the name yet. That's why I… What I'm trying to say is… What will we have a funeral with, if you see what I mean?"

"175lbs-worth of sandbags and some of his flying kit. Better for the family than the reality of it all."

As he marched out, Harper suppressed mourning - easy if he didn't know the man. Instead he set his mind wondering if it would be appropriate to attend the RAF funeral of a fallen fighter pilot on a German army motorbike. The black paint was still on – he hadn't had a spare minute – but it would only take one prolonged glance by one of the guests. So, no was the answer. Harper returned to Tiger's office.

"Sir, any chance I could borrow your car to go the funeral. My bike might not go down very well."

"Absolutely Harper. Go and have a look around it, by all means - I'll give you the keys in the morning. And don't crash the bloody thing."

There was a little activity at dispersal as Harper walked into the main area of the hut - the addition of a tannoy and a billiard table. Rhino had had a whip round. The effect on the pilots was out of all scale to the input. Immediately two teams assembled for a major tournament, accompanied by the music of Cole Porter. Harper deferred, more interested in having a look round Tiger's car. It was parked behind the hut – a 1932 Alvis Firefly Special. At first glance she looked like a 1920s Bentley sports car, just a bit more modern. The car was painted in British Racing Green of course. The winged motif on the top of the radiator was the give-away to the marque, surrounding a metal water temperature gauge ring with a needle inside it, visible from the cockpit. Alvis aficionados would also point out the inverted metal chevron stripes on the front of the radiator.

Harper looked inside the cockpit. The car had four forward gears in an 'H' and one left and up for reverse. The clutch, brake and accelerator pedals were in the right place for modern motor cars. On the right of the cockpit, underneath the instrument panel was a 'fly away' handbrake; squeeze the lever and ratchet it up to the park position, another squeeze and let it fly forward to release. The steering wheel was a four-pronged wire affair – at it centre was a large disc with a cruising throttle lever, advance/retard lever for engine starting and light switch, spaced out in a 'Y' pattern. The big starting button was on the instrument panel, not unlike the one in his Hurricane.

Jones caught up with Harper as he slowly walked round the beautiful machine.

"Got the de Wilde rounds in your kite sir." Jones was back from smoking his cigarette behind the hut.

"Eh?"

"I've loaded the de Wildes in your Brownings. Plus a few smokers at the end of the 9 yards, so you'll know when you're running out."

"Sorry I was distracted for a moment. What's 9 yards?"

"You've got 9 yards of ammo in each wing. And the boss said to put some tracer at the end so you'll know when you're running out."

"Right oh. Got that. And thanks - might be able to do a bit more damage eh?" Suddenly Harper could hear the phone ring on the other side of the hut. His heart started beating faster – this happened *every* time he heard a phone now, even the one on the bar at The Ship. Then the scramble bell was ringing, and he was running into the hut, colliding with someone on the way out, picking up his Mae West, throwing it on as he ran back out of the door, reaching inside his flying jacket pocket to check that his flying goggles were there, pulling them out and stretching them over his head, Jones wheezing behind him, losing ground.

18

What did 'multiple contacts' mean anyway? That's what the controller had just said on the radio. Five aircraft? Fifty? Harper tried to answer his own question as he climbed past 10,000 feet, and went into automatic again; clipping the oxygen mask to his face, selecting 100% on the regulator, arming his guns, testing them.

The tracer looked the same, the other rounds were still invisible, de Wilde or otherwise. The nose of the Hurricane recoiled down, just as before.

"Red section. Targets 12 O'clock. 5 miles."

"12 O'clock, 5 miles Red section" replied Tiger. Harper was Red 2, on his left. Gazzer, Red 3 on his right. And Smith T was Red 4, weaving around at the back - a Tail End Charlie. It was Group's answer to the criticism coming in from the squadrons about flying in Vics of threes. The proposal was that the Tail End Charlies' would look after the rear of the section as they concentrated on their attacks. Unfortunately no one would be looking after the tail of the Tail End Charlie. They would also tend to be the new pilots on the squadron, until they had honed their formation skills. Whatever the reality, Harper felt happier to have this extra ship weaving behind him.

"Red section. Bandits 12 O'clock high. Ten '109s! TALLY HO!" shouted Tiger. Harper couldn't see them yet, as usual. Tiger always saw them first. Ten? Two more unaccounted for. Tiger banked right then left to check underneath, and then started climbing, the other three following, instinctively widening out so that they could spend more time looking instead of formating. Harper checked the sun – it was so bright his eyes started watering, even behind his tinted flying goggles. He tried to block the sun with his thumb but it was no use – two fingers were better today. Nothing up there – he would check again in a few seconds.

Harper looked forwards again. YES! He could see them. Tiger was climbing and turning, Red section was now at the same altitude as the enemy but yet to accelerate, despite full throttle. The Messerschmitts had seen the Hurricanes too – they were turning and closing the distance. The closing speed was immense, despite the Hurricanes only accelerating slowly back to maximum level speed. At 1000 yards range – 3 seconds away - everyone seemed to start firing at the same time. Harper flinched as some tracer went just past his canopy to the right, each successive bullet getting closer. Then it stopped. In the moment taken for the Messerschmitts to flash past his cockpit Harper noticed that they had bright yellow engine cowlings and propeller spinners - inexplicably it made them look even more frightening - and he could see the face of the '109 pilot closest to him as he passed. All of that in a fraction of a second. The '109 arced upwards behind him at 400mph. Harper did the same - because he was slower he could loop tighter. He might get a chance. As he unloaded the stick at the top of the loop his vision came back. THERE! Right in front, a '109 rolling out to the left. Harper pulled and turned with it. No doubt that the pilot had seen him, its turn tightened to over 5G. A classic turning fight again. Harper took quick short stabs of breath and re-tensed his stomach between each one as he carried on pulling the stick. The '109 was accelerating away but it didn't matter. Harper was closing the turn, his nose now pointing out in front of the Messerschmitt. He hit the gun button – nothing for a moment, then tracer going the right way. And then he saw little yellow explosions dancing across the surface of the left wing, an instant before the most enormous explosion that Harper had ever seen tore the wing off, the fighter rolling and diving out of control.

"YES! Y E S!" shouted Harper to himself, a broad, amazed smile on his face. No time to waste though – he started looking up towards the sun, then over towards his tail as he unloaded the bank, just in time to see the vivid canon flashes on the yellow nose of a Messerschmitt. WHUMP! WHUMP! BANG! CLANG! CLANG! CLANG! Harper screamed with pain as his right foot was pushed off its rudder pedal, his leg straightened by the force of a bullet which tore through his calf, his shin smashing upwards into the underside of the instrument panel. An instant later a shell fragment sliced across the right side of his face – its sonic shock wave smacking him in the side of the head as it passed by. His mind went into a catatonic state for a second - a seizure in time and space - completely overloaded by stress and sensory inputs… Then Harper came back.

He was still pulling on the stick.

Something was wrong with the side of his face.

He wasn't being fired at any more.

Now Harper was back in a state of useful attention. He looked round – the sky seemed empty. The '109 had passed below and ahead of him after its strafing attack out of the sun, unable to get rid of the additional 150mph on top of Harper's airspeed.

Why didn't his leg hurt? Why couldn't he move his foot? Harper could taste blood in his mouth, the smell of hot coolant in his nose. Then he realised that he was slowing down. He rolled the aircraft onto its back and pulled the stick back. Suddenly he felt a wave of heat pass through the cockpit, front to back, a moment before he was thrown forward in his straps as the engine partially seized, individual propeller blades becoming visible as they rotated perversely slowly in front of the engine cowling. Most of the engine oil had gone down the side of the fuselage. The fighter was still diving at 250mph even with no engine power - Harper managed a glance at the Air Speed Indicator and decided to keep the vertical part of the dive going for longer - less acceleration without the engine meant that it would take more time to get to Vne. He finally pulled out of the dive at 2000ft and levelled off – Christ, his leg hurt - the aircraft slowing down but still a long way above stall speed, maybe enough time for him to find somewhere to land. He noticed that his right eye was closing, the side of his face throbbing in the same place where it had been hurting after his car accident a few days ago. A lifetime ago.

Harper looked down through a patchy layer of cloud. He was over a town. Which one? Who cared? Nowhere to land - absolutely nowhere. The Air Speed Indicator needle was winding back - soon he'd have to stick the nose down, or run out of flying speed and stall. How slow would he be able to go? Harper looked out across the right wing – it had two, 6in-diameter holes in the upper surface, just in front of the starboard aileron. Now Harper realised that he had been holding the right wing up with two thirds left stick. He wouldn't be able to come in slowly, the damaged right wing would stall well above normal speed. Still nowhere to land – why hadn't he jumped out? Harper knew why - because he was scared of heights. Like many pilots – ridiculous, but true. Maybe that's what the attraction of flying had been in the first place. Harper smiled for a second, his mind drifting. The fear was gone. This was it.

THERE! In front and below, a large field of allotments between two rows of Victorian houses. That would do! Harper pulled round in a wide right turn, the nose going down to maintain 90mph - as slow as he dare to go. Now he used full left stick plus some left rudder to get back to wings level – his right leg wouldn't have been able to push the rudder pedals if the turn and recovery had been the other way round. Harper put his right hand on the H selector and moved it right and down for flap. Nothing happened. No hydraulics. So, no flap – another reason to keep the speed up on the approach. He had already decided to leave the wheels up – if they dug into soft earth he could end up on his back, or worse. Harper lined up parallel with the houses and aimed to touchdown in the first third of the field, so that he didn't hit a 10ft high brick wall at the nearest end of it. The Hurricane glided in, nicely lined up – Tiger would be proud. He'd made the best of it. Then, at the last moment, as Harper pulled the stick back to reduce descent rate, the right wing stalled and dropped, clipping the top of the wall, the aircraft swerving to the right and crashing to the ground, ploughing sideways across the allotment field. Mud, fences, bushes, then something solid, a concrete bunker – the Hurricane hit it side-on. The aircraft stopped dead, Harper continuing sideways in the seat an instant longer - as much as his straps would let him - until he jerked to a halt, his head thumping into the side of the canopy. A cloud of dust slowly descended on the remains of the aircraft. The engine was steaming, smoking. The fuselage tank still had fuel in it, now leaking down the inside of the cockpit behind the instrument panel. Not that Harper noticed.

But he could hear something - the raised voices of excited children. It reminded him of being in a playground in his childhood. The noise was getting louder. Maybe they were getting nearer? And then an adult voice. Maybe it was the teacher?

"Keep away you little sods! There's a dead pilot in there."

19

At Dan's house, out on the lake in a little rowing boat: Harper was lying on his back, a cushion behind his head. He had a glass of champagne – he had to tip his head forward slightly to sip from the glass. Some of it ran down the side of his face.

A girl was there, rowing for him. What was her name? Lucy, that was it. No, no, no. Linda. It was Linda.

"What did you just call me?"

"I didn't say a thing - I was just looking up at the clouds." He decided to sit up.

"What did you just call me?"

"Oh give it a rest." He took a large swig of champagne. It was running down the side of his face again. How did that happen?

"What did you just call me?"

Harper touched the side of his face where it was wet. It didn't feel right. He peered over the side of the boat and saw his reflection in the mirror calm water – there was a large hole in his cheek, the champagne running out of it.

"CHRIFE" said Harper, opening one eye. He was in bed. He was in bed in a hospital. There was something in his mouth, he couldn't open his right eye, his right leg hurt like hell, he couldn't sit up. "WHAD THE FUCH?" exclaimed Harper, very alarmed.

"Calm down old boy!" said Gazzer. "All ok" beckoning a nurse whilst holding Harper down – one hand on his chest - gently but firmly. "You're not supposed to talk. So don't! They've put some padding in your mouth." Memories of the nightmare came back – Harper went to sit up again, the alarm rising.

"Stop it man. You're ok - just a graze. Your eye's ok too – you took a hell of a whack. And your leg." Harper was flailing his right arm. "Write it down old boy" handing him a pencil and note pad from the side table. Harper slumped back down on the bed, his memory coming back. He could feel his fingers and toes – all there, and the aching wound in his leg, his head, and his bloody ribs - it was like the death of a thousand cuts. Harper took the pencil and paper from Gazzer in his right hand, slowly turning onto his left side – Gazzer had let go of him – making a space on the left side of the mattress so that he could put the paper down. He began to write.

'How long have I been here?'

"Two days man. Sleeping like a baby."

'Where did I land?'

"Dagenham, just up the road from the base – not what I'd call a landing though" said Gazzer, trying to look stern, failing, and smiling.

'Am I ok?'

"Absolutely perfect. You were knocked senseless. Concussion." Gazzer was right. Now the whole of Harper's head hurt - not just one side.

'The others ok?' A short silence.

"Let's talk about it later man." Harper snatched the note pad back.

'Who?'

"Bloody hell old boy... Tiger." Harper's one open eye widened. "He went down at the same time as you did. We thought the world was coming to an end - we thought you'd both bought it. Bloody glad to see you!"

76

'Is he in here?'

"...When I saw ten of them, I thought there *must* be two somewhere we couldn't see, in the sun. I got it wrong – there were six. You got bounced and so did Tiger. Two of the fuckers, taking turns." Harper held the pad up and stabbed the last line he had written with the pencil. "He's in a burns ward – he's gone old boy."

A long silence then, forced, brighter; "New C/O came yesterday – Wing Commander David Cole. Getting on a bit (32) but a nice chap, in from 72 squadron." Harper didn't look like he was listening. His left eye was peering out of the sash window, across the lawn. "Rhino flew again this morning – good as he'll ever be! Got to get well soon – we need you. New pilots again today. We're running out of old boys. Think of all the brides you haven't had yet – that'll get you up and about. Every day you don't get back I'm going round Harper's Arse End on your bike, sideways."

"Sir, sorry but we've got another visitor" said the nurse. She and the doctor had been standing just out of the way behind a curtain. Gazzer had been doing a better job than they could. "Its only one at a time I'm afraid. Regulations."

"Not a problem at all" replied Gazzer. "Get well old boy. See you in a couple of days." Harper raised his hand and Gazzer held on to it for just a little bit longer than a normal handshake, before walking out.

The new visitor walked in. It was Jones - looking sheepish. He was holding a bunch of flowers with a clumsy, white tissue cone at the base. Harper nodded, smiling broadly, blown away.

"Evening sir. Good to see you." Jones waited until the nurse walked out of the room and then ejected the flowers onto the bed, unwrapping the tissue to reveal Harper's hip flask, slightly dented and filled with scotch. "Best medicine I've ever known. Private stash from the pilots."

Harper's eyebrows had already gone high when he saw Jones, in conjunction with a broad grin. Now they went higher. Then down.

"I know what you're thinking – I brought this" said Jones, rummaging into his overall pocket and producing a long, bent steel pipe wrapped in more tissue. "It's a fuel line!" Jones inserted it into the neck of the hip flask. "That'll do the trick." Harper put the open end of the pipe in his mouth to the side, like a tobacco pipe, and sucked on the smooth, amber liquid. It tasted wonderful.

20

Harper slept until well into the following morning. He had the nightmare about the burning Spitfire again in the middle of the night but it only woke him up for a few minutes - what was it about recurring nightmares that made them so creepy? - and then he had slept soundly. In the few minutes it took him to be fully awake he thought about Tiger - Harper felt guilty for mucking him around.

Ginger killed, Rhino injured, Tiger, now him. He hadn't had an incident free flight yet. Is this how it would always be? How many more would they lose while he was convalescing? What, who would be next, maybe another one of the new boys, or another of the old ones?

"Bruddy shuck up" Harper said to himself.

"I'm sorry?" replied the nurse at the bottom of the bed.

"Uuuurgh" replied Harper shaking his head from side to side.

"Good to see that you're awake... Look I think we can take that padding out of your mouth now. It was just to stabilise the stitches." The nurse walked round to the side of the bed, peeled back the bandage on the side of Harper's face, made a *good* noise, and then made him open his mouth. "Its probably best for you to pull it out yourself" she said, reeling back slightly. The gauze had soaked up some of the whisky from last night. Harper put his fingers in his mouth and pulled it all out in one go. The nurse gave him a glass of water and a bowl to rinse out the bits of cotton wool which had escaped from the packing.

"Christ that's better," said Harper, still spitting little bits of cotton. His cheek felt stiff, but didn't hurt as much now that skin wasn't being stretched by the packing. "I'm not vain or anything, but will I have a scar?"

"In your leg, a big one - front and back! Bearing in mind that you were hit in the face by a bullet, another in your leg, and crashed in a plane, I think you've come off lightly. You'll have what they call a duelling scar on your cheek. Don't worry, the ladies will love it." Despite his closed, blackened right eye, the bandages on his face, the bandaged ribs and a plaster cast on his right leg, Harper realised that the nurse quite fancied him.

Harper spent the day reading. First the papers; there was a good bit about Lord Beaverbrook - a brilliant businessman who Churchill had personally given the task of fighter production, knowing that he would bypass the petty bureaucracy of government and the upper echelons of the RAF. This was in the Daily Express – Beaverbrook owned that too. His son Max was flying Spitfires with 601 Squadron.

Then there were two letters from Eric – his younger brother – written months apart. The first one was addressed from his Elementary Flight Training School.

Only to be read by shits   *L.A.C Harper, E J*
                                              No 22   E.F.T.S
                                              Newmarket Rd
                                              Cambridge

Dear Tom,

There was a young man of Kent.

Whose tool was remarkably bent.

To save himself trouble, he stuffed it in double; instead of coming he went.

Since writing last, a great, a very great thing has happened. Eric has flown, Eric has spent a whole 2 ½ hrs in the air. And Eric Harper has done exercises 1, 1a, 2, 3, 4, 5, 9 (I've no more idea of what those numbers mean than you have.)

Continuing in pencil;

Pen has run out. Anyway, Eric was posted to above address on Saturday. He spent 6 instead of 7hrs at I. T. W and missed his navigation exam (a fucking good thing.) He was posted all by himself to a strange flight & has been feeling rather lonely. A bugger, actually, because six of us (all one room at aber) had just got used to each other. I mean 3 of us used to fight every night & the other 3 knew it was best not to interfere.

I arrived here on Sun: about midday, 12hrs: after the rest of the flight, after travelling since 6 p.m on Sat. I did fuck all on Sun & slept in a marquee surrounded by motor bikes, pee-buckets, benches etc : Last night & tonight I'm sleeping in a house on a bed with 4 blankets & its sodding cold. In fact I haven't had a decent night since Thurs. anyway, some of the sods in the flight aren't bad & I should be able to educate them a bit.

You'll be pleased to hear that we do Morse here. I can just get up to six's. We did it at I.T.W, not very seriously though & although had an exam, as the corporal who taught us also marked our efforts, it was in his own interests to see that we all got pretty near 100%. We have to pass out here at 8's (groups of mixed letters & figures) on the bugger, 6's on the aldis. With any luck; I should manage it.

We had a hygiene exam : at aber & one of the questions was; what are the dangers of Carnal Sexual Intercourse & how can they be avoided. You can imagine how we let ourselves go!

The grub here is bloody good! (For the R.A.F.) we get as much jam & bread & butter as we want. This was the chief shortage at aber. We get one day off per week , probably Fri: & get Sat & sun evenings. Other nights we're not allowed out of camp & have to attend "Evening Study" from 7.30 pm to ...

Harper couldn't read the next few lines - the letter had got wet.

...years. Still, wait till I bugger up Tonbridge High St in a Spitfire (some hopes!)

A lesbian maid of Khartoum

Took a nancy boy up to her room

Before she turned out the light

She said, "let's get this right:

Who does what, and with which, and to whom?"

Cheers you old sod

The next one was from quite a while later but still a long time ago –
Harper wondered why there had been a delay in posting or receiving it.
Also the airbase had been crossed out;

Just in case the censor gets it ➔   *R.A.F XXXXXX*

Nr. Cirencester

Glos.

Weds 19ᵗʰ

Dear Tom

*Now I come to think of it, I believe it's your turn to write to me. Still,
now I've started, I might as well go on.*

*Actually, I'm so glad to be alive, I feel like writing to everybody. Usual
trouble, of course, we crashed last night. My instructor & I had just
taken off, wheels up when we hit the ground again. We bounced up,
covered about 300x & then came down & folded up against a stone
wall.*

Harper was now sitting bolt upright in bed.

*I was perfectly OK, my instructor was cut about the face & concussed.
He just sat in the plane, swore for about 5 minutes: when we had
stopped, & then asked me if we had been landing or taking off!*

*I went out to look at the plane this morning, starb'd wing just isn't there,
starb'd engine is under the cockpit & altogether it's a helluva mess,
completely written off.*

*My instructor can't remember anything, I don't know what happened.
It's amazing the way these things happen at night.*

*I've still got to go solo at night, & do 9 night landings. With luck we
should be out of here by next Sat: week. Nearly everyone has about 1
crash or forced landing here, I feel I've had my share.*

I still feel a bit shaken, I was nearly sick when I saw the remains this morning. The Chief Flying Instructor was there, of course he shat on me, told me it was careless flying & I didn't manage to get a decent look at the plane. The C.F.I couldn't shit on my instructor, of course, as he's in hospital, so he chose the next best thing.

Mary's not going as well as she should be. I'm having a job trying to get the tappets adjusted. There's too much play at the moment and she's rattling a helluva lot.

We've had fairly decent weather here lately, done quite a bit of flying. One poor sod in our course was low flying on Sunday & beat up a Wing Commander from this station. He's been suspended & is waiting a court martial, bloody bad luck but a golf course on a Sunday is a silly place to choose.

We hope to get leave when we finish here, I expect I shall be one of the last to go now, they probably won't let me fly tomorrow night, just to be awkward.

Love to everyone

Harper decided to write back as soon as he could get some paper and a pen from one of the nurses. He hadn't been in touch with anyone since he was posted, not even his parents, even though he had promised. It felt to Harper as if he had been wrapped up in his own little war. He felt like he had grown in on himself - displaced, empty and alone. Rhino walked in just at the right time.

"God look at the state of you."

"Bugger off."

"Good thing I reckon – I'll get more chance pulling the girls when I take you down the pub."

"You couldn't pull the knot out of a shoe lace."

"Seriously, glad to see you're alright. That was quite a prang." Rhino was wearing his extra large flying jacket to cover his large body - like Gazzer he'd got to the hospital using Harper's motorbike. The flying goggles came in useful too. Rhino looked over his shoulder and then held out his arm as if to shake Harper's hand, but in an exaggerated fashion. "Little present for you." Up his sleeve was a bottle. "These are the tears we weep when we think, of the past, the present and the future" he toasted, as they chinked teacups filled with whisky.

21

The next morning Harper woke up late again. Depressed again. He lay on his back with his eyes closed, for the hell of it reciting a piece from Hamlet which matched his mood.

"I have of late, but wherefore I know not, lost all my mirth, forgone all custom of exercises; and indeed it goes so heavily with my disposition that this goodly frame, the earth, seems to me a sterile promontory, this most excellent canopy, the air, look you, this brave overhanging firmament, this majestical roof fretted with golden fire, why, it appears no other thing to me than a foul and pestilent congregation of vapours."

Despite his sadness, Harper was becoming mildly pleased with himself.

"What a piece of work is a man! How noble in reason! how infinite in faculty! In form and moving how express and admirable! In action how like an angel! In apprehension how like a god! The beauty of the world! The paragon of animals! And yet, to me is this quintessence of dust?"

Come on, don't blow it now. "Man delights not me: no, nor women neither, though by your smiling you seem to say so."

"Steady on - I'll slit my wrists." Harper opened his eyes and saw Rhino standing at the door. He stretched, sat up and yawned his first voluble words of the day;

"Have you been here all night? Bit keen." His eyes! - Harper realised that his right eye had opened as well. The bruising on the side of his face had spread out; black, red, and yellow around the edges - it actually looked worse to Rhino than the day before. But the swelling had gone down, and now he could see clearly out of his right eye.

"Yes I slept under your bed. Listen – I noticed you were a bit down yesterday. That's why I drove back again - I've got some news!" Harper could see that he was deliriously excited.

"You're getting married."

"Sod that! No, we're getting… we're getting…" Rhino trying to eke it out as much as possible.

"Out with it?"

"… Spitfires! We're getting Spitfires!" Rhino danced a little jig around the bottom of Harper's bed: a sweet dance for such a big man, all Spitfire snobbery forgotten.

"But how?! How does it work?" asked Harper, smiling so much that his cheek hurt.

"A call came in from Group yesterday. David Cole told us last night at dinner. He flew Spits on 72 Squadron so that might have something to do with it. I don't know. Abbo reckons its because we've bent so many Hurry's lately, and Beaverbrook's getting 300 Spits out a month - its easier to replace the whole lot! It means we can compete with the fighters. You've got to get well soon old boy – can you *imagine* what they must be like!" Rhino made sweeping gestures with one hand, a mug of tea in the other.

"Are there any two-seaters?" Harper was thinking about training.

"Rare as rocking horse shit - next year maybe. You just get in and go."

"Fan-bloody-tastic. I can't believe it!! When?"

"C/O said that the ATA will start delivering them in a couple of days if the weather holds. In another week we'll be a… *Spitfire squadron!"*

"I need a big favour. I need you to get the bus home."

After Rhino left, Harper spent the day writing letters; to his parents (to thank them for moving him to a private room), Jane (he was looking forward to meeting up again), Lucy (he'd heard about what happened in the pub and understood why she was so upset, but he really had finished with Linda and hoped that they could see each other some time), Linda (he'd heard what happened in the pub and hoped that she would bugger off) and another to the hospital administrator. He had a small dinner of bacon, eggs and chips, then waited until 'lights out' at 8pm before getting the pocket knife out of his flying jacket. It was on a hat stand beyond the bottom of the bed - quite a chore to get it quietly when hindered by a plaster cast from ankle to thigh. Harper opened the sawing blade. He started slicing across the knee of the plaster cast, slowly, religiously. He was surprised how quickly he went through what he had previously considered to be as impenetrable as concrete. He worked systematically, cutting through the ¾ inch coating, all the way around the back - that's where it got tricky. A couple of times he caught his skin with the blade and cursed quietly. Finally the top half came away in a 9 inch-deep ring. Then Harper started sawing down the front of the ring from thigh to knee. Finally he prised the ring open with his hands and pulled it away from his leg. The next part called for more courage. He wiggled his toes a few times to see what the wounds would feel like with the new freedom in his tendons and muscles. There was a slightly strange sensation from his shin - something tugging at something else under the skin. Best not wiggle them then. Still on the bed, Harper brought his knee up almost to his chin and started cutting the plaster cast around his ankle. This took a little longer – the plaster was thicker – but when he had worked all the way round the piece came off easily, like taking off a clog. Harper taped round the top and bottom of the cast with a reel of sticking plaster that he had stolen from a trolley earlier in the afternoon. Then he used the cutting blade of his pocket knife to slice up the back of the right leg of his uniform trousers - half way up to the knee - so that they would ride over the remains of the cast. Harper lifted himself off the bed and tried walking a few steps; that same sensation in his shin, fading, and a dull ache in his calf, growing. But good enough - Harper spent several minutes clearing up the dust and debris, and then continued to dress. Finally he put the letter to the administrator on his bedside table.

The drive on his R71 across to The Ship was Harper's most memorable to date (Rhino *did* catch the bus.) As the bike barked and blatted along the London Road he felt liberated, full of hope. The feeling increased the farther he got from Dagenham. Harper arrived at The Ship at 9pm – his subterfuge had taken exactly 1 hour. He parked the bike by the front door and straightened himself as much as possible to disguise his limp: he could feel a hot, sticky patch at the back of the plaster cast, but the ache was bearable. Harper trusted his own body to tell him if something was serious – one of the reasons why he avoided painkillers. Ironically the cold air had made the rest of him feel better, particularly his swollen face - it actually felt as if the swelling had gone down (it hadn't.) The yells and laughter Harper received when he walked through the front door of The Ship only served to intensify his feelings. Gazzer, Abbo and Rhino were there, drinking pints of bitter, Koval and Doogy, the two Polish pilots polishing off a bottle of Vodka between them. And in the corner, with a half, the new C/O.

"Boss, this is Flt Lt Tom Harper, fresh out of hospital!" said Gazzer. Harper leaned forward to shake David Cole's hand, and staggered slightly on his bad leg. The C/O looked slightly alarmed - the combination of bruising and bandaging on Harper's face and his ripped trousers weren't the best of first impressions.

"Sir, sorry about my uniform but I will telephone my tailor and", pointing to the bandage on his face; "…this is due off tomorrow."

"Ooh, I can't wait. I'll see you in the morning Harper. 0715, if that's ok with you?" as if it mattered to the C/O if it wasn't. Harper couldn't tell how serious he was. Whatever - he found a convenient chair to sit down on, a barstool to prop up his leg, and sank a very large whisky.

22

AT 0715, Harper was standing to attention in the new C/Os office. He had taken off the bandage to his cheek, revealing a long, thin scar across it with eight stitches. His face looked terribly bruised but still better for not having bandages. And now the swelling had gone down, a little.

"Stand at ease Harper. Would you like a seat?" asked the C/O, goading.

"No sir. I'm fine." Actually he wasn't comfortable at all – his right leg was aching, the sticky patch growing again.

"Don't give me that. Sit down." Harper did as he was told. "You look a complete mess. My adjutant woke me up at 0600 this morning – he received a call from the hospital in the early hours, asking where you were. And if you were still alive, no doubt! You discharged yourself - I was a headmaster before this job. I know how to deal with buffoonery."

"I didn't discharge myself sir. I transferred myself to my family doctor." The C/O looked confused. At once, Harper felt stronger.

"What *are* you talking about?"

"It's the right of every citizen of Great Britain to choose where he receives medical treatment. I chose my doctor. And he will send you a medical certificate if you want it. I'm fit to fly sir" - all bullshit of course.

"No you're bloody not! What does your family doctor know about the physical medical condition required to fly an aircraft?"

"My family doctor is a pilot. He taught me to fly sir"- this was true.

"Anyway I thought you were Irish" clutching at straws now.

"Not for well over a century sir, proud of the heritage though". And, labouring the point; "My great, great, great grandfather fought in the Napoleonic War, on the English side of course. He was a sergeant in a rifle brigade. After the war he came back with rather a lot of bounty and bought an estate, which…"

"Report to the M/O Harper! We'll let him deal with it and you! Dismissed!"

Harper marched out of the office as best he could, limped out of the hut – he could hear Cole Porter as he went through, this time with a scratch on the record - and climbed onto his motorbike. He drove past the medical centre, out through the gates and off to the local hospital. The roads were deserted and he covered the 5 miles in less than 10 minutes, sometimes driving at the bike's top speed of 60mph. At the hospital, after a painful trudge around the wards, he finally found Lucy walking out of the staff canteen.

"Christ Tom! What happened to you?"

"Don't worry – little bit of a crack up. I've got a nice new Spitfire to fly soon. I did send you a letter from hospital, (*this* hospital, posted about 5 minutes before) and I'm sorry about the ex' thing... Look, I need a bit of help. Would you give me a hand?"

After an hour's wait, Lucy got her morning break early and smuggled Harper into a private room through a side door. She cut off the rest of his plaster, checked and re-cleaned his leg wounds – his calf *was* bleeding, but not badly – and re-plastered his leg from his knee to just above the ankle, so that he could still use his joints. She used half the thickness of plaster than normal.

"This isn't going to be very strong. So if you fall over or bash it into anything you'll be back to square one - you could burst your stitches. And you'll have to come back in a few days to have them all out anyway." The plaster set hard in forty minutes. When he practised walking, Harper's limp had almost gone – he knew that he could

90

eliminate it entirely for a short time to fool the Medical Officer. Lucy used her medical kit to stitch up his uniform trousers. Then Harper drove back to base, directly to the medical centre.

The old (46) Medical Officer didn't even notice Harper's leg (he was only told to strip down to his waist,) concentrating instead on the facial wounds, and the vision in his bruised eye. The M/O said something about a detached retina at one point but then changed his mind.

"You'll be good to go in a couple of days," he said, finally. "Just be careful you don't damage the stitches with your mask. Rub a bit of antiseptic on it, just to be on the safe side.

"My face?"

"No, the mask! I'll have them out for you in a few days."

When Harper returned to dispersal, the C/O was less impressed.

"I will call the M/O personally this afternoon to check this. You're not going near another Hurricane - first Spitfire arrives in two days or so. Get your head in the books in the meantime. I appreciate your enthusiasm Harper, but you or anyone won't bamboozle me. I've got my eye on you."

"Sir."

"And one more thing."

"Sir?"

"Stay out of the pub. The general public seeing you like that – its bad for morale."

"Sir. Off to the tailor this afternoon sir."

"It's not the bloody tailor I'm worried about!"

As he walked back into the main area of the dispersal hut, Harper was greeted by the mute smiles and thumbs up of his comrades.

"Harper you need to meet the new ones," said Gazzer. "This is Flt Lt Jock McKay - transferred from 72' with the boss."

"Nice to meet you" said Harper.

"Bloody hell. Hello" said Jock. "Nice to meet you!"

"Only a scratch" replied Harper. He figured correctly that McKay was around 27. He was Dark-haired, 5ft 10in, wiry and exceedingly fit. Harper hoped he liked whisky.

"This is P/O Peter Pollock. Joined a while ago actually but been off sick." The man had dirty buttons on his tunic and wore his cap on one side of his head. He was dark haired, slim build and about 20. As much as he tried not to, Harper took an instant dislike to him.

"Blimey, you look like shit," said Pollock.

"Well thank you very much – glad to see you've played your own appearance down to match", replied Harper.

"And this is Sqn Ldr Bruce Hatton" added Gazzer quickly. "

"A pleasure sir" said Harper, looking for somewhere to sit down, thinking that Hatton was quite a bit older than the rest of them. Nevertheless, he still looked youthful, maybe fitter than some pilots in their 'teens.

"Bruce is a transfer from the Navy" said Gazzer. "Remember when I was a cadet? Bruce was one of the instructors. He's one of our most senior pilots."

"Here it comes," said Bruce.

"…He was one of the first naval aviators. He flew a hot air balloon off the poop deck of the Mary Rose." There was a general laugh. Hatton was 40.

"You'll be old one day," said Harper to Gazzer, hitching his leg up on an arm of the old settee that he was now sprawled across.

"No he won't" replied Abbo. "His heart has to work twice as hard as the rest of us, just to move that humungus mass around. I doubt he'll make 40."

"None of us will make 40" replied Smith T.

23

Harper went to bed early in the evening – it had been quite a long day after all - leaving the rest of the boys to visit The Ship for a session on the chance that the weather looked pretty rubbish for the next day, and any kind of flying was unlikely.

Suddenly Harper woke up again – he didn't know why. He checked his watch: 9.15pm. The luminescent dial illuminated his little part of the room. A beautiful woman was standing at the bottom of his bed in a nurse's uniform. Lucy. It wasn't a dream - she had been tweaking one of his toes, and now moved forwards silently, taking off her tunic and leaning down to kiss him. Harper let her. Then she rotated herself laterally and longitudinally from the side of the bed and up on top of Harper, carefully avoiding his plastered leg. She pulled up her white uniform dress, revealing brown stockings - no suspenders – and blackouts (uniform knickers, navy-blue, winter-weight cotton). Her free hand went down, pulling the sheets back.

"How did you get in?" whispered Harper, shy for a moment, lacking the Dutch courage that he was used to, unlike Lucy.

"Tried to catch you at the pub. The boys told me that you'd gone to bed early - very unlike you! Told the gate guard that I was checking on a patient, which I am!" her voice too loud – Harper motioned with his finger for her to *shush*. "Aren't we lucky that you're on the ground floor" as she opened the front of his silk pyjamas.

"I share a room" whispered Harper, grabbing her hand.

"Oh! Do you have a pet?" replied Lucy as she started to rub herself on top of him.

"Well...yes. A pet Geordie." Harper gave in. Lucy left as quickly as she came, going back out of the window just a few minutes before Gazzer fumbled at the door with his key and tiptoed in "...As elegantly as a hippo in a tutu" Harper whispered to himself, as he heard his friend trying, and failing to pee quietly in the bathroom.

Harper woke again at 0500, in time to catch a lift to dispersal with the main gaggle of pilots, rather than use his motorbike. Some of them looked in a sorry state, Gazzer one of the worst. The dispersal hut was freezing cold: a strong northerly wind had brought in a freezing, moisture-laden air mass from the arctic. Two boxes of provisions were brought in by Jock McKay whilst Harper lit the stove with broken up packing cases and old furniture, topped off with coal. Normally the stove would run all night; the last job of the day was to cover the burning embers with slack – tiny bits of coal and dust - and dousing it with a pint of water. In the morning there would be a tar-like black crust on the embers. Breaking it with a stoker would reveal a yellow-hot fire underneath. Except that everyone had forgotten, and now they were paying for it.

"Hurry up man," said Abbo. "I don't have Celtic skin like you. This cold will have me before they do" pointing at the Swastika over the door - during Harper's absence it had been joined by a complete starboard aileron from a downed Messerschmitt, courtesy of a late night recovery team spearheaded by Johnny, the one who had cracked it down.

"I'm surprised you weren't speared by the jealous husband of some native girl long ago," said Gazzer.

"If you were out there they'd tie you up - hands and feet – hang you over a fire and get the whole village out for a slap up meal."

"Old Spanish saying: for every pig there is a roasting" added Rhino, the chorus of laughs making everyone forget their hangovers and the freezing cold for a while.

"Come on Boy Scout. Look's like we're all counting on you," said the C/O, talking to Harper. A disparaging quip but never so icy as the day

94

before - perhaps he had been down the pub with the boys again? When DC wasn't looking, Harper caught Gazzer's attention and made a drinking sign with his right hand, frowning slightly and raising his eyebrows in a questioning way. Gazzer held a hand out in front with a fist and an extended thumb horizontally, held it for a moment and turned the thumb upwards. Harper mouthed a silent 'ah got it' and then carried on with the fire making. The flames started licking up inside the stove as they caught the wax layers on the old bits of furniture, illuminating the dismal room and Harper's face.

"Interesting scar you've got there, Harps" said Greg, the Intel.

"Why's that?"

"Well, it's obviously not a bullet wound. I think it's a shell fragment, judging by the small width of the scar, and the widespread bruising. You're lucky it was a '109."

"I don't feel lucky" replied Harper.

"The problem with the '109's Oerlikon canon is that its muzzle velocity is quite low. Its a shortened, lightened version of a much bigger weapon, modified to fit in the small cavities in the wings. Swiss weapon of course, and they're supposed to be neutral." Gazzer's eyes were raised to the ceiling in mock boredom, a few more of the boys chuckling. "The downside is that the muzzle velocity is lower, and sometimes the shells don't explode on impact – they just disintegrate. I think that's what probably happened to you."

"What would have happened if the shell had exploded?" replied Harper, realising the answer to his own question as he asked, and wishing he hadn't.

"You would have undoubtedly been shot down."

"You silly sod!" said Gazzer. "He *was* shot down!

"Well in a manner of speaking..." Greg drowned out by the laughter. Abbo was the first to speak after it died down.

"What I don't get is how they call you an Intelligence Officer."

Off it went again. And, when it died down again:

"Why don't we have canon?" asked Jock.

"They're working on it, believe me" replied Greg.

24

By 1700 hrs the squadron had been stood down for the day. Harper stayed back, studying his Spitfire notes, quietly proving to the C/O that he was fit enough to stay there all day. During the afternoon his leg had started aching quite badly, but the limp was easy to cover up on short visits; to the kettle for tea, and to the pee-bucket behind the hut. For the rest of the time Harper remained on his favourite sofa with his leg propped up.

"Would you like a lift Harper?" asked the C/O as he locked the door of his office. "I see you weren't up to riding your bike."

"Not at all sir. I was thinking of giving myself some exercise actually."

"So be it." Harper cursed quietly to himself as he realised that he *would* have to walk. He had forgotten that his motorbike was back at the mess. Harper waited until the C/O drove away before he left the hut and started making his way slowly across the airfield. After 5 minutes of walking he sat down on the grass to take a short rest and smoke a cigarette. All was silent, the low cloud suppressing all background noise, even birdsong - Harper wondered if the weather had been too bad even for them to fly.

Then, he fancied that he could hear an aircraft. No, surely not, he thought to himself. The cloud base couldn't be more than 500ft. Harper hated weather like this - the only time he didn't like flying, apart from when being shot at. Now he could hear the sound again. No doubt about it, definitely an aircraft and getting louder. Harper sat up and squinted towards the noise source. The sound was from a single Merlin – probably a Hurricane then. He reassessed the cloud base as he scanned the sky: more like 400ft in places he reckoned - terrible conditions for a fighter with limited blind flying equipment.

There, under the base of the cloud, he could see it, heading directly for the airfield. Louder, bigger, the unmistakable lines... of a Spitfire.

"Lovely" said Harper out loud, as the aircraft sailed straight over the top of the airfield at 220kts and 250ft. "Me soon" he added to himself as he turned and watched it fly off into the distance. But then he heard the engine note reduce, the aircraft banking hard to the left, slowing down and rolling out heading straight for the field again. At the last moment its gear lowered, followed by the flaps, and it touched down perfectly on all three wheels simultaneously, a *three-pointer*. All pains forgotten, Harper stamped out his cigarette and walked, considerably faster than he had since his crack up, towards the aircraft as it slowed to taxi speed. The pilot didn't appear to know where he was going to park, turning in a neat circle before he noticed Harper waving his arms. The Spitfire taxied up to Harper: he motioned for the pilot to follow him as he marched, jogged and hopped lightly back to the dispersal area and found a place for it to park. The pilot switched the engine off before he was in position, coasting the last few feet to a stop. Harper couldn't fail to be impressed by his judgement. The hood went back and the pilot unclipped his mask - he was wearing lipstick.

"Sorry about that, the engine was overheating. Wasn't trying to show off" said the woman's voice, the lips smiling, the goggles coming back up on top of the leather flying helmet.

"Is there... a problem with it then?" asked Harper, realising what she was, what this was: An ATA girl, with the squadron's first Spitfire.

"Not at all. With the gear down the radiator gets blanked and she'll overheat. You need to be airborne within 10 minutes from engine start" she said, climbing out and jumping down from the wing, "... and within 5 minutes after landing. Cripes! You ok?"

"Don't worry, getting better all the time. Flt Lt Harper - nice to meet you!" She was very beautiful, dark-haired, slim and also very small. Harper wondered to himself how she could reach the rudder pedals, except that she obviously could. "Can't believe you got here actually! The weather's... very mucky. Where did you come from?"

"Flew up from Waltham, sorry, White Waltham this morning in one of our 'Oxfords to Castle Bromwich and then sat around all day like a lemon."

"I thought Spitfires were built in Southampton."

"They are. Castle Brom' is the shadow factory - bloody shambles. There was supposed to be an improvement running east this evening: wasn't though. I think Letty turned back. Not here is she?"

"Definitely not, no."

"My name's Diana," extending a hand. "I'm supposed to take one of your Hurry's back to *the Bump* (Biggin Hill) but its not nice up there. Can I stay with you chaps?"

"Abso-bloody-lutely" he replied, motioning towards the dispersal hut. "I'll get some transport organised." Harper needn't have worried. As they reached the hut two cars, his motorbike and an ambulance full of pilots arrived. Diana was swamped with introductions and champagne – Gazzer had piled three bottles of it into the ambulance, the pilots not knowing what to do first; meet Diana or look round their first Spitfire. A small party developed around her, the champagne quickly consumed. Rhino blasted off on Harper's motorbike for more, the rear wheel spinning as he let go with full throttle in first gear on the grass.

"I know what that is," said Diana, looking at Abbo, the man all women tended to gravitate to in the midst of the rest of the Squadron. A safe bet.

"Yeah well, you need to talk to Harps about it. What you reckon it is?" his Kenyan accent poking through despite long-term English exposure.

"It's a Nazi motorbike" she replied. "I think we should give it a ritual burning". Abbo started laughing.

"I think we can organise that." Suddenly the conversation died, everyone looking westwards. Another Spitfire appeared out of the muck, flying straight over the field, this time at 100 feet and pulling up in a beautiful victory roll before rolling out, turning and landing in precisely the same place as Diana. The pilots were ecstatic. The Spitfire taxied in and parked at a discreet distance from the first, another small, female pilot climbing out. A loud round of applause broke out among the boys, Gazzer the first to greet her with a glass of champagne.

"Atta girls! Atta girls! Atta girls! Way hey!!" chanted Gazzer, all the boys shouting, clapping.

"Why thank you very much!" said the second pilot, swallowing the champagne in one go. "Got any more?" More yells and cheers. "Where's Diana?"

"Here Letty, honey." The two girls ran together and hugged, the boys in rapt silence. "Didn't think much of it up there, sweetie. Glad you're safe."

"Atta girls! Atta girls! Atta girls!" chanted Gazzer again.

"WAY HEY!!" replied the pilots in unison.

Rhino was back in a few minutes, the R71's panniers stuffed with Champagne, plus whatever food he could grab from the dining room table – it had been laid out for afternoon tea. The pilots took turns clambering into the cockpits of the new aircraft, the girls taking one Spitfire each, kneeling on the right hand wing root next to the cockpit so that they could show each of them round. Just before it was Harper's turn, something made him look over his shoulder – the C/O was approaching.

"Oh bugger," said Harper, trying to find somewhere to put his champagne glass.

"Sod it" said Gazzer, standing next to him, stuffing his glass into his flying jacket pocket, a barely discernible 'crack' as it broke at the top of the neck. "Bottle to throttle rule – no drinking within 8 yards of the aeroplane." Harper bit his lip, trying not to laugh.

"Diana!" shouted Dave Cole.

"Well I'll be…" said Gazzer.

"DC!" replied Diana, sliding down off the wing to greet him.

"Great to see you! Delivery with style. Glad to see that the boys are looking after you. Are you joining us for dinner?"

"Of course darling."

"How's Waltham ticking along?" Their conversation continued.

"Darling?" said Gazzer to Harper. "Blimey. Right, we're out of bubbles again. Its Beer O'clock - back to the mess!" The party travelled in the ambulance and the two cars. Diana accepted Harper's offer and rode the motorbike to the mess with him on the back – he figured that, if she willed it, the boys would happily set fire to his bike just to please her. Thankfully, on arrival at the mess, Diana told Harper that she liked it after all.

25

The next day had better weather. The low cloud was replaced by a cold front with clear skies and fluffy white cumulus clouds, which would build into rain showers later in the day. The ATA girls departed at dawn for Biggin Hill with two Hurricanes. Half an hour after sunrise two more Spitfires were in the circuit - the Squadron turned out to a man to watch them land. The first one landed in exactly the same place as Letty and Diana the evening before, into wind and pulling up in less than 500 yards. The second made a fast approach, went around, made a second approach slightly slower and went around again. Inexplicably, the last approach was made at right angles to the first two, slightly downwind, mostly crosswind and still too fast. The Spitfire touched down at a ground speed of nearly 100mph, bounced, skewed left into wind, touched down again hard and tipped forward onto its nose. Then, the aircraft finally dropped back onto its tail wheel as it came to a halt in a cloud of steam from the ruptured cooling system, and dust from the rotorvated airfield. The squadron boys were already running before the Spitfire had stopped, followed by the blood wagon and a fire engine.

Doogy, the taller of the two Polish pilots reached the aeroplane first. The canopy was still closed, the male ATA pilot inside had his head in his hands, crying his eyes out.

"Open silly shmuck" shouted Doogy, rapping his knuckles on the canopy. The pilot looked up suddenly; his face went bright red and then he started crying again.

"So sorry, so sorry" he sobbed, the rest of the boys (apart from Harper) reaching the wreck more or less together, seeing what was going on and then turning away quietly and walking back to the dispersal hut. 30 minutes later, as the wrecked Spitfire was towed by its tail wheel away from the landing field, the C/O called for a meeting. The other ATA pilot was already sitting in a Hurricane, prepping it for a return to White Waltham.

"Right chaps, I'm going to non-op myself this morning and talk Spitfire to you" said DC. "Abbot, Sqn Ldr Hatton, Kowalski, McKay, Smith and Tyler: you're on first standby for a scramble. Bruce, you'll be section leader of course. The rest of you will sit tight, unless we get a big scrap. So, Spitfire…" he revealed a large cut away drawing of the aircraft on an easel as he spoke, pointing to the picture with a tapered wooden dowel, definitely from his days as a headmaster. There were a few sniggers and giggles from the audience, despite the mutual love of the subject. "The main difference between the Spitfire and the Hurricane is that the Hurricane is effectively a rag and tube biplane from the '20s with one wing missing." There were a few murmurs of disapproval. "Yes, yes I know we all love our Hurricanes but, *the Spitfire* is a different kettle of fish. Firstly it has a stressed skin construction – the aluminium skin, as you probably know already, is the main structural component of the fuselage. The wing has a thick skin forward of the spar and round the leading edge making an incredibly strong wing – no one's been able to pull them off of one yet."

"Nor the Hurricane's" piped up Smith T.

"Yes, yes I know that," DC slightly annoyed, Harper and Gazzer nudging each other, their mirth increasing in proportion to his temper. "The wing is elliptical, giving a perfect distribution of lift. Most of the lift is in the inboard part of the wing, where it's thicker and stronger, progressively reducing out to the tips which are the weakest part of any wing. Practically its not so different from the Hurricane, similar engine for instance, lighter on the controls, much faster, just doesn't like crosswinds particularly."

"Why's that sir?" said Smith T.

"The Hurricane's wheels retract inboard from what seems to me to be an arbitrary position out on the wing. The Spitfire's wheels retract outward from where the wing is thick enough to house the retraction mechanism. This means that with the wheels extended the distance between the Spit's is much less than the Hurry's. Which means that, on the ground, the aircraft wants to swap ends a little more readily than the Hurry. The aircraft is also nose-heavy on the ground. Don't, whatever you do, move the stick forward with the engine running on the ground. The tail will lift and that'll be that."

"So is it more difficult to fly?" asked Abbo.

"Certainly not. It's just a much hotter ship. Better power to weight ratio, better aerodynamics."

"So why did Atta boy crash then?" asked Smith T.

"Because he's a bloody idiot." All of the pilots started laughing, except Atta boy - who also heard the slur - sitting outside the hut, waiting for a lift home. DC had telephoned his base and told them that he wouldn't release a Hurricane to him. "The good news, if you want it is that the Messerschmitt 109 is much, much harder than the Spitfire to land. To the point that, we're informed by our intelligence (more suppressed laughs from the audience – they associated the word with Greg and Abbo's joke) that they're losing more airframes in landing accidents than they are in combat. Keep it up chaps, keep shooting them down and we'll run the bastards out before they chew us!

"I'm not convinced," said Smith T. The room fell silent, Gazzer biting his fist, Harper's shoulders rising and falling as he tried not to laugh. But he couldn't help himself.

"What did you say, Smith is it?" exclaimed DC.

"I said I'm not convinced sir. I prefer the Hurricane." Harper uttered a loud guffaw and then shook with silent laughter again, luckily not noticed by the now enraged C/O. Harper's laughter was infectious, the rest of the pilots now giggling like schoolboys. DC was losing control of the mob.

"You're as bold as bloody brass!" said the C/O. "But woefully misguided - get me my fucking helmet Jones, if you please!" to the fitter, standing by the door smoking a cigarette, the swearing strangely at odds with the pleasantry. Jones, jumped to attention and then dived into the C/O's office, coming out a few seconds later with his hands full of Mae West, helmet, goggles and kid-leather flying gloves, his cigarette dangling from his mouth. DC grabbed his belongings, issued a quiet 'thank you' to Jones and stomped out of the hut. The pilots jumped up as soon as he had left and gathered by the door and windows as they watched him climb into the nearest Spitfire, start up and then taxi across to the take off point.

"What's going on!" said Rhino, laughing deliciously as he watched the Spitfire stop, turn around and then open up for take off, heading straight for the dispersal hut. The aircraft was airborne in just 400 yards but stayed low, the wheels retracting, the Spitfire accelerating past 200mph as it roared 10ft above the roof of the hut.

"Bloody marvellous!" shouted Gazzer, drowned out by the noise, the pilots now spilling out of the hut so that they could keep visual contact with the beautiful aircraft as it translated into a climbing turn to the left. Up and up it went, then it rolled to the right, almost inverted, before diving straight down at the hut again. It pulled out at the last moment, levelling off 10ft above the hut at nearly 400mph.

"Christ almighty" said Smith T.

"You asked for it" replied Harper, mesmerised by the Spitfire's performance. The aircraft pulled up into a 2000ft-diameter loop, completing the manoeuvre 20ft above the grass and pulling up once again, this time into a vertical climb, disappearing into the cloud base 3500ft above the airfield. Ten seconds later the Spitfire came back down vertically, way above Vne, a 6g pull out to tree top height one last time, two high banked circles around the airfield to lose energy, followed by a perfect circuit and landing. The Spitfire taxied in, accompanied by the whoops and cheers of an ecstatic squadron. DC jumped out, to a round of applause - he walked straight up to Smith T.

"Now go and get your kit. And go fly it, or I'll post you to a Hurricane squadron as far away from here as possible."

Smith T thought for a moment and then walked into the hut, emerging less than a minute later with his flying equipment. It wasn't what the boys were expecting - now they stood back and watched with growing respect as Smith T climbed into the aircraft and strapped in. The C/O climbed up the left wing behind him and squatted down.

"Its got a very similar Merlin to the Hurry so it starts the same way, same pitfalls too, so don't over-prime when starting a warm engine or you'll end up with a carburettor fire. Remember, stick back at all times. You've got less than 10 minutes after engine start to get airborne or it'll overheat so don't hang around. This one's warm so make that 5. On the take off, just feed the power in slowly, even more slowly than the Hurry, raise the tail and she'll fly off when she wants to. Coming back in you want 85mph over the hedge and she'll land at just below 75mph."

"But that's like the Hurricane?"

"I told you it's a good wing. When you taxi in shut down immediately or she'll overheat again."

The C/O slid down off the wing, and stood back. Smith T gave a thumb up to the fitter and then turned the engine. The blades went slowly at first - it was brand new after all - then the Merlin fired up a few cylinders at a time, settling down into a heart-warming, rumbling crackle - or heart-stopping, depending on where one was sitting.

Smith T's fitter pulled out the trolley battery and kicked away the chocks. The aircraft taxied out, slowly at first, then a little faster. Harper could see that Smith T had the stick hard back, because the elevator on the tail plane was in the full up position. With the elevator held hard up, the huge prop wash from the Merlin, even at idle, was enough to create a down force on the tail plane. Harper was focussed completely on the sight of the aircraft as Smith T taxied with growing confidence into the distance – and so he didn't immediately register the ringing telephone in the hut

"Blue section scramble!"

Bruce, Abbo, Koval and Smith A were in and out of the hut in less than a minute, four Hurricanes firing up and chasing across the field to where Smith T was doing his engine run and pre take of checks. Smith T let them take off first – just in time, because his glycol temperature was on its limit. Harper watched as Smith T lined up and opened the throttle slowly, keeping perfectly straight as the tail lifted. By the time he had full throttle he was already airborne, in less distance than the Hurricanes before him. He flew a smooth, wide circuit with the wheels down and throttle well back to keep below the gear limiting speed, coming into land at 85mph over the hedge, 75mph at touchdown, a perfect three pointer, and then opening the throttle progressively to take off again.

"Well done Smith" said DC, standing next to Harper.

"Its Smith T sir, we've got Smith A as well; he doesn't say much though. Lost his friend, first day on the squadron."

"This one does the talking for both of them by the looks of it - I hope his flying matches his attitude."

"I think it does sir." Harper went inside the hut, laid out on his favourite sofa, lit another cigarette and started sulking. He wanted to be up there with his friends – it didn't matter that only four were up, the rest in the hut with Harper. He felt left out, redundant. His leg was hurting and so were his ribs where he had just sat down too heavily.

Harper reached inside his flying jacket and pulled out another letter from Eric – no date at all this time.

L.A.C Harper

Block 48 Room 4

R.A.F S. Cerney

Nr Cirencester

Gloucs

To My dear Tom,

The fellow who:-

Bust the chain of my motorbike, Mary.

Smashed all my trains on countless occasions.

Dented my silver pencil &

b- - ed about in Ferdies, etc, etc & Yet I still love him.

Oh! Happy days!

Well, the reason for all this is that today we finished the Wings exam. Whether I passed or not is another matter. But after a couple of week's swotting in this place, I feel so browned off I couldn't even fuck a pros: if it was free. Anyhow, if I didn't pass, I simply take the bloody thing again & nobody cares.

Thank you for your letter & all the usual…

Sorry this is in pencil, I'm in bed, waiting for the other chaps to finish playing cards, its no good trying to go to sleep yet.

Its only 11.30pm. anyway We get up about 7 a.m here now, its one consolation for this place.

all we have to do now is to sit back, do a bit of flying & wait for our Wings. Or so we hope. There is not much risk of being suspended now, we're too far gone (I don't mean what you mean) actually, altogether I've done 82½ hrs: flying & about 10 more hrs: passenger.

I like the story about Sam, don't be surprised if I shoot the same sort of thing before long. After all, I'm 18 now, you know, & getting quite a big boy. By the way, I believe it's your birthday soon, many happy returns & I shall have to find some suitable literature.

I'll admit that Cambridge is simply lousy with R.A.F, poor show, isn't it, & also with very loose women but they're even looser in Cirencester.

I don't think I shall be home until the end of the course when I may get 7 days. Fuck it we got 24 hrs: at Christmas, it was hopeless to try & get home, the R.A.F training command as generous with leave as my asshole. I've been in over 5 months now & only had 3½ days. Some poor sods haven't had that.

I'm seriously thinking of getting a car. I hate to think of getting rid of Mary, but I'll be a sarge or even a P/O before long & then it will have to be a car actually a sergeant is much better off than a P/O for cash which is one consolation.

I was looking through "Flights" & "aeroplanes" the other day. I see that J.A.F Sowry and J Woolridge (the oldest one D.F.M) have got commissions. I believe J.A.F Sowry was the older or was he the younger? I pity Peter if he was a flight mechanic, all they do is start up aeroplanes & can aeroplanes be sods to start up.

We had a fall off during the night, which has buggered up flying for a bit. So we continue to do f. all, one wouldn't think there was a war on if one came to S. Cerney.

The press came down a few days ago & took a lot of pictures. Three of them have been published in local papers so far but none of me although two or three of self were taken. There have been 2 or 3 articles in Sunday papers recently, one about S.F.T.S's. all absolute balls of course & pure journalism. You needn't believe a thing they say. Godfrey Winn even said we drink nothing stronger than Shandy!

I return Lord Byron's effort. actually we came to the conclusion that it wasn't quite up to Byron's standard, the poetry of course I mean.

Love to all. I only hope it isn't my or your last.

"Harper, can I have a word?" said DC. Harper jumped up, forgetting his leg, and went into the office.

"Slight change of tack. I'd like you to take that Hurricane back to Waltham for me." Harper could barely contain his excitement. "You're bound to do a better job than that idiot out there, but you haven't got one over me - so don't start thinking that you have. Get them to give you a lift back in an 'Oxford. I don't want you travelling on public transport, scaring people."

"Yes sir, I mean no sir. Thank *you* sir."

26

The flight to Waltham was superb. Harper flew north-westwards initially, to avoid the barrage balloons on the outskirts of London, then turned west, tracking to the north of Stapleford. He tuned the radio to the controller frequency to hear how Blue section were getting on but he couldn't hear any voices, just the occasional transmission of white noise - he was too low and too far away. The cumulus clouds had developed during the morning and were now several thousand feet deep, the cloud-base still at 3000ft or so. Harper climbed to 4500ft and then started gently rolling and turning around the edges of the clouds, enhancing his sensation of speed. Then he tried to loop round one of the smaller clouds; the top part went fine, but pulling G at the bottom of the manoeuvre made his leg hurt like hell. He relaxed the back pressure and let the aircraft pull out of the dive more slowly, coming down to 500ft in the process and then sitting contentedly at this height, the speed washing back from 320mph to a slightly more sedate 250mph. Within a few minutes the built-up areas north of London were replaced by the gentle hills of the Chilterns. Harper spotted Amersham, with its triangular-shaped field on the hill between the old town and the new town, where its martyrs had been burned in the Middle Ages. Harper turned south-west, next flying past Beaconsfield and over the sprawling, smoggy, filled-up valleys of High Wycombe, a stark contrast to the beautiful riverside town of Marlow. It had a distinctive suspension bridge – Harper had been out on a rowing boat with a girl there before the war. He knew he was very close to Waltham now but he didn't know what to look for, and so couldn't see it. He carried on flying towards Reading for a couple of minutes, then turned back and followed its arrow-straight railway, the London/Bristol line heading north east out of the town. On Harper's chart it looked like the airfield had the railway as its northern boundary, and that's the way he found it. Tracking along at 500ft with the railway line just to his left, a huge grass aerodrome appeared ahead, with fighters, bombers and transport aircraft littered all over its southern and western perimeter. Now he wondered how he'd missed it in the first place.

Harper pulled up to circuit height, throttled back to lose speed, and rolled left into the circuit pattern dictated by the windsock. He used the 'H' selector to get the wheels and flap down in quick order and set the aircraft down on the largest piece of uninterrupted grass he had ever seen - possibly with the exception of the pasture behind his family home.

He shut down next to the 1930s, 'art deco' control tower on the north side of the field and limped into an office marked 'ATA – Pilots Only'.

"Can I help you?" asked an austere, middle-aged man, sitting at a desk and smoking a pipe. He was wearing a new uniform shirt and tie, and an old jacket with faded wings, the braiding worn out around the edges.

"Yes I'm Flt Lt Harper. Brought back a Hurricane for you. One of your boys had a bit of an incident with a new Spit this morning."

"Ah yes. Very cheeky chap your C/O if you don't mind me saying. Told me that he wouldn't let *my* chap fly one of your old crates back. Its not really his job to tell me what *I* can and can't do with one of *my* pilots.

"Are you the C/O?" asked Harper, checking the stripes on his sleeve – there weren't any.

"In a manner of speaking yes. It's cocked up the schedule completely of course. I needed my man back here to get back up to Castle Brom' and deliver another Mk1. The Cosford lot should normally look after that one but they're a bit short-handed, not up to full strength yet, which is why we've been roped in. I suppose you're going to ask for a lift?"

"Well I, I only started flying again today. Been off for a few days - had my own little incident."

"Yes I can see that" replied the 'C/O.' "What did *you* do then?" Harper could feel the tension in the room, his own temper rising with it.

"I got shot down."

"Oh I see." The tension diffused immediately. "I was in the first one: two kills and a probable." His jacket looked to Harper like it came from the same era. "Hope someone got the bastard for you." Harper realised that he didn't know, or couldn't remember if he'd been told. He stayed silent. "Well, I suppose we can get someone else to go up to Castle Brom'... I know, what we'll do is put you on the same 'Oxford, drop you off, pick up my chap and fly on from there. That'll work!" he added, as if he'd just solved something complicated.

"Yes I suppose it will!" replied Harper brightly, adding "numpty" quietly as he limped out of the office to find a mug of tea.

"Oh and Harper?" Harper wondered why people always had something to say to him after he had walked out of a room.

"Sorry about my chap. He's been delivering bombers for weeks. That was his first fighter."

"What, his first fighter since the bombers?"

"No, his first fighter."

"Don't you have a two-seater?"

"There aren't any two-seaters – maybe next year."

There wasn't anything more to say, so Harper didn't say anything. One hour later he was back with his squadron, the return journey in the 'Oxford taking exactly twice as long as the ferry flight. He managed to sleep for most of it, despite the noise, and felt refreshed as well as satisfied when he walked – no limp - into the dispersal hut. One by one the boys looked up at him, then down again quickly, no smiles.

Abbo took the lead, jumping up from his seat and motioning for Harper to come back outside with him. Not just outside, but 30 yards out across the airfield, before he stopped and lit a cigarette.

"Not here Abbo – the C/O."

"Fuck the C/O." replied Abbo. Harper noticed that his hands were shaking. "There's no easy way…"

"To what?"

"Smith went in."

"T?" Harper had visions of another Spitfire crash.

"No, A." Harper felt a wave of relief, and then immediately hated himself for it. "…And Gazzer."

"Oh, please no!"

"He's posted missing. Bruce watched it - didn't see a parachute." Harper was silent, and still, for a moment, and then started walking to his motorbike, keeping his head turned away so that Abbo couldn't see the tears starting to roll down his cheeks.

"Thanks for having the balls..." his voice cracking with emotion.

"You off somewhere, Harps?"

"Down the pub."

27

The squadron was stood down at 8pm, the boys immediately making for The Ship. The C/O let them take two ambulances with drivers and left them to it, figuring that they could properly let themselves go if he was absent − it was very much appreciated. The ambulances parked a few yards down the road from the pub so that no one would be alarmed, and Harper wouldn't have false hope. Abbo took the lead at the door, wondering, worrying about what he would find inside.

Harper was playing darts.

"Are you winning old boy?" asked Abbo, walking up to him, smiling gently.

"Of course. I'm playing myself."

"What about the locals?"

"Polished them all off hours ago" replied Harper, nodding across to three farmers with their elbows on the bar: three smiles and a couple of raised pints back.

"Bit of a shitty old day."

"Started well, shame about the ending. Did we get any of the bastards?"

"No. We need your help Harps. Its Smith T − he's not doing so well." Abbo was boxing clever.

"He'll get over it."

"Come on old man. Behind that hard, ugly exterior, there's a little, hard, ugly Harper trying to get out."

"All right, all right." Harper pulled his darts out of the board and limped across to Smith T, slumped in a chair by the fire with a pint - and not drinking it."

"Come on Mr T, its not what our mates would want. They're up there on their little clouds looking down here at you not drinking that pint, and wondering how they can start a brewery." No response. "Anyway, every cloud has a silver lining."

"How does that work?" replied Smith T, looking up angrily.

"Well, from now on we can call you... Smith!" A few of the boys drew their breath through pursed lips and turned away, grimacing. Then Smith T smiled, and started laughing, Abbo starting to laugh with the others, looking at Harper and moving his head from side to side.

"Smith T's fine, thanks" said Smith T. "I've taken to it."

The pilots drank heartily for the next couple of hours, beers supplemented with whisky chasers at Harper's insistence. The evening tracked on in the same pattern as a classical Irish wake; periods of quiet conversation interspersed with wild laughter – the release of tension – the quiet periods reducing and the laughter growing as everyone had more to drink.

"So tell me," asked Harper to the smaller of the two Polish pilots, when there was a quieter moment; "why are you called Koval?"

"Because I'm 'The Blacksmith.'"

"What, you're like a blacksmith? Like you do a girl like a blacksmith does, or something?"

"No. I am a blacksmith."

"Right oh. And what about you, Doogy?" Doogy didn't say anything: instead he grabbed his trousers by the crotch and lifted it. Koval started laughing.

"What, you've got big balls?" Koval started laughing even more. The boys started to crowd round, trying to get it.

"No. He has long dick," said Koval. The squadron erupted with laughter. Harper wanted to know more; even though, and probably because, he was drunk.

"So 'Doogy' means 'long dick?'" Somehow Harper's earnest enquiry was even funnier, the boys collapsing with laughter.

"It means long anything." replied Doogy. "My dick is long, I am long."

"Well that's bloody marvellous! From now on if I shoot the hun down from more than 250 yards I'm going to call it a 'Doogy!'"

"Three cheers for Doogy!" shouted Jock.

"Hip, hip, huzzah! Hip, hip, huzzah! Hip, hip, huzzah!" shouted everyone. And then they all started laughing again.

"Well, fuck me." said Rhino, dropping his beer glass - it shattered onto the floor, spilling half a pint of bitter. The laughing died quickly, all the pilots turning to Rhino, and then turning to where he was staring.

Gazzer was standing at the door.

"Hello chaps!" said Gazzer.

"AAAAAAGH!!" shouted the pilots as they rushed towards him, bundling him to the floor, and then lifting him horizontally and running him to a space between the bar, the fireplace and the chairs, where they lowered him to the ground and then dived on top of him again.

"Stop it! I'm hurt! I'm hurt!" wheezed Gazzer under the weight of the bodies. Everyone climbed off and backed off instantly, a couple of 'oh shits' exclaimed as they did so, leaving Gazzer on his back, on the floor, alone.

"Only joking."

"AAAAAAGH!!" shouted the pilots, bundling him once again, Greg Ball explaining to the worried barman what was going on. Harper pulled enough of them off to clear a space, then took a running jump and dived on top of the lot of them.

"Get off of me you… poof!" shouted Gazzer.

"No bloody way!" replied Harper. Eventually the boys helped pull Gazzer up – he sat in the chair by the fire, quickly supplied with a pint of bitter and a scotch.

"Not too much for me, had rather a lot of rum on my cruise."

"What the hell happened?" said Harper.

"Well, it started when God spent 6 days making the world and rested on the 7th. And then Dinosaurs roamed the earth."

"Believe me. I will personally shoot you if you don't explain yourself."

"Simple story actually old boy. Don't happen to know what went on between getting a good old shelling at the back end, and finding myself on the end of a parachute."

"Yes but Bruce said he didn't see a parachute?"

"Maybe I only think I'm still alive then. He *is* getting on a bit though, failing eyesight and all that. Anyway I drifted down for a while. Then I went through some cumulus and it felt like I was going up again. Got very cold actually. Then came down in the sea. Biggest break was finding a buoy to cling to. Couldn't inflate my Mae West, no matter how many breaths I put in - I nearly drowned trying to blow it up, kept inhaling seawater. Later I found a bullet hole in it - can you believe it? Then a trawler came by but one of the fuckers thought I was foreign – he wanted to stick a boat hook in me."

"You are foreign - you're a Geordie."

"Shut up. Anyway I adopted a BBC accent and persuaded them I was a southern poof like you lot and an hour went by before I was picked up by the most beautiful ship I ever saw – it looked like it could fly. The HMS something or other - I'll never forget it, as long as I live."

"He's gone soft," said Abbo. "Exposure to seawater."

"And then I was picked up in an ambulance with busted suspension. Did me more damage than being shot down and dunked." Gazzer produced a small fish from the pocket of his flying jacket, holding it by the tail and wiggling it, to shouts of laughter. The flying jacket was dry, a replacement - a spoof then, but still wildly received by the boys. "Sorry I couldn't find a shoal of potatoes, otherwise I would have organised some chips." There was another organised bundle instead.

28

In the morning Harper fought off his hangover with a shave and cold shower, woke Gazzer up – he was snoring as usual - and then drove to the hospital on the R71. He had a quick cup of tea with Lucy in the canteen and then she took him to the private room. Harper stripped off to his shirt and underwear whilst Lucy got the plaster ready.

"Eight days should be enough, so we'll get the stitches out of your leg, then reset the plaster, and while that's drying I'll get those stitches out of your cheek." Harper laid back on the table with a rolled up towel behind his head - Lucy couldn't resist leaning down to kiss him before getting to grips with the other end. To Harper, the cast looked relatively undamaged but he couldn't be sure. It had certainly done its job though.

"I can't believe it! You haven't damaged it. You've really taken care. What a good boy you are." She kissed him again. Harper decided not to tell her about jogging across airfields, flying aerobatics in a Hurricane, getting riotously drunk and bundling Gazzer in the pub. Lucy started cutting down the side of the plaster with a large pair of snips, careful to avoid coming into contact with the two wounds. When she got to the end she opened the cast. A smell not unlike dirty socks wafted up.

"Er, sorry about that. It's not my feet." Lucy looked up at him, her expression read by Harper as 'I'm a *nurse,*' and then carried on with her work. She doused the front wound with alcohol on a cotton swab and then cleaned the surrounding area with more alcohol and a larger cotton cloth. As it evaporated it cooled Harper's leg – the feeling was sensational. He leaned forward to give it a good scratch but Lucy smacked his hand. She ran a scalpel up inside each stitch to cut it – the effect was to snag the rest of the stitch underneath the skin before the thread parted. The trick was to have a steady hand and a new blade – Lucy had both. Once each stitch was broken she took a pair of tweezers and gently pulled the stitch out from the knotted end – Harper found the sensation strangely satisfying. When she had finished she cleaned the wound with more alcohol, re-packed and dressed it, got Harper to lay on his front and then repeated the process.

"The entry wound is better than the exit wound," she said. You'll know all about that I suppose."

"Not really. I know the stitches hurt more at the front though."

That's because you've got more nerve endings there, and more disruption. Honestly Tom, an inch to the left and I don't know..." When she was finished Lucy added water to the plaster, mixed it up to a consistency of double cream and dipped the bandages before plastering his leg to the same thickness as before. While it was setting she cleaned up the room, careful not leave a trace.

The stitches on Harper's face were another matter – removing each of them seemed to hurt more than the previous one. Despite Harper's wincing and groaning, Lucy got on with it as quickly as possible, and then doused the wound with more alcohol. By the time she had finished cleaning up, the cast had set.

"You look good!" she said.

Harper rubbed his face with both hands for the first time since the crash – apart from the dull ache in his leg he felt normal again. The side of his face was still badly bruised, his eye still black, but the swelling had gone completely. Even his ribs were better.

"Its good to feel well again" he said.

"I must say you look it. I've got used to being careful with you because of all the damage." Harper was sitting on the table with his legs parted. As Lucy walked past he grabbed her arm, pulled her close to him and kissed her ever so slightly more roughly than he had before. "Getting a bit frisky now we're better, are we." Harper kissed her again, his left hand around the small of her back, squeezing her closer, his right hand climbing up the back of her leg - Lucy let it go up far enough to squeeze her bottom, and then grabbed his arm with a free hand.

"Not here. I'd get away with this if I was caught, because it's for the cause, but I wouldn't get away with *this*." She pulled back, still smiling - Harper let go and then started getting dressed again.

"That's not what you said last time."

"Last time was different."

Don't know what I'd do without you," said Harper, trying to pull her to him again.

"Start playing with yourself, probably."

Harper laughed, then went quiet and turned round to face the window. Lucy went to speak, but he put his hand up. Lucy waited for a moment. A few seconds went by, then a distant 'crump.' Nothing for a few more seconds, then: 'crump' 'crump.' Harper jumped up and put on his trousers and shoes.

"What is it?"

"I think they're bombing the bloody airfield!" he said as he picked up his jacket and goggles and ran out of the door.

"Be careful of your leg! It's not set properly!" Lucy shouted after him. As he ran out of the side entrance, Harper could hear more distant explosions, and the drone of multi-engined bombers at high altitude, the engines unsynchronised so that they made a faint *wa wa wa wa* sound. Only German bombers sounded like that. Harper jumped on his bike and roared back to the base as fast as possible.

For the first few minutes Harper couldn't see anything but, as he rode the last couple of miles he spotted rising columns of smoke.

"You fucking bastards!" he shouted, his voice lost in the wind and the engine noise from his flat-out motorbike.

As Harper got near the gate he was flagged down by the security guard.

"Get down the shelter you!" shouted the guard.

"Bugger off!" replied Harper, swerving round the back of him and laying flat on the tank as he drove under the barrier. The infuriated guard tried to draw his gun, but he hadn't unbuttoned the holster for weeks and couldn't get it open in time - it's magazine was empty in any case. Harper went for the short cut between the two main hangars and then straight across the grass towards the dispersal hut. The bombs had fallen in the next field but at the far end of the dispersal was a huge fire being put out by two fire engines, the crews running forwards and backwards as exploding ammunition went off, popping and banging.

All but one of the Hurricanes (The C/O's) and all of the Spitfires were airborne.

"What's wrong with that one?" Harper shouted to the C/O's fitter as he ran across to the hut.

"He took his Spitfire."

"Is it serviceable?" Harper shouted. In the background was a steadily increasing whistle.

"GET DOWN!!" shouted one of the fire crew. Everyone dived onto the grass and put their hands over their ears. Harper remembered to open his mouth so that a shock wave wouldn't burst his eardrums. An eternity of waiting, then five massive explosions shook the ground from underneath him – Harper felt like he had lifted a couple of inches into the air. His ears popped, the left one painfully. After a few more seconds he opened his eyes and looked up. The stick of bombs had landed straight across the airfield, a perfect hit. There were five mushroom clouds of smoke: earth and dust raining down across the field.

"LOOK... AT... THAT!" shouted the fitter, pointing upwards. Harper looked up to see a bomber emerging from the clouds, falling vertically, on fire from wingtip to wingtip. The crews started cheering as it came down, crashing on a ridge 2 miles to the north of the field and sending up a huge black cloud of smoke and earth.

Harper ran, hopped and jogged across to the Hurricane. It was armed – eight red patches were in place over the gun muzzles. He jumped up on the stirrup and leant inside the cockpit, switched the battery on and tapped the fuel gauge. It was full.

"ANOTHER ONE!" Harper looked up to see what was obviously a Heinkel minus some of its tail, spinning out of the cloud. The crews were supposed to be putting out the fire but instead they were mesmerised by the action above them.

"Put out the bloody fire!" shouted Harper, but they ignored him – this was the first fighting they had ever seen. Harper ran into the hut, found his Mae West and ran back to the Hurricane. There was no trolley battery connected but he tried a start anyway. According to the temperature gauge the engine was cold, so he primed the fuel for a cold start. Jones was running over to him now, thumb in the air. Harper gave him a thumb back and hit the starter – three blades later and engine roared into life. Jones climbed up the wing and checked that Harper had managed to get his harness connected. He leaned down and plugged in the radio lead from Harper's helmet for him – Harper had forgotten.

"Thanks Jonesy!" he shouted, above the noise of the engine. "Chocks away." Jones jumped down and pulled the chocks out. Harper taxied carefully so as not to drop into a bomb crater, or hit one of the huge chunks of earth and concrete scattered across the airfield. Visibility was down too – dust and smoke everywhere. He taxied past the fire that the crews were still trying to put out - only then did he notice that it was a burning Spitfire.

Harper lined up into wind and opened the throttle smoothly, bringing the tail up earlier than usual so that he had a better view forwards. At 70mph he pulled the stick back slightly too hard and wallowed into the air, immediately raised the gear, accelerated and rolled into a tight right turn as an evasive manoeuvre in case something was coming down to attack him. Then he put the radio on – it was silent. Harper headed south until he had climbed to 3000ft and then started circling as he gained altitude. He didn't want to come up under the action with a lack of airspeed or altitude, but instead would climb up above it and attack from the south with the sun behind him. Harper looked back at the airfield in time to see another stick of bombs hit home, one of them blowing out and collapsing one of the hangars that he had rode past on his motorbike just a few minutes before.

Suddenly a Messerschmitt 109 came down out of the clouds directly in front of him, a Spitfire on its tail - guns blazing. Harper froze for a moment – nothing he could do – then carried on climbing up into the thin layer of cloud and above it into the blue sky.

"Jesus Christ!" said Harper. There were fighters and bombers everywhere, curving vapour trails, parachutes descending – he couldn't tell from what side. He fought off the urge to start flying towards the melee – it would have been futile at best and suicidal at worst. "Come on, come on!" he shouted at his aeroplane. The altimeter wound up through 10,000ft. Harper spotted a formation of bombers heading south east, back to Northern France or Germany – they must have dropped their bombs already. He couldn't see any fighters attacking them. Harper was enraged by the thought of his airfield being bombed - for the very first time, the anger completely swamped any fear he had for his own life. He couldn't let them get away with it. Harper turned east so that he was on a converging heading. Only a thousand feet of height left to go and he would be at the same level. He armed his guns but didn't fire for fear of the tracer giving his position away. As he arrived underneath the bombers he turned right again, heading south east. Just above him were five Heinkels in close formation, one streaming smoke from its starboard engine and dropping back slowly. A little jink left to right and he was underneath and behind it. He waited until he was only slightly under and 100 yards behind, before aiming and hitting the firing button. The de Wilde bullets sent their dancing yellow flames into the belly of the bomber, which hesitated for a moment and then rolled right and pushed out away from the formation. Harper carried on firing, following the bomber's flight path. His aim was perfect. The roll continued until the bomber was completely on its back and diving for the ground, flames streaming from its fuselage. Harper could see someone trying to bail out, the body dropping away from underneath the bomber, no parachute, the figure decelerating and flying back up and behind the Hurricane. Harper broke off the attack, and pulled out of the dive. His leg hurt like hell as the G built up but he carried on pulling the stick until the aircraft was pointing skywards again. He was checking his 6 o'clock automatically as he brought the aircraft around heading east again but he had lost sight of the other bombers. Harper reasoned that they had dived for the clouds – that's what he would have done.

Two Messerschmitt 109s suddenly appeared in front of him, coming the opposite way. He was back to 200mph – still climbing - and slightly below so no chance for a fight unless he went for a head on attack. One of the fighters had seen him and peeled away, hard to port and down, the other lined up on him and started firing. Harper did the same, the two aircraft closing on each other at 600mph. In that instant in time Harper could see the flashes alternating between wings and nose – he was completely unmoved by it as he pressed the firing button. At the last possible moment he pushed hard forward, fancying that he saw a few puffs of smoke from the Messerschmitt as it screamed over the top of him. Harper carried on pushing until the Hurricane was vertical, its engine coughing, failing and then coming back to life as the negative G reduced to zero in the vertical dive. He kept the dive going all the way down to 3000ft before bracing himself, and starting the long, agonising pull to level flight. He levelled out a just a few hundred feet above the River Thames – he couldn't look at the altimeter for fear of hitting the ground, but he recognised a ferry as he passed over the top of it. His subconscious told him that he must be near Dartford. Harper transitioned into a zooming climb, the vertical speed needle hard against its stop, at 6000 feet per minute – another check on his 6, all clear. His leg wasn't hurting so badly as the last time - he wondered if it was getting better, or maybe that he'd done even more damage to it. Harper looked over and behind him yet again – nothing seen.

When Harper returned to the airfield he initially had problems recognising it. The whole of the north side was ablaze; two hangars flattened, the officers' mess in flames, the sergeants' mess, the machine shop. Harper had trouble finding a clear landing strip – there were so many craters. He finally elected to land cross wind, bringing the Hurricane to a halt in a curve at the end of the landing roll to avoid a particularly large crater, and shutting down where he had stopped rather than negotiate the numerous holes and divots on the way back to the parking area. He got out of the aircraft and walked the 200 yards back to dispersal.

Harper walked towards the hut, looking at but not immediately appreciating the smaller holes and divots in the grass as he did so. He walked through the doorway to find the boys in a huddle in one corner – that familiar, furtive, up and down look, and look-away as he walked in. Gazzer was the first to hold a gaze.

"Well done old boy!"

"Yeah well, I don't suppose DC will be pleased," Harper thinking that he might get a hard time for taking the boss's Hurricane. This time Gazzer looked away. Abbo motioned for Harper to leave the hut.

"What the fuck is it now?" asked Harper.

"Smith T."

"Bloody no!"

"He got nailed out there by a '110" said Abbo, looking out to the burning aircraft.

"Are you... jok...? Everyone else ok? Am I bloody ok?"

"You're ok." replied Abbo. "You're always ok."

29

At 1900 Harper was called into the C/O's hut.

"Long list today Harper. Where shall we start?"

"I don't know sir. Suppose you're a bit raw, I mean upset, about me borrowing your Hurricane."

"Yes, I suppose that would be a good place to... How did you think you got on up there?"

"Well, I got one kill – Greg, sorry, Intel approved it – and one damaged."

"And what about my tailplane?"

"Don't know anything about it sir."

"Well, it's got bullet holes in it."

"Probably the Messerschmitt sir."

"Ah yes, the Messerschmitt. What happened there then?"

"Head on attack: I was a bit slow so I couldn't engage from a normal firing position."

"What if I told you that you got him?"

"I'd be very pleased sir."

"Well, you did. Rhino was trying to get to him – right behind when you pressed home and pushed away. He said that it went into a vertical dive and cracked down. Bang on Rhino, I say – he could easily have claimed it as his own. Why do you think that is?"

"I… I don't really know why."

"No nor do I. What I do know is that you're making your mark." Harper stayed silent. "And what would you say if I toyed with the idea that I was thinking of recommending you for a DFC and promotion?"

"I'd… be amazed sir."

"Yes, well I'm amazed by the idea too. I sat here last night for at least 10 minutes while the station commander chewed my backside off about a certain gate guard trying to shoot you."

"Sorry sir."

"No you're bloody not. But seeing as our head of the chair-borne division spent another 20 minutes berating me for beating up the airfield the other day, I find myself in the same camp. And seeing as this is the same camp comedian trying to regulate air battles so that they coincide with meal times I find myself even more in the club called 'subversive, ex-paddy, shits.'"

"Didn't know you were Irish sir."

"With a name like Cole? Get a grip Harper. Its ironic to see the blarney hasn't escaped the five generations or whatever you tell me it is since you turned Brit. So, yes I am recommending you for the DFC. But not for promotion until I see a marked improvement in respectability, discipline and general awareness of your impact on those around you, beyond your seemingly insatiable appetite for action, skirt and whisky. Do I make myself clear?"

Under his breath; "Fuck me" and; "Absolutely sir! And thank you, sir."

"Don't thank me Harper – it's my job to encourage those officers who I feel have a positive impact on the morale and effectiveness of the squadron." Harper couldn't help but think it sounded like a quote from a manual. "…And now, I will ask you to perform your first task as a soon-to-be decorated officer."

"Er, yes, carry on sir."

"Its Pollock, Bollock, whatever his name is." Harper suppressed a laugh, but the name would stick. "He turned back today."

"Sorry, I don't understand sir."

"No, I didn't think *you* would - its anathema to you. He complained of an overheating engine – highly convenient. Bearing in mind that: he joined the squadron nearly a month ago, went straight to the M/O with a temperature of 102 – no doubt the old Zippo lighter under the thermometer trick when he wasn't looking - then went home and got his local doctor to extend the sick period. Ever had ring twitch (fear of combat) have you?"

"Every time I go up. Of course I do. I think I might have… pissed myself sir, the first time - if I'm honest. Not that it stopped me firing at the bastards."

"Well at least you admit it. I had a skid mark in my pants the first time I went into combat. A very unpleasant experience."

"I can only imagine sir (except that he didn't want to.)"

"The point is we're all scared out of our wits most of the time, but we signed to do a job, and we have a bloody job to do here. Why the hell Pollock joined up escapes me. I knew I'd have a problem with him first time I met him."

So what would you like me to do?"

"Very simple. Talk to him. See what kind of man he is. Or not, as the case may be. If all else fails, read the riot act. He was tail end Charlie today and left our boys exposed. Bloody liability."

"I'll do my best sir." Harper walked out the door.

"Harper?" He came back in again.

"Well done."

"Harper drove his bike to The Ship, finding the boys in a wake for Smith T and getting drunk again.

"Wey hay Harps!" shouted Gazzer as he first saw him and instantly cheering up, followed by rolling cheers from the rest of the boys. Harper took the whisky that he was offered and scanned the bar for

Pollock - he was chatting to a local girl. It looked to Harper like he was bragging.

"I'm sorry to bring it up chaps, but what happened to Smith T?" asked Harper. Gazzer pulled back from the crowd.

"He hadn't even started his bloody engine. We got the go and legged it out there, Smith T was first off the bat. Bloody '110 came in over the hedge and strafed us (Harper experienced a moment of clarity – burning Spitfire, exploding rounds, divots, holes in the turf.) Two fitters were killed as well, one injured: blew his fucking leg off. Put the wind up the lads a bit, especially *that* one" pointing to Pollock.

"Oh really?" replied Harper, disingenuously. "Why's that?"

"We'd just taken off and formed up. Went up through a cloud layer and spotted them, thirty bombers and about the same number of fighters – more than I've ever seen in the air. Scared the bloody hell out of me actually old boy."

"Me too."

"Anyway, that c**t turned back – said his engine was overheating. But it wasn't, I checked with the fitter afterwards."

"Which fitter?"

"Jones – trustworthy (Harper raised his eyebrows, pursed his lips and put a thumb up). It's the second time, out of two. He's been off sick for nearly a month already. We think he's the wrong Colour for our work."

"I'm sorry?"

"Yellow. He's fucking yellow."

"His name is Bollock actually. DC says so." Gazzer turned from hatred to jollity in an instant - his natural state. "Don't think much of the girl. Bollock must have his beer goggles on." The girl was rather plump. Rhino overheard the last part of the conversation.

"You'd have to drink her pretty. Top tip from me: don't go out with a girl whose bum is bigger than your own."

"You'd be alright there then!" replied Gazzer, their laughter drowned out a few seconds later by a rising commotion from the doorway, halting Harper's line of thought - he decided that he would tackle the Pollock issue in the morning.

"Laydees an genlemenn." Said Jock. "camp comedians, landed gentry, noblemen. Without further ado …"

"Get on with it man!" shouted Rhino.

"…I bid you three cheers for…"

"For god's sake" added Rhino.

"… Flight Lieutenant Tom Harper! D! F! C!" All the boys cheered - massive approval. Harper took two of the many offers of whisky. Doogy voiced the most vociferous of approvals.

"You are bad leg, inspiration for small pilots."

"Why thank you!" replied Harper. "Unfortunately, neither of my kills were *Doogies*. One, *half-Doogy* maybe.

"All of your kills are long," said Doogy.

"Well, here's to long kills" raising his glass.

"I can't believe it," said Gazzer. "The way things are going I'm going to have to call you sir. Can you imagine it – Group Captain Harps."

30

At 0730 the next morning, DC called for a meeting in the dispersal hut.

"Firstly I have something to tell you about the war effort. Last week the allies withdrew all troops south of Trondheim, a retreat. And I can now confirm officially that Germany has invaded France. I don't know what fighter ops will be conducted at this stage, or how any of this will affect squadron concentration here in the south, but there's no doubt in my mind that the war is going to hot up from here on in, as if yesterday wasn't an example. The Station Commander has asked me to ask you to carry your tin hats and gas masks at all time when not on ops. And to obey the instructions given by our Gestapo...shit...our military police, who, I'm told, are here for your safety." DC glanced at Harper and then back again to his notes.

"And in case you didn't already know, and I'm sure most of you do, I am very pleased to announce that Winston Churchill is now Prime Minister!" Cheers and clapping from the boys. "Yes well, I hope it turns the tide."

"We've occupied Iceland and the Faroes – at least that means our Empire is still growing!" said Intel.

"Oh really? Thank you Greg. I've got some more bad news as well, I'm afraid. I'm sorry to tell you that Tiger passed away, peacefully in his sleep last night. Seeing as I was his replacement I never met him but I realise that he was very well liked and respected by all of you. We'll have a minute's silence now, if you please."

"I was always told to finish on a high note, especially by my music teacher." The joke fell flat. "...We've got the last of the Spitfire deliveries today if they can find somewhere to park. That should make ten but as you've probably noticed we've only got eight. So we'll continue to fly four Hurricanes plus spares until we're completely up to strength on the Spitfire front. Abbot, Harper, Kowalski, Tyler, you will operate as an independent section for the time being, because you won't be able to keep up! Abbot you'll be Section Leader. Harper you can have my Hurricane, seeing as you already stole it yesterday and nearly had the bloody tail off." A trickle of laughter went through the hut, Harper disappointed at not getting a Spitfire. "And I have decided to adopt Group's recommendations about combat formations to the letter." The room went silent again. "This means that we will continue to be flying three ship formations with a weaver. *Completely coincidentally,* this equates to two pairs, if you think of number one and two as a pair, number three and tail end Charlie as a pair. I want you to fly these formations as badly as you possibly can, at different heights and spaced out. But the pairs will miraculously stay together at all times, get it?" The boys had warmed up, some of them started laughing. DC was effectively telling them to fly *finger four* formations. "I know that Tiger was pushing for it, plus several other Squadron Commanders. It was ignored. My orders conform to Groups' recommendations – any questions or arguments? No I didn't think so!"

"Good on you boss!" said Abbo.

"Tip top bloody tastic!" said Gazzer to Harper, sitting next to him.

"Can't believe it" replied Harper. "I thought he was going to be a bloody martinet."

"And lastly, We've had some comings and goings recently and its been difficult to keep up with it all but I'd like to introduce you to three new pilots; Flt Lt Steve Pipe, Flt Lt Jack Tinley and Fg Off Lexy Smith, all of them already qualified on the Spit. Please make your introductions, show them round and help them get settled in as quickly as possible." A round of applause went up, for the C/O's tactics, not the replacements.

The meeting broke up and Gazzer took charge of tea making. Harper looked for Pollock. He was sitting at the back of the audience, his hat still on and skew whiff, no tie, dirty buttons. Harper approached and stood in his vicinity, courteously, cautiously.

"I say chaps can anyone tell me what all that 'wa wa wa' is about with their bombers."

"I can, actually" replied Intel, as usual. "Unlike our bomber boys, typical German, they don't, *apparently,* want to accept the reduction in performance you get if you pull back the faster engine to synchronise it with the slower one - full throttle all the way! The 'wa wa wa' is the interference pattern between two sources of noise." Gazzer looked up from the stove and started laughing. Greg ignored him. "Its Good for us on the ground because it makes them so easy to recognise. It's also comforting to know that *our* chaps show a bit more sympathy with the locals that they're about to bomb." Murmuring and approval from the boys.

"That's very interesting, thank you professor" replied Harper. "Tell me, Pollock, What range do you think our guns should be set at for optimum firing?"

"I don't know."

"Oh, ok. Not a problem - what are yours set at?"

"Don't know," said Pollock, looking up menacingly. The pilots around him became embarrassed, and started to find reasons to turn away.

"Can I have a word?"

"What about?" Pollock seemed to have a residual smirk on his face when no other emotions were apparent.

"Oh you know, stuff... outside if you don't mind?" Harper motioned towards the door.

"Don't mind if I do." Now the flavour was belligerent. After they got through the doorway, Harper carried on walking around the back of the hut. Pollock followed a few paces behind.

"You want cigarette?" asked Koval, leaning against the back of the hut, dragging on a *Capstan Full Strength.*

134

"Thanks very much, will save it for later though" replied Harper taking the cigarette and putting it in the breast pocket of his tunic. Koval looked over Harper's shoulder, immediately got the picture, stamped his cigarette out and left them to it.

"How did it go with your new bride last night? Assuming she *is* new, seeing as you've not been around here much."

"Shagged her silly. Not really my type though. Prefer them skinny."

"Oh well, me too. Hope we don't end up competing."

"That's not going to happen, is it?"

"Oh, really! Why's that then?"

"Toff like you. You've got money written all over you. Don't suppose you've worked a day in your life." Harper tried not to rise to the bait.

"I think you'll find you're about a quarter of a century out of date. It's been very hard on the estate since we lost all our lads in the first war. My family have to work hard, get their hands dirty."

"It must be terrible." Another smirk; a menacing smirk, even.

"Actually it's not what I want to talk to you about."

"I don't give a fuck what you want to talk to me about."

"Well, it's quite simple. You either listen to me. Or, one way or another, you'll probably end up facing a court martial."

"I got the bit about the gong, didn't hear anything about you becoming Marshal of the bloody Royal Air Force."

"Look you... Right, listen up! The C/O asked me to talk to you on a quiet, friendly basis." Pollock smirked again and raised his eyes - Harper tried desperately to ignore it. "So I'm trying to give you some quiet, friendly advice."

Pollock walked up to Harper, nose-to-nose: "fuck off."

Harper took a couple of steps back, pulled his right arm back and punched Pollock in the mouth: he crumpled backwards onto the grass. Harper squatted down – hearing a loud 'crack' beneath him as he did so - lifted Pollock by the collar with his left hand, and drew his right fist back ready for the next one.

"I'll have you for that" spluttered Pollock.

"You compromised the boys yesterday - *my* friends. They had to go in, outnumbered and with no tail cover. Don't you realise we're all scared? You've got to deal with it. You signed up for this; you've had the life, the best booze, no rationing, the women. Now you've got to pay for it. Turn back again and it'll be one of us who's shooting at you. Don't even worry about the hun." Pollock struggled to retaliate. Harper twisted his grip on Pollock's collar until he started choking.

"I'm... going... to... kill... you."

"Hear me well - each and every one of us is watching each and every move you make. Turn back and you'll get the whole nine yards." Harper released him and stood up quickly, ignoring the tugging feeling in his leg. He stepped back a couple of paces to a defensive position, fists ready.

"Like I said, I'm going to fucking kill you for that" said Pollock, getting up.

"If I were you I'd think about deserting. It'd be much better than compromising us."

"Are you calling me a coward? I'm going to..." lunging forward. Harper swung a right hook – Pollock went straight down again, and stayed there. Harper walked, limping slightly, back into the dispersal hut, and straight into DC's office.

"Had a chat with Bollock did we?"

"Oh yes, went very well. We had a nice chat about it. I... corrected him on a couple of things. He'll be probably be complaining of a bit of a headache but it's legit' for a change. Happy to take his Spitfire off of him in the meantime."

"No, you stick to Hurricanes for the time being. We'll get a nice new Spitfire for you Harper. Be good to see what you can do with it."

"If you don't mind sir, could I have an hour off to go to the hospital. Just for a quick going over."

"To see, Lucy is it? Is that what we're calling it these days?"

31

"Jesus Christ Tom! Doesn't it ever stop!" Harper's cast had cracked neatly down the outside of his leg, where the calf had flexed. Lucy snipped and broke the remainder of the cast away, cleaned the wound, repacked it fore and aft and then re-plastered it again, just slightly thicker. "This is the last time, I swear. Really Tom! I *could* get sacked for it you know."

"I'm trying to stay on ops! I'm doing my best, but it's not all fun and games!"

"You should still be in hospital - this is still a serious wound! And you're bloody flying with it like that. I don't get it!"

"Lucy, we've lost a handful of pilots already. I've been introduced to another bunch today – I don't even want to be friends with them for god's sake. Sometimes the new ones don't last a mission! Christ, I'm new. I've just been lucky."

"You call this lucky? You could have lost your leg! How is that lucky?"

Tiger just died! Burned to a crisp. Thank god he *died*! Smith T yesterday, Smith A before that, and Howell, their friend, on his first mission, Ginger, Gazzer shot down – we thought he was dead. Then find out he's not, for now anyway. It goes on and on for fuck's sake."

"Right! You sort this out! I'm finished. I've had enough!" Lucy stomped out of the room, starting to cry.

Harper waited for another 30 minutes, propping his leg up against a radiator to help the plaster set - trying, and failing, not to think about Lucy - then he cleaned the room and walked out. The ward sister gave him a strange look as he passed her in the corridor but he beamed his best, most confident smile back.

"It's ok, its gone hard" he said, realising what he was saying as he said it. The sister scurried on, blushing. Harper rode back to the airfield, just in time to see four Spitfires take off. He slowed down well before the gate to watch them as they formed up in two pairs – they looked more menacing, like '109s. For Harper, Vic formations looked like they belonged in an air pageant. He glanced back down in front of him to see the gate guard staring back – the same one as the day before, hand on holster. Predictably, Harper was stopped, his papers examined and the lights on his bike checked to see if they were properly blacked-out. Next; tyres pressure and tread depth – as he walked round the bike, the guard muttered something about 'bloody German crap.' Harper made a mental note to get round to the job of stripping the paint off at the earliest available opportunity, to uncover the BMW labels and German camouflage. Next the guard retreated to his gatehouse, purportedly to make a phone call concerning the use of personal transport while ops were taking place. Harper toyed with the idea of ducking under the gate, deterred in the end by observing that the guard now wore his side arm unclipped, his rifle slung over his shoulder instead of in the gatehouse. After he was finally let through, Harper accelerated to well above the 20mph speed limit whilst still in visual range of the guard and rode as fast as he could to dispersal. Short cut again, between the hangar and the heap of twisted metal girders and sheeting which used to be the other one. Greg flagged him down as he reached the hut.

"You're ok. Just those four."

"Who's up?"

"DC, Johnny, Doogy and Lexy - one of the new boys."

Harper dismounted and walked into the hut. The atmosphere didn't feel quite the same. Pollock was sitting back where he had been to start with, trying to latch onto the other new boys. Harper went straight to the food boxes by the stove and made himself some bread and jam, and two mugs of tea. Then he went outside to sit in the deckchairs with Intel.

"You ok?" asked Greg.

"Had a bit of a row with Lucy" replied Harper, handing over the second mug. "One sugar, right? I thought she'd be a little more on-side, seeing as she's dealing with this sort of thing every day."

"Yes, but she's at a civilian hospital. Most of our boys have gone to RAF Halton, most of the serious ones anyway. It's still a phoney war to most people, especially if they don't live near an airfield or army camp."

"Well she does live near an airfield – this one. A lot of our casualties went there yesterday. Halton - is that where Tiger ended up?"

"Yes." Harper stared into his tea. "What else is bothering you?" Harper didn't realise that he was such an open book – to Greg, anyway.

"Two things, I suppose. We've got a problem with one of the new ones. Except he's not that new – joined around the same time as I did, pretty much."

"I can't keep track with all the postings and replacements. Do you mean 'Old Yellow.'"

"Maybe, Pollock, Bollock?" Greg nodded. "C/O asked me to sort him out. I did, of sorts. Ended up biffing him on the nose."

"Good on you!" laughing. "And the other thing?"

"I know it sounds cheesy, but I don't like being down here when they're up there."

"Not cheesy at all - far from it. So you've got the opposite problem to Yellow. Don't worry, there'll be plenty to go round. Unlike you scally wags, I read the papers. I can see it coming."

"Listen, I need a bloody distraction. Fancy a game?" Harper was referring to Billiards: Greg agreed, but they only got so far as setting the balls up before the telephone started ringing, and then the scramble bell. Harper shot a glance at Intel, his expression a clear 'you're always right.' Not *quite* right this time - it still wasn't Harper's turn. Hatton, Rhino, Jock and Pipe ran out of the hut and towards their Spitfires.

"Look's like something's brewing," said Greg. "Might be you next." Now Harper was even more uneasy, the waiting always worse than the callout. Next the air raid siren went off. Harper, Intel, Gazzer, Abbo and Koval raced out of the hut, heading for the bunker, along with the majority of the fitters. And then the scramble bell rang. The boys ran back again. Jones saw Harper and turned on his heels, going straight for his new Hurricane. Harper ran into the hut, grabbed his flying gear, and back to the aircraft, panting, realising for the first time how much the past two weeks had taken a toll on his fitness. Jones helped strap him in, connected his headset – he had forgotten again - and then ran round to the wing, thumb up. Harper hit the starter button: the engine cranked ten blades but didn't fire. He released the starter button, primed again and hit the starter button once more. A muffled 'whump' accompanied a bright flash from the left exhaust stubs as unburnt petrol caught fire in the carburettor. Harper had over-primed. He kept his finger on the button, cranking the engine, trying to suck the fire into the inlet manifold as Jones shouted at the top of his voice to another fitter standing nearer the portable fire extinguisher. Five blades, six', seven', eight', nine' - Harper was thinking about getting out, when the engine suddenly coughed and barked into life, the flames immediately sucking back inside the cowling around the exhaust stack and disappearing.

"Blimey!" said Harper, collecting his wits before giving Jones the 'chocks away' signal – both fists together with thumbs pointing in opposite directions and then fists moved apart. Jones was laughing so much that the unlit cigarette that he had in his mouth fell off his lip - he dived under the wing and pulled on the rope, which was tied to both chocks, pulling them clear of the Hurricane. Harper looked across to check on Abbo, Gazzer and Koval: all engines running. He started to taxi but then saw a red flare go up from the control tower. And another.

"Ok Yellow section. Knock it off," said Abbo on the radio. "Shut down. I say again, shut down." Harper experience a flood of relief, followed by crushing disappointment - he had mentally geared himself up for going into combat. Now he had a surplus of adrenaline and nothing with which to use it up. He put in a small burst of power with the throttle and booted the rudder, bringing the Hurricane round in a neat 180-degree turn, taxied 20 yards, and then shut down. Jones and another fitter pushed sideways on the tail, castering the tail wheel of the Hurricane round to point the aircraft in its original direction. Jones bent down to retrieve his dropped cigarette.

"Jones?" said Harper. He looked up, expecting a telling off. "Can you roll *me* one."

Twenty Heinkels and fifteen '109s had been successfully turned back by Red and Blue section, with the help of nine Spitfires from Biggin Hill – one Spitfire and its pilot were lost. All eight Spitfires of Red section and Blue section returned safely to base, Johnny's losing its tail wheel in a rut from what remained of a filled-in bomb crater, also causing minor damage to the rudder. Doogy bounced heavily on landing due to oil on his windscreen, impairing his vision. No more aircraft were called out during the day, the weather deteriorating rapidly early in the afternoon.

DC stood the squadron down at 1700 so that the boys could go to The Ship. To their third wake in three days.

32

The boys assembled at the pub at 7pm. Doogy had something to celebrate, but the boys weren't in a party mood, even though they were trying to be.

"Come on, tell us how you got him, Doogy" said Gazzer.

"We are 5000ft. He comes in from my right, up in the sun. I am watching the flashes, not realising they are bullets."

"What did you think it was!" said Rhino.

"Confetti" added Johnny

"I don't know this word."

"Belt up and let him get on with it" said Abbo.

"So I am turning towards him and firing back. He pushes down, I roll, pull and down we are going. Then I am behind him. I am shooting again, and missing again. So I stop firing and say a prayer. 'Jesus, Mary, Mother of the...'"

"Yeh, yeh, we all know what a prayer is" said Gazzer, some of the boys sniggering.

"Shut! Up!" said Abbo.

"And the prayer make me shoot straight." All the boys started to laugh, even Abbo. When it had died down; "I shoot once, half second burst. Tailplane struts come off, brup! Shoot again, canopy blows off, BRUP! Nearly miss me."

"You mean nearly *hit* you?" asked Harper.

"Exact! Shoot again, engine blow up."

"BRUP!" shouted Gazzer. Abbo stood on his foot.

" Oil all over my screen. Now I am not seeing so I pull. Pull, pull, pull, very quick." Doogy shook his fists together between his legs. "Then I am flat, roll round, look down. Big bang! Big hole in ground!"

"Three cheers for Doogy!" shouted Gazzer. The boys cheered and clinked glasses, rising to it.

"Anyone else see it?" asked Intel.

"Yes, me" said Johnny. He was lying.

"It's a kill then. Well done Doogy. Come and see me next time or you won't get them awarded. You're obviously a crack shot!"

"In Poland, I am always shooting like this. Birds, rabbits. Germans invade, we starve. I kill as many as I can."

"Birds, or rabbits?" asked Gazzer.

"Germans." Harper slapped Gazzer on the back, laughing.

"Famous saying, can't remember who though," said Greg. "'God is not on the side of the best battalions, but on the side of the best shots.'"

Rhino to Harper; "Nice to see you with a smile on your face. You didn't seem yourself today."

"I think this has been one of the most frustrating days of my life. I think the highlight was punching Bollock."

"Heard about that. Well done!" shaking his hand: "...Notice how he was the only one who didn't climb into an aeroplane today?"

"Yes, well that's just as well because I think I gave him a headache. We didn't do anything either. Taxied 20 yards and shut down again after nearly setting fire to the thing."

"Eh?"

"Carb' fire."

"Ah, you've got to watch that. We don't have any trouble like that on our Spitfires of course." Rhino was joking, the engines were virtually identical.

"You bugger. Tell me what it's like."

"No, don't think I can help you there, we're a secret brotherhood."

"You're a secret shit!"

With nothing in particular happening at the pub, and no one feeling able to fully celebrate the dead or the living, the boys decided to go back to base early and save themselves for the weekend. Two days of peace would make all the difference. The damage and state of repairs to the officer's mess was so bad that many of the pilots had taken the option to sleep in the dispersal hut for the evening. Plus it meant that they didn't have to get up so early. Once again the catering staff had defied the Station Commander and supplied trays of sandwiches, a joint of ham, three chickens and fresh vegetables. The log burner had been redundant for a couple of days and now was fired up again. Greg was the most ingenious, making a chicken rotisserie out of wire coat hangars, except that after a few minutes the wire softened and the bird descended into the fire. Most of the pilots opted for cold roast ham and boiled vegetables rather than charcoal chicken. Harper settled down to an early night, still wearing his uniform and flying jacket between sheets and blankets on the floor.

Harper woke again early, with first light coming through the slit from the partially open door of the hut. He found the crumpled cigarette in his breast pocket that Koval had given him and tried to smoke it, but it was too strong – he aimed the remaining half into the stove and pulled a letter from Eric out of the pocket of his flying jacket:

Block 48 Room 4

R.A.F. South Cerney

Nr Cirencester.

Gloucestershire

Dear Tom

> *We've been in this 'ole about two weeks, & I'm just beginning to poke my head up thro' the top most layers of red tape & see daylight. As a warrant officer said, the only reason the Jerries haven't bombed this place is because there is so much bull shit around that they think its a farmyard*

But, really, we're treated like children. We're told to march to flying and lectures. If we don't want to, we simply don't. We're meant to be in by 9.45 p.m. We can simply walk straight in at any hour we please. And, on the whole, once one's learned the tricks of the trade, its not such a bad place.

> *Dad brought Mary back. He came over last Friday about 7 p.m & we went back to Brize Norton. I left him there & went on about another 20 miles to spend the night with the tart I knew in Ramsgate & had met quite accidentally in Cheltenham the week before. I played my cards right and got asked up to her place on my day off. Anyhow I got there about 10 p.m, it had rained all the time & I was soaking wet. I came back on sat: night. Mary's running O.K, pinking a bit but that can be remedied. Daddy certainly put a couple of dents in her petrol tank O.K, fucked up her appearance good & proper.*

By the way. I did the first 20 mls: on Fri: pillion, I never realised before that its so uncomfortable. I don't know how you stuck it.

> *Did you hear the one about the girl who was playing with her boyfriend's tool in the theatre. He was getting pretty excited & finally it came right into 'er 'and like.*

"What shall I do with this," she said.

"Oh, you'd better chuck it at the orchestra," said the boyfriend. Consequently the 'cello player received the packet smack in the eye. "Hey", he shouted to the conductor, "Someone's thrown a fuck at me!" "That's O.K" said the conductor, "You've been acting like a c**t all day."

> *Filthy isn't it.*

> *We're flying 'Oxfords here, they're pretty good fun & probably mean bombers. They're much more complicated than Tigers, of course, with*

pull-up undercarts, etc, & twin engines. By the way, I can make a marvellous Heinkel note by unsynchronising the engines, it almost scares me.

Harper laughed at the coincidence.

One of my instructor's pupils went & killed himself yesterday. He got lost, got into filthy weather & was apparently flying at about 200 ft, the silly fool. Of course, the poor bugger didn't realise the 200 ft: on the altimeter was set for his own 'drome & he creamed his plane into a hill near Stroud. I didn't know him actually, he was a Canadian. Actually, there is a high %age of accidents at F.T.S, we're getting down to business now.

Would you be a pal & try & get hold of a copy of "The Enchantment" for me. I'm reading a book "First Passion" at the moment. The following quotation, by Byron is on the Fly. Sheet:-

"In her first passion Woman loves her lover.

In all the others all she loves is love."

Cheers you old sod & give my love to Jerry, etc: I did intend to come home on my day off sometime but now that I've found this new attraction, . . . Well, its too good to miss. I'm afraid I've got to give her lunch next Sat: & yours faithfully will soon be broke again.

Good luck with your flying.

Harper drifted gently back to sleep for a while, with memories of comfort, hearth and home.

33

Harper woke up to the smell of roasting chicken. Greg was busy at the stove with a new, improved rotisserie. It worked, and the pilots were treated to a breakfast of chicken sandwiches to supplement their bread and jam, boiled and scrambled eggs.

"Ok squadron, up the lot of you!" It was the C/O. "I want you to form up outside for shotgun drill at 0730." Gazzer had been asleep a few feet away from Harper – unusually, the snoring continuing despite the delicious cooking smells. Harper nudged him awake.

"Get up old boy, we've got shotgun drill."

"Shot what? Shotgun what?"

"I say chaps!" said Harper. "...Looks like Flt Lt Tyler doesn't know what shotgun drill is." Neither did anyone else.

The pilots formed in a line outside the dispersal hut at 0730. DC marched out in front of them with two guns, one over each shoulder. He put one on the ground and broke open the other.

"This, as you will all know I'm sure, is a shotgun. Hands up who hasn't fired one." Lexy, Pipe and Pollock put up their hands. "Well we'll soon change that. This is my own gun, a particularly nice Woodward that I saved up for, but I'll be happy for you to try out." He closed the gun, placed it on the ground, picked up and broke the other one.

"And *this* is a Merkel. Anyone guess where it was made?"

"Germany" said Greg.

"Correct! And, if you look on the stock here" moving closer to the boys: "…you can see a pair of *Luftwaffe* wings, embossed. A very good friend of mine found it in the back of a downed Heinkel. Why do you think that was, anyone?"

"In case the gunner ran out of ammunition for his machine gun sir" said Gazzer. The boys started laughing, quickly suppressed by a stern look from DC.

"Its 'special issue' because the Germans give their pilots shotgun lessons" replied Greg.

"Correct again, Intel. That's because to be an effective shot you need to learn about and practise deflection shooting. So that's what we're going to do. Its *particularly* important when flying a Spit because, unlike the Hurricane with its sloping nose – which I like very much by the way - when you point the nose ahead far enough to shoot the hun, the Spit's long nose can blank him out. You need to have the instinct to know where you are going to point a Spit before you do it. I've got a couple of clay traps rigged up at the fire dump, and so if you'd like to join me in a morning's shooting gentlemen, Jerries permitting of course."

The Squadron arrived at the dump to find a fire engine with its ladder up and extended, and Jones standing at the top with two, Ely clay pigeon traps lashed to the support rail. Over his shoulder he had a newspaper bag filled with clays, which he supported by raising one leg onto a higher rung and balancing the bag on his knee. And he had still managed to light a cigarette.

"Look at Jonesy!" said Gazzer to Harper, standing too closely to DC when he said it.

"Yes, how kind of him to show us the wind direction" replied Harper elbowing him in the ribs. Gazzer elbowed him back, Harper clutching his side and doubling in pain. The first two called up to shoot were Rhino and Harper, who handed over to Abbo while he recovered. The rest of the squadron huddled round behind so that they could get an idea who was pointing at what.

"Abbot, you take both shots to get the first clay, and Rhinde, likewise for the second," said the C/O. "PULL!" Jones delivered the first clay, followed by the second, 2 seconds later. Abbot aimed, fired and missed, fired again and missed again. Rhinde got the second clay with his first shot, and the first with his second.

"He wiped your eye. Well done Rhino" said DC. "Abbot, you were high and behind. Again please." Jones delivered again; Abbot missed twice and Rhino got both clays. "Bloody excellent!" said DC. "Abbot, high and behind. Swing through the shot, like a golf swing. Don't stop and shoot. Squadron, take note. Again please." The exercise was repeated with the same result. DC stepped in, got rid of Rhino and took his gun. "AGAIN JONESY!" DC hit his target and Abbot missed.

"For Christ's sake" said Abbot.

"JONES, LIGHT ANOTHER CIGARETTE, IF YOU PLEASE" said DC. And to Abbo; "Now watch the smoke, it's behind the bird so you need even more deflection. JONES, ONE CLAY ONLY, PLEASE. PULL!" Abbo missed with his first shot – same level, just behind – and hit with his second. The pilots roared and clapped their approval. "AND AGAIN, TWO CLAYS. PULL!" Abbo got them both - a bigger roar of approval. "Right, next two." Harper and Gazzer went up. "PULL!" Gazzer missed and Harper got both clays.

"Oops, sorry" said Harper, Gazzer laughing.

"Beers on me" said Gazzer.

"No, on me" replied Harper, quickly reloading his gun and firing at the next two while Gazzer was still trying to reload. Harper relaxed and let Gazzer go for the next – he missed them both.

"Low and behind Tyler. Well done, and bugger off, Harper. Give your gun to Hatton" said DC. Harper was relieved – the recoil was hurting his cheek. "Tyler, you need working on boy. Keep the stock of the gun at your waist, the end of the barrel on the horizon. When you see the clay bring the stock up to your shoulder, run the gun along its trajectory, pull the trigger once you've passed it and keep swinging the gun. Just like a golf club after you've hit the ball. Don't stop the gun and shoot, keep moving past the target and complete the swing." Gazzer reloaded. "TWO CLAYS JONES. PULL!" Gazzer took aim, fired and hit the first one, aimed again, fired and got the second. The boys cheered their approval.

Then a loud 'POP' made everyone turn round. A green flare had been fired from the control tower. "OK chaps, look's like we're needed" said DC. "We'll continue with this later." Two ambulances roared across the airfield to collect the boys - Johnny and Lexy were small enough to share pillion on Harper's motorbike. As Harper reached the hut and switched his engine off he heard the phone ringing. Even though he knew they were being scrambled, the sound of the phone still made his heart skip a beat and then start thumping.

"I think I'm becoming 'telephonophobic'" said Harper to his passengers as he climbed off the bike and ran into the hut to collect his flying clothing. Lexy didn't know any better, but Johnny's look said it all.

34

The patrol initially climbed to 14000ft and headed north-east, out across the Blackwater estuary in Essex. Abbo was Yellow Section leader, Koval, Yellow 2, Harper, Yellow 3 and Gazzer, his wingman, Yellow 4. DC, Johnny, Doogy and Lexy had been scrambled as Red section and were already 5 miles out in front due to their Spitfires' speed advantage.

Harper listened intently to the radio. His nerves were raw – his hands shaking and his knees knocking slightly. He had got used to being away from battle, but the two-pair formation gave him a sense of security. And if he went into an attack he knew that he could trust Gazzer to look after his tail. Harper looked over his shoulder and gave him a little wave – Gazzer smiled back and stuck two fingers up.

"Red section, 30 plus bombers 10 O'clock low! Tally Ho!" It was DC. Harper's reaction was immediate - what about the fighters? Surely there must be some escorting? A few seconds of silence passed. Harper squinted ahead but he couldn't see anything, they were just that little bit too far away.

"Ten plus '109s coming in from the sun Boss!" Harper didn't recognise the voice. And he didn't feel anything good either, about his own instinct or their situation. He leaned forward in his straps, as if bringing himself a few inches farther forward would make a difference to what he could see. Ironically now he *could* see – a faint black, curving smoke trail going downwards, still too far to see the aircraft though.

Harper switched on his gun sight, armed the firing button and tried a half-second squirt. All ok. Then he saw the tracer from Gazzer's guns going forward.

"Yellow section check your sights and arm your guns" said Abbo - two more squirts from the other two Hurricanes. "Yellow section, multiple targets straight ahead! Go for the bombers. Tally ho!" There! Harper could see a few black spots just below the horizon, a few bigger ones underneath. There was another curving smoke trail too, a big one, maybe a bomber. Unlike Red section, Yellow section was in a perfect firing position, the trap from their fighters already sprung. Harper checked over his shoulder again - Gazzer was still there watching his every move. Now Harper could see the bombers clearly, still in formation and heading inland. He wondered about their target – Duxford or Cambridge maybe - and then forgot about it as he chose which bomber to attack. Abbo started a shallow descent towards the bombers *still* in formation – it looked like they hadn't noticed the impending attack. Either that or they were the most disciplined pilots Harper had seen so far. Abbo turned left slightly, he was obviously going for the starboard group. Suddenly all the bombers started firing together, the tracer from sixty machine guns curving up in a huge dome, like a massive birdcage. At once Harper was absolutely terrified. He turned slightly to the right, aimed for the nearest one, told himself to wait and, despite it, started shooting before he felt he should – he couldn't help himself. The tracer went the right way, towards the glass-panelled nose of the Heinkel 111 but he was still too far away to see any damage, despite the massive closing speed, the sum of the airspeeds of the two aircraft. At the last moment he started pulling up, raking the gunfire along the top of the fuselage – now he could see the dancing yellow flames and puffs of smoke from the incendiary bullets as they hit home. A split second later and the bomber had passed underneath. Harper aimed again and raked the aircraft behind it in the same way. His finger on the firing button was like a countdown timer: 12 seconds of ammunition left, 11,' 10,' 9,' 8.' Out of the corner of his eye Harper sensed Gazzer peeling away to starboard – something was happening behind him but he couldn't turn to look for fear of hitting one of the stragglers at the back of the formation. An instant later and he was clear of all aircraft. Now he pulled hard on the stick and rolled right to make another attack from the rear left quarter. Harper looked over his shoulder – nothing there. As he completed the turn he checked the stick to neutral and then pushed, translating into a shallow dive. A quick check of the sun: no one up there. The formation was breaking up and a bomber - one of the two that he had just attacked - was now rolling slowly onto its back, smoke and flames spewing from the fuselage. Harper selected a bomber turning blindly away from him and pressed the firing button again; 7,' 6,' 5,' 4,' – the shells hosing along the side of the fuselage, bright yellow flashes from the rear upper gun as it fired directly at him, the tracer going wide and to his right. Another burst; 3,' 2,' 1' with continuous tracer, and then his guns stopped firing. Harper pushed and rolled to the left, diving away to the deck. Another furtive glance behind – nothing there – he was being lucky. He kept the dive going all the way from 14000ft, the throttle still wide open, and levelled off a few hundred feet from the ground before turning for south-west for home, the speed washing back from Vne to a high speed cruise. Harper trimmed back so that he could release the stick, and then noticed that his right leg ached, he was panting, bathed with sweat, his knees knocking and his thumb still pressing on the firing button.

"Silly bastard" he said, laughing.

35

"One damaged and one probable. Can't be sure it was the one I hit that I saw going down" said Harper, sitting outside the dispersal hut with a large mug of tea with two sugars in his left hand, a piece of bread and jam in his right, both his hands still shaking. As he spoke, Gazzer walked nonchalantly across the grass, put up his extended forefinger to his fitter and then bent it, imitating a pistol being fired. The two other Hurricanes from Yellow section were just shutting down.

"We'll get the reports from the others and collate" said Greg. "See what the they have to tell. Well done though."

"I feel well done all right. I was scared silly. What happened to Bollock?"

"Wasn't scrambled. I think the C/O's got the nod on him. I did notice him being sick round the back though."

"I don't have a problem with sick, piss or shit - just as long as he does the job. We all know what he's about. He's trying to get himself posted to a nice fluffy training squadron where he can show his fighter pilot's wings off to the birds at the local."

"Be that as it may…" the phone interrupted them. Harper jumped again slightly, spilling his tea. Greg picked the phone up.

"BLUE SECTION SCRAMBLE!"

154

Hatton, Rhino and Jock came running out of the hut, followed by Pollock.

"As if by magic!" said Harper. Greg smiled and then wiped it from his face, deciding that he wasn't being impartial-enough. "This'll be interesting."

As the four Spitfires fired up and taxied out, Red section was returning at the same time - all four of them, the last one trailing smoke. The first three landed safely, the last came in with its wheels up and landed on its belly, sending up a spray of earth and dust as it came to a halt. Harper knew by the small yellow circle on its nose that it was DC's aeroplane.

"Hope he's alright," said Harper, taking a swig of his tea, and then realising how callous it might look.

"You really like him, don't you," said Greg.

"Too much." The blood wagons and a fire engine were quickly in attendance to DC's aeroplane. Harper and Greg watched intently, relieved finally when the canopy was heaved back and DC climbed out, unaided. Harper felt a tap on his shoulder.

"Beers on you old boy!" It was Gazzer.

"Why's that then – I thought we'd already agreed."

"Not for wiping my eye you silly sod! I'm talking about the bandit I got off your arse."

"I had no idea! I saw you peel away though!"

"Christ man! He was right up your chuff! I peeled away and reversed the turn, came up behind him and shot him to pieces. Didn't you see the tracer? He was blatting away at you like a good one."

"No I didn't. Not a single hit on my old crate. Well done ... and, thanks, of course."

"You ok old boy?"

"Its that bloody phone, makes me jumpy."

"Tell me about it."

Greg, Harper and Gazzer watched as the four Spitfires got airborne, and then went into the hut – it was getting a bit chilly outside. Harper warmed himself by the stove while Greg put a record on the gramophone and wound it up. Cole Porter, with a scratch again.

One hour went by before the boys heard the sound of Merlin engines and, one by one, walked outside to watch them come back in. Two Spitfires showed up, landing perfectly and taxiing to their allotted stands at dispersal. Just two.

"Bloody hell" said Gazzer. "Please, not again."

"Wait, wait and see" replied Harper. But no more came. The Spitfires shut down and their pilots climbed out: Rhino and Jock. They walked back to the hut, quiet in their manner.

"Oh no" said Gazzer, again.

As they got closer, Harper noticed that Jock had tears in his eyes, embarrassed because of it.

"Rhino?" said Harper, questioning.

"Fucking Pollock" replied Rhino, throwing his flying helmet at a chair, and missing.

"Christ, what happened?"

"He peeled off, *engine* problems! Bruce tore him off a strip, told him to come back in formation or he'd have him court martialled. He came back in all right. Collided with Bruce – took his bloody tail off."

"I don't bloody believe it," said Gazzer.

"Believe it" replied Rhino.

"Any parachutes?"

"If I'd seen a parachute from Bollock I'd have shot him to pieces, trust me."

"No, Bruce!"

"I don't know. Cross your fingers."

The boys made tea and sat in a circle outside the hut for another half an hour. No one said a word in that time, until the phone rang. Everyone jumped, some more than others. Greg answered.

"Yes? I'm Ball, Intelligence Officer. So, yes you can. HE IS? Thank Christ for that! I mean thank you very much, sir. Good... great... oh really! Thanks again!" The Squadron was as one in its complete attention. "It was the C/O of 601'. Bruce got out! All fine! Bruised his backside a bit evidently!" The sighs of relief spread out across the lawn.

"I swear to all of you, if Bollock turns up I'll put a bullet in him" said Rhino, his right hand resting on his service revolver.

"You'll have to get in the queue," said Harper. He sat down on a deckchair, smoked a cigarette and contemplated his feelings towards this man. The mutual lack of respect meant that they could never have been friends. Nevertheless, Harper surprised himself for feeling absolutely no remorse or regret of any kind. Not even for punching him on perhaps the last day of his life. Harper's attachment to his squadron was as strong at this moment as he was to his own family, its pilots as close to him as his brother. And Pollock had compromised them. As time continued it became more and more obvious that Pollock wouldn't be turning up, especially considering that they had collided over land rather than sea. When the squadron was stood down, the boys decided that a return to The Ship was called for, and this time they were in the mood to celebrate.

36

The pilots slept in the dispersal hut for another night after they returned from the pub. Harper had retired early, feeling tired. Consequently he was up early, and made a breakfast of omelettes or fried eggs and toast for the rest of the boys, some of them nursing hangovers.

"Harper, can I have a word?" asked DC. Harper walked into his office. "Well done yesterday. I think we can properly call you ace soon (five confirmed kills)! How are you getting on?"

"Like the *ace* bit, thank you. Never felt better sir."

"Well, I don't know about that. I've got another job for you. I need a Hurricane delivered."

"Great, which one?"

"Yours. Don't get your hopes up about Spitfires though. We're even more down after yesterday. Three weeks away from full strength I was told by Group – and that's *without* further losses."

"Sorry, I don't get it sir."

"I want you to deliver your Hurricane somewhere, for two days. And then you can deliver it back again. Think of an airfield that's long enough, come and tell me and I'll sign off the trip for you. Need you new chaps to practise your navigation skills."

"But I... What about the others?"

"Don't worry about the others. They'll get a turn. You're an asset and you need a couple of days off."

"I don't sir."

"You do. Don't oppose me Harper. I hear I'm a martinet! According to you! It all gets back, believe me. At least you won't be frightening children and old ladies – I can see the bruises have died down. Go and get a tan for a day or two and they'll look even better."

"But what about our section? We need four."

"We've got two fully serviceable Hurrys in the hangar. Might even fly one myself actually. I'll court martial you if you repeat this, but I'm realising that in some ways the Hurricane makes a better gun platform than the Spit. More stable in turbulence – except at high speed of course - better concentration of fire (the Hurricane's guns were close together, the Spitfire's spread out across the wing) and better viz. And it absorbs a lot more punishment. Just a shame about its top speed. Anyway, I'll shuffle the pilots. Now bugger off in case I change my mind."

"I don't know what to say."

"Well don't say anything. You are dismissed!"

Harper couldn't believe his luck. This would be his first leave since joining the Squadron - it felt like years since – and what a way to take it. A pang of guilt about leaving the boys for a couple of days came and went – leave was different to being off sick. The destination was easy to choose: he would go and stay with Dan in Norfolk. He'd be able to land on Dan's strip at the house, maybe even catch up with Jane.

DC signed off Harper's flight and he rode back to the mess on his bike to pack a small bag – his own clothes this time – before returning to his aeroplane, refuelled and rearmed, just to be on the safe side. As Harper walked out to the Hurricane, Abbo cornered him.

"Hey you, where you off to?"

"Friend's pad in Norfolk, meet up with a girlfriend too if I'm lucky."

"I got you something." Abbo pulled a brown paper bag from the pocket of his flying jacket. It contained a red & white checked silk scarf.

"It's the nicest thing that anyone's got me. Er, apart from the car of course, and the ... hmm. Thanks!"

"Have fun. And don't forget, there's only enough blood in your body to keep one head working at a time."

"Eh?"

"It means that when the little head comes up the big one stops thinking."

"You've got me to a tee."

"Have fun old boy, lucky bugger!" added Rhino.

"Rhinde, come here please" said DC. He was getting a leave pass too, and a Spitfire to go with it.

Harper chose a different route from the last time. He flew east until he crossed the Thames estuary at 500ft past Southend and then dropped down to 50ft above the water, tracing the coastline of Essex and Suffolk, past Shoeburyness, Clacton, Felixstowe, Aldeburgh and Lowestoft. Where the sea was relatively calm he brought the aircraft within a few feet of the water to try out something he'd heard discussed in the bar. He wanted to experiment with the bow wave produced by the form of the aircraft pushing through the air at high speed. With the Hurricane perfectly in trim to fly hands-free, the propeller tips less than six feet from the water, the bow wave was squeezing between the sea and the wings of the Hurricane. Harper took a leap of faith and loosened his grip on the stick. The bow wave gently pushed the nose up and he started climbing again. He tried it several times in case it was just his imagination, but it was there for sure. Then he nearly hit a squadron of low-flying seagulls and decided to climb back up to 50ft again.

· At Great Yarmouth Harper turned inland, and climbed to 500ft, heading west until he saw the A11. As he passed over it he could make out the four turrets of Dan's house sticking above the trees. Harper descended to just below tree top height, banked around the back of the

160

wood on the south side of the lake, turned in to skim just above the surface and barrel-rolled over the house. No milk floats this time. He flew a neat circuit with a curving approach and landed on the 750-yard strip, which ran from north west to south east, perpendicular to the approach road. Harper taxied up through a gap in the hedge at the end of the strip, taxied up the approach road and parked on the lawn in the courtyard at the front of the hall, next to the clock house. Dan had been out on the back lawn above the lake watching the fly by, and now raced through a side door in the west wing and into the courtyard, clutching a bottle of champagne with two glasses sticking out of his jacket pockets.

"Now that's what I call arriving in style!" said Dan, expertly popping the cork from the bottle as he walked round the back of the trailing edge.

"I know, I can't believe it myself!" said Harper, jumping down. "28 minutes, from take off to touchdown! Bit quicker than horseback. I think we should toast my Commanding Officer."

"It was great when dad parked the Moth here, first time. But I never thought I'd see a fighter on the lawn! I'm going to call everyone I know in a 10 mile radius and hold a party here tonight. *Don't* tell me you can't stay."

"I'm most definitely staying," replied Harper, taking and gulping down his first glass. "I'm not going anywhere for two days, if you'll have me?"

"Christ, you can base it here permanently if you like. I'll tether a blimp from the lake and get some anti aircraft guns installed in the turrets."

"The C/O said he expects me to return with a suntan" said Harper, topping up his glass.

"You're in Norfolk, not Nigeria - might have to get the shoe polish out. Hope you brought your country shoes by the way!"

"Oh of course, I've got a special shoe compartment fitted in here. Its next to the picnic hamper." Dan had a good look round Harper's Hurricane and sat in the cockpit for a thorough description of the controls and instruments before his father arrived in the Rolls' and took pictures with an ancient camera. A few people arrived by mid afternoon, followed by another group at teatime. By 7pm a party was in full swing, guests taking turns to be photographed in the cockpit - every conceivable combination of people, house and Hurricane as the subjects.

After a while Harper started to tire, deciding to take a walk and liven himself up rather than nap – he worried that he might not wake up again otherwise. As he reached the end of the approach road at the gatehouse he saw a bus pull up, full of factory workers. They were from the CRO, and Jane was among them.

"Hi hon! Long time no see! You look better than I thought you'd be. Dan told me about your... prang." Jane hugged him and then kissed him firmly on the lips.

"I was going to call. Only just got here myself. You look better than ever."

"Its ok, Dan invited us, told us you were here - he's a lovely man. You should see my biceps. I'll give you an arm wrestle later and probably win. I'm an expert with a rivet gun."

"Love to, but I think you will. I'm as weak as a kitten."

Predictably, the evening descending into chaos, everyone drinking as much as possible, particularly the CRO workers, who had been used to nothing stronger than pale ale for months. And Dan had a very large cellar. When darkness fell the CRO workers went back in their bus – apart from Jane - and the party started to move inside. But Dan had a plan.

"Tom, I've got a little idea but I wanted to pass it by you. Yes means yes and no means no, so no problem."

"Go on."

"Well, seeing as we've got a few hundred acres out front - no problems with livestock, that sort of thing - what about a little half second burst on the guns? Please the ladies?"

"Hmmm... brilliant idea! Let's make it better. Lift the tail up and we'll shoot at something."

Setting up took 20 minutes, after which the guests were reassembled on the front lawn in the courtyard, the Hurricane tethered with its tail lifted onto a hay bale, courtesy of five workmen from Dan's estate.

Harper got a leg up onto the wing – it was considerably higher up as a result of the elevated tail - climbed into the cockpit and switched on the battery and the gun sight.

"Left a bit please!" said Harper. The workmen lifted the tail and brought it a few inches to the left. "Sorry, no right a bit please,"– he wanted the nose to go left, not the tail. "Bit more. Got it! Tail up a bit more. Stop! Ok, push the chocks in behind the wheels (the guns' recoil would push the aircraft backwards.) Now stand clear all of you."

Harper turned the ring from 'safe' to 'fire' and hit the button. For eight seconds.

The entire courtyard was illuminated with blazing light and deafening sound – the withering effect of eight .303 Browning machine guns with incendiary bullets decimating an old tractor parked 200 yards away, a quarter way down the drive. One of the elderly ladies fell backwards in a complete faint, caught by her husband. Another stood and rocked slightly, a puddle forming at her feet. Harper released the firing button - a deafening silence followed, any background noise stifled by the spreading pawl of smoke. Then wild shouts and laughter built steadily from the audience, the applause reaching a massive climax. Dan ran, ankle-deep in shell cases, up to the cockpit as Harper was switching off the gun sight and the battery.

Between coughs and laughs: "Tom, I've… led a privileged life and… seen a lot. But I will never… forget this moment, as long as I live."

"It's a shame that I'm not going to let you tell anyone, or that lot for that matter! Until I'm dead, or the war's over, whichever the later."

"If they ever build a two-seater I'm going to sell this house and buy one. Christ! What about the ammunition?" The shell cases were absolutely everywhere.

"Don't worry, I've got a tame fitter."

37

Harper woke late. He was in the same room as when he last visited, with the same sounds of the country coming in through the sash window. But no sunlight, and no girl. Jane had decided not to stay the night because she was working – Harper had got Dan's butler to take her back in the car at midnight.

For a few seconds, Harper couldn't remember what had happened during the evening. But then he *could,* and he started smiling. The gunnery demonstration had seemed to have a wild effect on the guests, especially some of the women. The party really had descended into chaos, everyone drinking more than before, a few of them had stripped off naked and skinny dipped in the lake before streaking around the lake shore. Jane had literally jumped Harper in the tree house in the main garden. It was quite unexpected – beforehand he'd quietly dismissed the idea of getting anywhere, he had thought she'd seemed a little too 'decent' last time. Then Harper started laughing, when he remembered taking her from behind whilst she was waving out of the tiny window to the guests passing by below – they couldn't see what was happening of course. Wild, tree house memories came back in his mind and he squirmed around in the bed, thinking of what they had been up to together, his plaster cast snagging on the silk sheets as he kicked and stretched out.

"You're coming off," said Harper to the cast in a sudden burst of activity, as he got out of bed, dressed quickly and then walked out of the house, across to the combined garage and tractor shed behind the clock house. The place was deserted, most of Dan's workers were out in the field. Harper found a pair of tin snips among the boxes of tools – they looked almost identical to the plaster snips which Lucy had used the last time she removed it. Harper had a quick look round and then whipped his trousers off, raised his leg to the bench and had the plaster off in less than a minute. There was that familiar 'bad socks' smell again – he was glad that the place was deserted. Then he removed the dressings underneath the cast, and doused the wounds with a bottle of white spirit which he found on a shelf. Afterwards his leg looked, smelled and felt much better, the calf muscle atrophied only slightly from disuse. Harper decided that he would borrow some long socks from Dan and use two of them as a dressing, changing them every day, otherwise getting as much air to the wounds as possible. He went back to his room for a bath and shave before dressing again and going out for a walk.

Harper marched out of the courtyard, past the pink cottage where Dan's parents lived and onwards to the main road bordering the edge of the estate. He managed just over 2 miles before his leg started aching, but he carried on, taking 5-minute breaks and then walking for 10 more. After 4 miles he arrived in the town and found the local pub, still stuck on the back of the church. It was open for lunch.

"What can I get you to drink?" said the barman as Harper limped in.

"Oh, let me see, could you mix up lime and lemonade in a pint glass?" replied Harper.

"This is a pub, not a gymnasium. Now what do you want to drink?"

"A glass of red wine and a packet of crisps please."

Harper sat down to read a copy of the Telegraph, propping his leg up on another chair and kneading it occasionally with both hands, as rewarding an experience as scratching an itch ignored for a week. He read about himself on page one, about his squadron repelling a large formation of bombers over Essex. The kills were exaggerated, the losses underestimated. He wondered to himself that, seeing as this was a piece of journalistic bullshit, government propaganda, or both, how much of the rest of the news might be broad fiction. Another piece explained that German forces were now occupying The Hague. In complete contrast to the upbeat nature of earlier stories, it went on to imply that the fall of France was inevitable, but Harper couldn't understand why, even though he reread it three times.

"Good to see you're getting down to the arduous business of complete relaxation," said Dan as he walked in, ordering himself a glass of wine. "Personally, I can't do it without exercise or at least a faint trace of alcohol."

"Hello old chap! Been so busy I haven't had time to catch up with anything. Eric's been writing me letters though, getting on fine. Looks like he'll be on bombers. Don't know how mum is going to cope with two of us in the air. Or dad."

"…Yes I know" pausing for a few seconds. "It was a brilliant night last night. You livened the place up a bit - understatement of the century! I have never heard anything like that in my life!" Just for a fraction of a second Harper thought that Dan was referring to his performance in the tree house. "Its just awesome, the *firepower* of the beast. What's it like Harps? You know, combat… I'm sorry, shouldn't have. I learned not to ask silly old shit like this with my uncle – he served in the first one."

"Not at all. Not what I'd talk to any old Tom or Dick about though."

"What I mean is, are you scared?"

"Out of my wits, every time."

"How do you, you know, *deal* with it?"

"We go to the pub a lot. Not always the answer though. I thought I'd be getting used to it by now, but I don't seem to. My last battle, the one in here (folding and pointing to the piece in the newspaper). Absolutely terrifying - when people used to say that their knees were knocking when they were scared, I thought it was a figure of speech. But its true: happened to me several times. We've changed our tactics so we've always got someone guarding our tail but it still gets hairy. I was being shot at when I was shooting and didn't even notice."

"How's that?"

"I was being attacked from behind when I was shooting at a formation of bombers. My wingman got him."

"Who? Got what, sorry?"

166

"The fighter that was attacking me. He shot it down and I didn't even notice. If he hadn't I'd be brown bread."

"How's everyone else getting on? Your friend Gazzer?"

"He's ok. He ditched last week but got picked up. Most of us have had something happen to them by now, you just get on with it." Harper decided not to tell him about Pollock.

"Don't know how you do it old boy. Really I don't. Very proud though." The two clinked their glasses and ordered another glass of wine each. "Tell you what though - sod the estate - if it carries on much longer I'll be signing up."

38

Harper spent the rest of his time at the estate walking, reading, eating well and not drinking. He'd noticed the yellowing of the whites of his eyes, the semi-permanent bags under them and a certain sallowness of his complexion. He had even noticed a few burst blood veins in his nose, but he didn't know if that was the effect of alcohol, rich food or G force. On the morning of the second day Harper still felt drained and tired – secretly he'd felt relieved that Jane hadn't showed up the evening before, even though she had promised to.

There was another drive growing within him - guilt. He was starting to be aware of a desire to get back to the Squadron. It threatened to become overwhelming. His logical mind told himself that he deserved this leave, it was right for him to have it. But a deeper, unstoppable force was telling him to get back and support his family, his band of brothers. The feeling developed all morning on day two, until at lunchtime Harper could stand it no longer. He packed quietly and took *French leave,* taking care to leave the house without detection – he didn't want to have to explain himself to Dan. As Harper climbed into the Hurricane he tried to make himself laugh, remembering that the French called the same thing *English leave,* but he wasn't laughing. The attempt at humour couldn't dissipate the lump in his throat as he started up and taxied quickly out of the courtyard before Dan could intervene. As Harper taxied the aircraft down the drive, he did a quick check of the magnetos and carburettor heat, rolled onto the strip and opened the throttle up – he didn't look behind him.

The aircraft used just over half the length of the strip. At the end, just above the ground he selected wheels up and rolled into a steep right turn to fly across the lake, in time to see Dan running down the garden waving both hands. Harper waggled his wings in farewell, stayed low, and turned left, heading south until he picked up the A11, then turned right to track along it, all the way down to Duxford. Then he turned south again and stayed on that heading for a few more minutes until he could see the Thames running west to east ahead of him.

Harper ran through some of the pre-approach checks as he first caught sight of the airfield, his feelings a mixture of relief to be back, and apprehension as to what he might find when he got there. But then he saw something else - a fleeting glimpse, out of the corner of his eye. He wasn't sure at first, a black spot snaking along the north side of the river, leaving a black smoke trail. It was alone, no sight of friend or foe. Harper checked his fuel and then turned south east to make an interception. As he got closer he could clearly see that it was a Dornier 17 bomber, flying level at about 2000ft, its port engine streaming smoke. Harper weaved right then left, armed his guns and came up behind the right engine, giving it a three second burst – continuous tracer, he was nearly out of ammo - before pushing down and left, cursing himself for being such a stupid show off at the house. When Harper considered that he was well clear he pulled round in the turn until he was heading east again, closing in on the bomber. Now both engines were streaming smoke, the bomber descending. As Harper closed in the rear gunner baled out, his parachute streaming. He throttled well back - he could slow up and assess the damage now without fear of someone shooting at him, the bomber now flying, half-gliding at less than 150mph. Harper formated on the right wing, adjusting his attitude to start a shallow descent – the fuselage was literally full of holes, the pilot sitting bolt upright in his seat, either dead or wounded, because he didn't look round. Then a pair of legs appeared from the hatch underneath the fuselage – probably the navigator. He protruded as far as his waist, paused and then started thrashing his legs. Harper realised that he was stuck. He suddenly felt physically sick, but then he snapped himself out of it, thinking of the people down below, cowering in their air raid shelters - perhaps these bastards had already dropped their bombs, killing and maiming. The legs still wriggled and thrashed, the man trapped in a doomed aircraft, with a dead pilot at the controls. One of the boots came off, and then the other. There were no socks, the feet bare. To Harper the scene was pathetic.

They were down to 1,000ft. The navigator would be cut in half when the Dornier hit the ground, and Harper couldn't allow it. He dropped back a few yards, kicked in the rudder, held the yaw with opposite stick so that the aircraft was flying slightly sideways but tracking across the ground in the same direction as the bomber, and aimed just ahead of where the man was sitting on the right side of the fuselage. He hit the gun button, peppering the fuselage with his last few tracer rounds. The legs became still.

The pilot must have been dead or completely incapacitated. He made no attempt to flare and belly land. In slow motion, Harper watched as the aircraft sailed just over a line of trees. He could see a little boy in one of them, his face looking upwards in terror, another one running away across the field. The aircraft cracked down into the next field, disintegrating in a yellow fire ball, several pieces sailing up in the air and about to hit Harper's Hurricane until he pulled back on the stick and soared above them.

As he transitioned back to base along the north of the Thames, Harper realised that he hadn't been in the least bit scared, merely revolted at what he had felt obliged to do. The feeling reminded him of the first time he had gone shooting with his father: he had knocked down two pheasants without experiencing any emotion other than the jubilance of success. But then he had winged the third, sending it crashing onto a reed island in the middle of a stream. None of the dogs had been able to get to it. Harper had watched and listened to it dying for the next few minutes, unable to finish it off because this would have meant aiming below the tree line - a threat to the beaters - before he shot it anyway. And this had felt the same, even though he had just despatched a human being instead of a bird. Harper started with round 2, chastising himself for comparing the life of a man to a pheasant. Suddenly he removed his mask and slapped himself round the face.

"PLEASE... SHUT! UP!" he shouted as he pushed hard on the stick, diving the Hurricane down to just above the surface of the Thames and then pulling up in a victory roll over the Dartford ferry. Harper levelled out, thought about the Squadron pilots, and crossed his fingers.

39

As Harper walked in across the dispersal, he counted the aircraft on the line. There were ten Spitfires - two with no markings on the tail yet, so they were new - and four Hurricanes, plus his own. He paused at the door of the dispersal hut and steeled himself before walking in.

Everyone was there. Including Bruce. Harper breathed a sigh of relief before speaking:

"Hey you! How's your backside?"

"Hello Harps! It's about the same colour as your face. Where have you been?"

"Just visiting a friend. Just shot something down on the way back actually!" Harper checked himself - false jollity. "Have you chaps been flying?"

"No one here yet. Not today, anyway. What did you get?"

"That's good; might mean I get the whole thing then. Dornier 17."

"How so?"

Well, it was full of holes when I got there. But no one around: I just finished it off. 3 second burst."

"Did you see it crash?" asked Greg.

"Yes, in a field, near the oil refinery, south of Stanford le Hope. I followed it down. Must have already dropped its stick, or I'd have been blown out of the sky."

"Well you shouldn't have been so close then! I doubt if you'll get all of it, but I'll phone round and find out for you."

"Everyone ok here?"

"They're all good – must be if they're arguing." Harper wandered across to where the boys were grouped. Gazzer was making a point.

"Hey ho!" said Gazzer. Then, back to Rhino: "You've got that all wrong. What school did you go to?"

"Harrow."

"So that explains it! The only good thing about Harrow is that if you climb to the top of the roof you can see the spires of Eton."

"Winston Churchill went to Harrow!" replied Rhino, in mock resentment. "What school did *you* go to?"

"Eton, of course. All the clever geordies go there, didn't you know?"

"So, you must have been the only one there then," replied Rhino, the boys laughing, including Gazzer. "What school did you go to Greg? You're the brightest one here."

"It was called 'Mary, Mother of Jesus and All Saints' School for The Neglected" replied Greg with his cut glass accent. "Its behind Catford Bus station." Rhino looked serious for a moment, until the rest of the boys dissolved into laughter.

"Ah, you don't know do you!" said Gazzer to Harper. "Come out here old boy!" He grabbed Harper's arm and pulled him out of the dispersal hut and round the back. A few yards away, parked on its wheels was a shabby, camouflaged caravan, a pile of bricks propping up each of the corners. Outside the door, on the grass were a foldaway table and two deckchairs. Harper's bike had been parked next to it.

"What's this all about?" asked Harper.

"It's your Uncle Percy! He heard that we'd been bombed out of the mess and had this delivered. Keeping an eye on you he is. You've got your own dispersal hut old boy! It's even got an Elsan in it. No more pee buckets, rattling away in the middle of the night."

"Good old Uncle Percy!" said Harper as he climbed inside. "Crikey, two bedrooms, very fine indeed."

"Yes, I've moved into the other one."

"No way! You snore! *And* fart."

"Only temporary old boy. Mess should be fixed up by next week. Then we can take it to the seaside!"

"What, towed on the back of my motorbike?"

"No, towed on the back of your *car*."

"Eh?"

"You're supposed to say pardon. Your father sent you one," said Gazzer, feigning disinterest. "Only an old banger, came with the caravan. At least it's got a tow bar."

"Where is it?!"

"Over there," pointing to what looked like Tiger's Alvis, parked deliberately as out of the way as possible, at the far end of dispersal.

"Hold on, what's that doing back here?" said Harper, straining to see.

"It's yours."

"What?"

"Your father has bought you an Alvis, that Alvis. It's the same as Tiger's, a year newer maybe. It came yesterday, with the caravan!"

"But, how could he know? Know that I liked it!"

"Just a bit of secret correspondence from me to Gray" said Gazzer, exaggeratedly tapping his nose with his finger. "Started when you went in, and I gave them a progress report!"

"Christ Al-bloody-mighty. Is this the bit when the shell comes in and leaves a pair of smoking boots where I used to be standing" said Harper, before running properly – for the first time since his crash – across the field to his car.

40

Harper sat upright in bed, in his caravan, unable to sleep from excitement. It was just past 0500, Gazzer snoring in the next bedroom. Harper dragged out his flying briefcase, desperate for anything to read. He wished he had amassed a collection of books or magazines, but they always seemed to end up on the floor of the dispersal hut in tatters. Finally he found an insert in the front of his logbook. He went through it on the pretence of interest, trying to ignore the crashing noise of his friend: the sound coming out of his lungs like that accompanying the death throes of a dying man.

FLYING ITINERARY - PRIMARY TRAINING SYLLABUS

1. Air experience: for pupil.

2. Effect of controls.

3. Taxiing/ handling of engine.

4. Straight and level flying.

5. Stalling, climbing, descending & gliding.

6. Medium turns with and without engine.

7. Taking off into wind/ cross wind.

8. Approaches and landings.

9. Preliminary action in event of engine fire; stopping and starting engine.

10. Spinning.

11. First solo.

12. Sideslipping.

13. Further action after engine fire.

14. Low flying - dual only.

15. Steep turns with/ without engine.

16. Climbing turns.

17. Forced landings.

18. Landing with & without engine.

19. Instrument flying under blanking hood.

20. Stopping & starting engine in the air.

21. Crosswind take-offs and landings.

22. Aerobatics/ tail chase *.

23. Air navigation.

24. Forced landing test.

25. Cross country test.

* Further training as required at operational unit.
(Revision 3/1935.)

Harper's experiences of flying training felt as if they had been in another lifetime. His very first type had been the Tiger Moth, an under-powered biplane with design roots from the First World War. Harper remembered how he had to prime it under the engine cowling which lifted up sideways like the ones on Dan's Roll Royce. And then, before start he had to switch up the little external magneto switches – two sets – just in front and on the left of each open cockpit. The engine had to be started by hand, the 'armstrong' method as they called it.

Harper had never got used to the fear invoked by hand-starting a propeller - even now the thought of a flailing arm or leg being hit by a prop blade made him squirm in his bed. He remembered the smell inside the cockpit: an amazing mixture of leather, petrol, hot oil, and hot Bakelite. Harper had always thought that he'd be able to make a fortune if he could bottle it. Series two in his perfumery range would be *Essence of Steam Train.*

Harper wondered how he'd rate if he had to do another flying test now. There was no such test. The bad and inexperienced pilots would be killed on ops, plus some of the good ones - Tiger's face suddenly flashed up in his mind. That was the current state of grading and assessment. He wondered if he'd fail a driving test too, if he took it again.

Finally Harper couldn't stand the noise any longer. He would go for a drive. He put his flying clothes on, climbed out of the caravan and walked across the dewy grass to his car. The sky was starting to lighten but the sun was still well below the horizon, the air at its coldest now until half an hour after sunrise. Harper didn't notice the cold, he'd been used to the freezing water in the big old house that he grew up in – he could never be bothered to wait for the hot water to run through from the boiler, always opting for a cold shower instead. Harper took a rag with him to wipe away the moisture from the windscreen, seats and controls. He turned the little brass handle on the cockpit door, opened it rearwards and sat in. Harper pulled out the ignition button to the left of the steering wheel, checked that the gear lever was in neutral, set the advance-retard lever on the left of the steering wheel centre to 'retard,' turned the choke rotator switch round a quarter clockwise, pumped the throttle a couple of times with his foot and hit the starter button. The engine fired immediately, a quiet blat emitting from the exhaust pipe running along the skirting board. As soon as the engine was running smoothly he moved the lever back to 'advance' and switched the lights on with the little lever on the right of the column.

Harper drove slowly out of the dispersal area so as not to wake anyone, and then round the perimeter track and out of the base. As soon as the guard let the barrier up, he gunned the throttle and blasted out onto the country road.

The cold air made Harper's eyes start streaming almost immediately and he pulled his flying goggles down, before changing up from 2nd to 3rd gear. The speed advantage over his bike was a surprise, but Harper quickly acclimatised, going up into 4th and gunning the throttle again as he wound up through the hills towards his Arse End. The Alvis was so much better than his old MG, which ironically had been newer. This car was superior in every respect, even though it only had an old rail chassis - like a ladder held horizontally, a wheel at each corner - and leaf spring suspension. Before a turn, Harper noticed that he was better off braking while still going relatively straight before releasing them and turning in – classic racing driving. Otherwise the Alvis would fishtail and wallow through the corners. He took the start of the bend flat out, dropping to 60mph at the apex, and getting only slightly sideways as he opened the throttle fully at the exit. It was a beautiful car to drive.

"Thanks dad!" shouted Harper to the slipstream, resolving to write as soon as he got back. Eric too – he still hadn't got round to it.

When Harper got back to dispersal, the area was alive with activity. The fitters were running up the engines of the Hurricanes and Spitfires, arming their guns with belts of ammunition fed out of long wooden boxes with rope handles, the bowser driving from aircraft to aircraft, topping the petrol. As Harper pulled up outside the caravan, Gazzer was just emerging; bare-chested, a towel round his neck, a dash of shaving foam on his left ear -

"Have a nice drive old boy?"

"Tip top tastic! Goes really well, much better than the Midge. Look, do you have some writing paper – I've got to do some letters; Eric and Gray. And mum, I suppose. Or will one for both do?"

"One for both."

"Harper can I have a word?" It was DC, peering round the side of the dispersal hut. As Harper walked back towards him, he could see him peering over Harper's shoulder. Then, as Harper reached the hut: "What's Gazzer wearing? Some funny vest? Is that something to do with caravanning?"

"No, that's his, err... chest hair, sir."

"God, he's like half man, half beast! I've never see anything like it in my life." Harper's shoulders started moving up and down. "Anyway, I've been talking to Intel and he says he can't find any of your combat reports. We need them to sign you up for your gong."

"Oh right, I wonder where they might…"

"Who did you hand them into? Intel?"

"Err, no sir."

"Well, who then?"

"…I didn't sir, hand them in I mean."

"Into my office now!"

DC stomped in right behind Harper, slamming the door. "This is exactly what I'm talking about, it's the nitty gritty, the detail that makes the R.A.F tick. And you miss it, every time!" DC was firmly back into *headmaster* mode, rummaging in a draw as he spoke. "There. Take a look at that," handing over an A4-sized form.

"Now look here. This is a proper combat report. It even details how many rounds were used in the attack. And what type!" Harper looked incredulous – until he started reading it. All of it.

COMBAT REPORT.

Sector Serial No..	(A)..
Serial No. of Order detailing Flight or Squadron to	
Patrol..	(B)......... 613 8570...............
Date...	(C)......... 4th May 1940........
Flight, Squadron..	(D) Flight:Cockle..Sqn:...... ...
Number of enemy aircraft.............................	(E)...........one.....................
Type of enemy aircraft.................................	(F).......... JU88.. ....
Time Attack was delivered............................	(G)......... 0300.. ....
Place Attack was delivered...........................	(H)..........EastSussxcoast....
Height of Enemy...	(J)..........10,000ft...............
Enemy Casualties.......................................	(K).........three killed......... .
Our Casualties.................. Aircraft............	(L)..........nil......................
Personnel..........	(M).........nil......................
GENERAL REPORT..................................	(R)..

Took off 0134 in Beaufighter R251. (4 cannon and 4m/s.) We were
vectored at 0245 hours on to a bandit travelling out to sea in an
easterly direction. We were at 10,000ft and were instructed to
fly at a speed of 180mph. At 0255 hours radar reported a blip, a
bandit 10,000ft ahead and 10,000ft alt. Arrangement was made to
draw up to enemy aircraft's starboard side and at same height in
order to get a silhouette of it against the dawn glow. Visual was
obtained on the enemy aircraft 600ft ahead and slightly left and
below. Identified it as a JU88. Fire was opened from dead astern
at 100/150 yds range, and after a 2 second burst the e/a blew up
in the air, fragments hitting our port wing and fuselage. Further
examination showed unmistakable traces of human remains on the
port wing, with numerous blood splashes on the port airscrew,
fuselage and tail plane, and damage consisting of about 2 feet of
the leading edge of the port wing (outboard of engine) stoved in
as far as main spar. This e/a is claimed as destroyed. Type of
sight fitted - reflector; range 100/150 yds; total of 50 canon
shells (26 20mm ball & 24HE incendiary from 4 cannon guns, and
286 rounds of .303 (145 incendiary & 141 ap)

O.C. Section/   *Ian Edgerly* W/Cdr I.C Edgerly.

"Harper? HARPER!"

"Christ! Oh, sorry boss. I was just reading this er... Have you read this sir?! I mean, all of it?"

"Yes. Now go and get the typewriter and put down each and every detail of your actions; number and type of enemy aircraft, type of attack, number of rounds used (Harper winced as he thought about the evening at Dan's house,) the whole bloody 9 yards."

"Absolutely."

"Promotion, Harper? Remember our little chat? Obviously, not. Now bugger off! Dismissed!"

"Yes sir, terribly sorry, really I am." Harper saluted, left the office and went straight across to see Jones, still reeling slightly from reading the report. Jones was sitting on top of the nose of the Hurricane as if riding a horse backwards, with one leg each side of the cockpit. He was cleaning the windscreen with a cloth and a special liquid compound to take the scratches out. It was the colour of milky coffee and smelled like brass cleaner. Harper jumped straight up to the wing without using the stirrup.

"Can see you're doing a bit better sir," said Jones.

"Yes, thank you, well, no, actually. Look I'm in a bit of a dwang with the C/O. Can I ask you, does anyone keep a record of how much ammunition we use?"

"How much taken from stores? Yes, every round."

"Sod it. Thought you were going to say that."

"What's the problem?"

"Well, between you and me... I *can* trust you can't I?"

"'Course."

"Well, I used up most of my ammo showing my friend how the guns work while I was up in Norfolk. Trying to impress the ladies, you know!" Jones moved his head slowly from side to side. "And of course now I've gone and told everyone that I only used a three second burst knocking down that bomber, plus a few more for... something else.

And of course I came back empty." As he thought about it, Harper dropped his face forwards, closed his eyes and started moving his own head from side to side a little faster than Jones.

"I think you're very much mistaken sir."

"Sorry?"

"Well, let's see, it's about 24 rounds per gun per second, call it 200 rounds per second for all eight guns. I can only remember having to put, er, 1000 rounds in the breaches last time I loaded it? Will that do? 5 seconds?"

"You are bloody brilliant! Thanks! But how will you, you know?"

"The armoury thinks they're really fucking clever by making us sign for each box we take, and bringing all the empty clips back. But it ain't... clever I mean - they don't count the returns, the left over rounds. So we... take care of 'em."

"Jonesy, I owe you enormously. If there's anything I can do for you just ask."

"No you don't boss. Hold on a minute – one thing, could I borrow the bike, just for special occasions, Sunday best, seeing as you got the car now." Harper raised his eyebrows and put his thumbs up. "You know, impress the ladies."

41

The early sun and pink sky had been the precursor to a false summer day. By late morning a low overcast with fine rain descended on the airfield. Harper had borrowed the squadron typewriter and taken it back to the caravan, earnestly starting with the first of his many combat reports. But, after a couple of hours he got itchy feet and changed tack, writing instead to his mother and father, Uncle Percy and then Eric. The postman came at midday, ironically delivering another letter from his brother. Harper wandered from his caravan, back into the dispersal hut.

Rhino was sitting next to the stove – symbolic only, since it wasn't lit – and smoking a pipe.

"Sorry, got a little busy yesterday. How did you get on with your weekend away?" asked Harper.

"Pretty good! I flew all the way up to a little strip near Cumbernauld to see my bride. Spent the night in Edinburgh. Then back down via the Lake District. Beat up the Ullswater ferry quite nicely, on the way back."

"Me too! Mine was at Dartford. Doesn't quite have the same ring about it though, does it."

"Ah, Harps, there you are" said Intel. "Quick word?" handing him another letter from his brother.

"Sorry about the reports – writing them now – just taking a break."

"It's not that, actually. I let the C/O do the bollockings around here. Its about your kill, no one claimed it. Mind you, it might be because they were shot down subsequently - sorry to have to elaborate." Harper thought for a moment.

"I don't have a problem with it – someone's got to have it. I lost out to Ginger... a while ago (another one of those *lifetime ago* moments.) This balances things up."

"Well... it's yours then, ace! Well done anyway."

"Why, thank you (Harper hated himself for that false jollity thing) - I'm not feeling all that proud for now. Maybe it will kick in. No flying today by the looks of it," he said, trying to think of something else to say. Harper sat down, becoming bothered at the thought of anyone else talking to him while he tried concentrating on Eric's letter.

> *L.A.C Harper E*
>
> *Room 4 Block 48*
>
> *L.O.V. S Cerney*
>
> *Nr Cirencester*
>
> *Glos*

My Dear Tom

I passed the fucking wings exam! Actually, I was top in navigation, 90.5%, & 2nd in the whole exam. But it makes bugger all difference, they're not giving me a commission from here & considering that both the chap who failed & the one who came bottom have got them I'm feeling pretty fed up. Actually it seems to depend a lot on noise" some of the chaps who have got commissions aren't fit to shovel shit. Still, as I always say it is the sergeant pilots who are going to win this war, not the P,Os, F,O's Flights and Sqn Ldrs.

Not in bomber command anyway – so, present company excepted you old sod.

We've done practically no flying this month. There's a helluva fog again today, although we did a bit yesterday. We're still meant to be doing ground exams. An instructor turns up for about 1 in every 5 & altogether we've not exactly been exerting ourselves.

We went out drinking last night. I got the other two gloriously tight. One was simply very sleepy & didn't say a word after 5 or 6 rounds. The other became marvellously merry, I nearly shat myself laughing. He did his best to get shoved in the clink but didn't quite manage.

He wouldn't get up this morning so we tipped his bed over & then took his pyjamas off.

Auntie wants to sell her Austin 7, open, & I may be able to get hold of it. The only trouble is that it is at Hastings at the moment, so that I don't suppose I shall be able to get it until I get leave & also Gray may decide he wants it, which will be a nuisance.

A chap was trying to sell his bike to a Polish sergeant & buy his car last night, it was impossible!

There's no more news, its been snowing a bit again, so I might get leave.

Harper thought, if he sent his own letter now, how many weeks or months would pass before it would get there.

Give my love & X X X X To all & I hope keep a check of yourself with all these fags about

Ps How's the pimping racket these days? I'm thinking of setting up an agency at the camp

   "You want the Sexiest prosses: We have them"

"Sexual Satisfaction for sensible students."

Filthy, isn't it.

Bungho, & may your F.L have a hole in it

Eric .

Harper noticed a change in the tone of the letter. As if his brother was becoming a little disillusioned, maybe just bored. He wandered back to the caravan and re read his own letter, eventually deciding to screw the lot up and start again from scratch, even though it meant that the combat reports would be put back even more.

Harper T. A. Flight Lieutenant

c/o Operations – Dispersal

p.s please send c/o dspl, not off mess   60X Squadron

R.A.F HXXXXXXXXX

Essex

17th May 1940

Dear Eric,

Very sorry for nothing before: what can I say except I've been a bit of a shit. Been a little bit busy with ops, but sod you about officers! Utter nonsense - Cut the attitude and they might even make you one. I'm expecting a smart salute in full dress uniform when next we meet, total decorum. Doesn't make sod all difference out here on the line of course. We don't display our rank, except it's a shame when we go to the mess for drinks and the Sarges can't join us. We just go down the local instead.

Check out advancements, pensions, etc etc and you'll have a different opinion about it.

Sounds a little dull where you are but believe me its better to be bored in safety, than in at the sharp end. It's fucking terrifying most of the time. I don't know where you'll end up but you'll have your moments, without a doubt so enjoy the calm.

I'm Sure that Gray & Co told you about what happened to me (I'm completely out of kilter about when you've been up to what you've been up to: is it the censors, post office, or do you write it and forget to post it?) I felt like your flying instructor in my crack up – didn't know what the day was, or the few after, as a matter of fact.

Much Better now though & I have a lovely 'duelling scar on my cheek to prove it. Plus a couple in other places but I'll save that for my girlfriend: no bride, tool or wedding tackle jokes thank you.

I don't know if I'll ever get used to the combat. It's not like in the flicks: do you remember when we went to see Aces High?! How ridiculous that is compared to it. I had a very terrible time the other day when I had to shoot a poor bugger who'd got stuck in his hatch, trying to bale out of

185

his bomber, which I shot down by the way. One got out & I let him go –
I heard some stories about them shooting at us in our parachutes: not
good is it. Pilot was stone dead, still sitting at his controls. Any way I
shot jack in the box before they hit the ground. It just missed a little boy
in a tree, looked like about 5 years old if he was a day. I could see the
expression on his face –he didn't look very happy to have a ringside
seat. Funny what the human eye can see in a hundredth of a second:
especially when your blood's up.

I was chilled to the bone by the whole thing, believe me. Some of my
chums piss themselves every time they fly and a few go that little bit
farther. The fitters know the shitters, so they stay clear until the
necessary has been sorted out.

On the up side, think I'm an ace officially by now but it's so unfair, who
gets what etc etc

And my crowd are a scream, makes it all worth while really. Except we
just get down to some semblance of normality when another one gets
himself shot up. We had a terrific C/O called Tiger: we all loved him
(don't worry I'm not turning fag) and then he went in: I can't even begin
to tell you how sad I was, and it was worse because he went down in the
same fight. I cried my eyes out, and I don't care if you tell everyone. At
one point, I put my service revolver in my mouth and nearly pulled the
trigger.

New one has his moments but then he was a headmaster and you can
tell: he'd have us bent over with our trousers down (I don't mean what
you think) and caning us if it were allowed. Top chap - has our respect
of course, if not always our co operation. We've got the Eton types,
Harrow types and rugger buggers like us here so its all standard ops
really, like the old place I suppose.

By the way don't worry about this Austin 7 from auntie thing – I got a
lovely present from m & f the other day so I reckon you'll get yours – or
have already got it, probably - but I won't tell you what mine is until our
leave combines because you'll get hugely jealous and it'll ruin
everything: (You know I pranged Midge of course – here's a quiz;
rearrange these letters to make four words N. A. T. U. M. A. I. C.) I
might even do a swap with you for a while. Got a nice bike on loan from
Uncle Percy too, a real Luftwaffe or army motorbike: don't even bother
to ask how, when, what:

There's an old lady, a young lady, an Englishman, a Frenchman and an Italian in a train carriage. It goes into a tunnel and the lights go out. Then there's a scream and a loud slap, and when the lights go back on the frog has got a red mark on his face (like me). The old lady's thinking 'I bet that frenchy grabbed that young girl's leg and she slapped him.' The young girl's thinking 'I bet that frenchy grabbed that old lady's leg and she slapped him. The Frenchman's thinking 'I bet that Italian grabbed that young girl's leg but she thought it was me because I'm French so she slapped me.' And the Englishman's thinking 'I hope we go into another tunnel so I can give that Frenchman another slap.'

Which leads me to tell you ....We'll be on French ops any day now, maybe even a posting, and everyone says it'll be bloody carnage. We're on the run out there. Its just about alright now because they have a peck and we have a stab, but when its all out we'll be out there outnumbered, running out of fuel and ammo just like their fighters are with us.

Take care you bugger and keep the letters coming. Give me a ring (!) if I can help with the ''7 except you've probably already got it of course
X Tom

The rain was coming down in sheets now, battering the top and one side of the caravan. Harper started to relax, sure in the knowledge that there would be no flying. Until he jumped at the faint sound of the telephone ringing next door.

"Orange section scramble!" Abbo, Gazzer and Koval were already running out of the hut as Harper reached the doorway, perplexed. He ran in behind them, picked up his own pile of equipment from the corner, and ran back out into the rain, shielding his head with his Mae West.

"Head east, angels ½!" shouted Greg behind him as he sprinted towards his Hurricane. Jones was in position as Harper used the stirrup to get up onto the wing - it was too wet for one of his leaps. Jones' roll up had been extinguished by the rain but he still had it dangling out of his mouth.

"Can't believe they're sending us up in this!" said Harper.

"The controller ain't got a window in his ops room" replied Jones, getting completely soaked in the short time it took to help Harper with his straps and then jump back down to plug in the trolley. The engine fired after three blades – Jones pulled the plug out – no permission - and Harper taxied out behind the other three, slightly ahead. Abbo went first.

"Listen up" said Abbo. "Stay close, and below cloud. Anyone loses contact, immediately turn back for base. I don't want a collision in this soup." The cloud was down to less than 800ft feet as the four aircraft took off in trail formation, one after the other. Harper closed his canopy as soon as he was airborne to stop the rain getting into the cockpit. With his wheels up he pushed the nose down to level off and accelerate, still at buster, to catch up before he lost contact with the front three. They were already becoming faint, the rain reducing the visibility straight ahead to just a couple of miles. Finally Harper throttled back as he tucked in, loosely, on the right of Gazzer's right wing, the four aircraft in an echelon to starboard, like migrating birds, Abbo at the front.

"Orange section, request." said Abbo to the controller.

"Go ahead."

"Orange section viz is 2 miles max. What and how are we intercepting?"

"Multiple targets south of Southend, attacking convoy. 8 miles ahead and closing from the right. Stay below cloud."

"Wilco, Orange section."

Occasionally a wisp of cloud obliterated Gazzer's Hurricane but Harper stayed in position, ready to peel away to the right if the visibility didn't return in a couple of seconds. In his peripheral vision he was aware of small groups of ships in the estuary underneath him. Then nothing but merging shades of grey: water, cloud and rain. Finally Harper was aware of the pier at Southend passing by beneath, followed soon after by the boom south of Shoeburyness.

"Orange section turn right heading 140 degrees. Targets will be at 3 miles."

"Orange copied" replied Abbo. The echelon turned right neatly, just as they entered cloud. Each aircraft had to throttle back more than the one ahead to stay behind the leader, because the radius of turn was progressively shorter for each aircraft. Harper had to come back to half throttle, since his radius was smallest. Nevertheless he was moving ahead of the pack − he carried on rolling right - the three aircraft disappearing under his left wing as it came up - to break away from the formation and then tuck back in behind them. But, when he reversed the turn, they had gone.

"Orange 4 lost formation, clearing right" said Harper, rolling right again until he was heading west, so that he wouldn't inadvertently crash into the others.

"Orange 4, R T B" replied Abbo. As Harper rolled level he pushed the stick forwards, clearing cloud at a height of 500ft. There, straight in front and just below him was a Stuka, a German dive-bomber, flying level from left to right.

"Well fuck me!" said Harper as he looked down, rotated his arming ring from safe to fire and then looked up again, rolling left so that he could come round behind.

"Orange 4, lone enemy sighted south of the pier. A Stuka − attacking!"

"Do your worst" replied Abbo. Harper counted to five and then turned right again to come round behind the Stuka. He was closing fast − at least 100kts quicker than the painfully slow dive-bomber. Harper opened fire at 200 yards. He missed, paused - he had overestimated the deflection on such a slow target - and then fired again. The Stuka made no attempt to turn and evade. It was as if the crew were concentrating so hard on the weather and the ships that they didn't have enough spare capacity to look for interceptors. Another spray of bullets, this time hitting home. The fuselage of the Junkers exploded without precedent, its wings folding together perfectly like a butterfly's - there was no way anyone could have survived. Harper watched as the enemy aircraft folded in on itself, diving into the sea and creating a huge splash, pieces of the wreckage skipping across the surface of the water.

"Enemy destroyed!" said Harper, punching the top of his left knee with the fist of his left hand and then quickly scanning for another target. His knees weren't knocking but he noticed that his left hand was shaking as it went back onto the throttle. Suddenly Harper noticed another huge splash out to the left. It was a bomb dropped by another dive-bomber, missing the ship that it was aimed at, but Harper couldn't see the attacker. At least the Stukas were having a hard time of it – they normally dived in vertically from a couple of thousand feet, instead of lobbing them in at a shallow dive from a few hundred. He turned left to get closer, heading south, and immediately flew into a cloudbank.

"Christ!" said Harper, pushing down to 400ft before coming back out under the cloud again. He was almost across to the southern bank of the estuary and now turned west to run along it. The weather was getting worse, solid masses of cloud regularly engulfing him even down this low. "I'm getting *paid* to do this," he said to himself, trying to laugh, as he dropped down yet again, 200ft now, and just below the indistinct base. "Orange 4, R T B. Weather bad – tell you how I get on."

"Thanks '4. Orange section continue patrol." Harper followed the estuary west, until it curved away to the south, and then continued inland where he knew the terrain was low and flat, pretty much all the way back to the airfield if he got it right. But if Harper overshot he would quickly be over London, with its towers, masts, barrage balloons and cables. He pulled the throttle back and slowed to 120 knots so that he could give himself a little more time.

"Orange section come right, heading 090 target will be at 12 O'clock and 5 miles."

"Copy, right 090 Orange section." It sounded to Harper like they were chasing themselves round in circles, so easy for the dive-bombers to jump into the cloud to avoid detection. Just to the right of him, in the murk, Harper could see the junction between the A13 and the old roman road that ran north to Brentwood. He turned right - he would head 290 degrees for 3 minutes, at 2 miles a minute. That should take him to the airfield. If he got to 4 minutes he would turn back and try something else, maybe divert. Harper leaned down between his feet and moved the glass bezel top of his compass round to the next line past '28,' turned the aircraft gently right and then levelled out, the inverted 'T' engraved on the bezel top now lining up with the compass needle underneath it. He was still at 200ft. He checked his watch and peered forward, wondering if it was his imagination, or had the visibility got worse. Then the rain intensity started to increase.

"Orange 4 heading inland, changing to tower, cloudbase 300ft and heavy rain."

"Thanks '4." Harper slid back his canopy, despite the rain, so that he could see better the ground ahead of the leading edges of his wings. The time passed slowly – any minute Harper was expecting to see a looming tower, or to be dragged sideways as a balloon cable sliced through his wing. 3 minutes passed on his watch - still nothing, just grass fields, telegraph poles, unidentifiable roads, a line of houses… and a few upturned faces from a pub car park. The Ship! Instantly, Harper knew where he was. And there! Just off to the left he could see the airfield, a red I/D beacon on the top of a 60ft mast at the north west corner, flashing *dot dash dot* for 'R,' every 6 seconds. Harper dropped gear and flaps, and then made a left turn, heading west, into wind, and touching down on three points, his sense of relief slumping him half a foot lower in the cockpit than he had been for the entire flight.

Ironically, as Harper taxied in, the rain stopped - he'd been in the worst of the cold front. And, as if to tease him, by the time that Harper had shut down, unclipped and climbed out of his Hurricane on the dispersal line, the first rays of sunshine were breaking through the cloud.

42

Harper was in a deep sleep. He had dried off two of the chairs outside his caravan and sat down in the warm sun, his backside on one and his feet on the other. He jumped awake again when the telephone rang, scrambling four Spitfires - DC, Johnny, Doogy and Lexy - to a point farther out in the estuary. Harper quickly drifted off to sleep again, and woke again, more gently this time, to the sound of Hurricanes coming in across the fields from the north east - two of them. As they taxied in, Harper could see a line of bullet holes on one, stitched along the left side of the fuselage and rudder. It was Abbo's aeroplane. Harper walked across to meet him as he shut down, a few of the fitters grouping around the back end.

"Looked like you saw a bit," said Harper. "Where's..." trying to work out who was missing from the tail letters on the other Hurricane: "...where's Koval?"

"He's ok. He got a Stuka but it got him back. Put down at Rochester."

"On the airfield?"

"Yeah, dead-sticked it in (landed without power), clever boy."

"What about you?"

"Same thing - I got him but he got me." Abbo jumped down and walked to the back of his Hurricane to see.

"So we *aced* three between us. Not bad, considering."

"What, the weather? No problem, it's just like Rhodesia," said Abbo with a straight face – until Harper looked up questioningly, whereupon he started smiling. "Anyway, you got it wrong there mate. I got two! This one (pointing to the bullet holes) and another one flew into the sea trying to get away from me."

"Crikey! Well done! Ship it is then."

"I could ship a couple right now given the chance."

"Sorry about losing you."

"You did the right thing. If it had been Pollock…" his voice drifting off. Abbo had forgot that Pollock wasn't around anymore – its what the survivors always tried to do, put bad news behind them as quickly as possible.

The four Spitfires returned in 30 minutes – their interception had been called off just as they got past Southend pier, the remainder of the enemy being turned away with the help of another squadron.

Inexplicably, Johnny came in low and landed with his flaps down but his wheels up, despite repeated red flares from the tower instructing him to go around. The aircraft arced round in a spray of mud, its propeller blades bent back double, the flaps and radiator ruined. DC shut down and waited patiently for Johnny to walk across from the wreck, in the opposite direction to the fire engine and blood wagon, which arced round behind him and brought him back.

The two of them went straight into DC's office. The boys in the hut tried to appear not to listen, but no one spoke of their recent action – highly unusual – so that they could all earwig. Predictably the voice behind the wall got louder and louder as time went on; something about 'expensive government equipment' and 'bloody slovenly' followed by 'DISMISSED,' the sound of marching feet and a roughly opened door. Newspapers and magazines flicked up and three pilots attempted to make tea with one kettle as Johnny walked back into the room. Then, another one-sided conversation in the office – a telephone call – another raising of a voice, and a loud 'BOLLOCKS' at the end. Lastly, Greg was summoned.

"Hello chaps, C/O would like to call a meeting in 5 minutes" said Intel. Harper went to the caravan to drop some of his things off and came straight back to the hut.

"Ok everyone, three things. I don't know who taught you what but its standard ops in my squadron to fly echelon port or starboard in bad viz. What did you Hurry boys do?"

"Echelon starboard" replied Abbo.

"Good. It's also standard ops to land with your wheels down, so that's what we're all going to do from now on. Next man not to do it will face a bloody firing squad.

Next thing, I know we're only 36ft up from sea level here, but I still want you to unwind that 1 millibar off your altimeters when you come back into the circuit. You have sea level pressure set when you're going cross-country, and airfield pressure set in the circuit - always. It'll stand you in good stead for when you have to divert to Biggin Hill, which we all know is 600ft up. Otherwise one day you'll go stooging around in the clag thinking your 600ft above the airfield and suddenly you'll get a tree in the face. By the way I'm very pleased that the camp comedian allowed the I/D beacon to be switched on. You can only expect it on days like today, and never at night, no matter what. Sounded like you Hurrys needed it more than we did, clearance coming through like that. And last but very much the least, you've all been invited for tea!"

"Ooooooh!" said a few of the boys at the same time.

"Yes, at the station commander's request, sort of reopening ceremony. Aren't we lucky! So go and have a shave the bloody lot of you! 1645 here for transport or 1700 at the mess."

"Bloody meet and creep" said Johnny, quietly.

"Meet and greet dear boy, meet and greet" replied Rhino.

"Christ, I've just realised what a state I look," said Harper, examining his reflection in a window.

"That's what living in a biscuit tin does to you" replied Gazzer. "You've become *caravan man.*"

"And you've become bloody ungrateful" said Harper. "Anyway if the mess is open I'm moving back into my old room. We can turn our tin into the games room instead. Install a full size snooker table."

"I say! I'll borrow a tin opener from the mess," said Gazzer.

194

"How about a bowling alley" said Rhino.

"Rowing machine" said Jock.

"And a little swimming pool" from Lexy.

"I think we should turn it into a whore house" said Pipe.

"Christ can you imagine that!" replied Gazzer. "With you at it in there, it'd shake itself off the bricks." Pipe was even bigger than Gazzer.

"If that isn't a pot calling a kettle black then I really don't –" added Harper, his sentence interrupted as the phone rang. It wasn't a scramble.

The only person not to add something was Johnny.

His silence continued at the tea party, despite the forced sociability of the occasion. Officers were expected to make polite conversation but Johnny sat the event out, a cup of tea on his lap, the cup tinkling against the saucer for a moment, each time that he raised or lowered it. The sound of it was very subtle, but every pilot in the vicinity noticed it. Harper looked down, and raised up his own hands. The left one was shaking slightly. He took out his hip flask and topped up his half-empty teacup with whisky.

"Never seen that done before old boy," said Gazzer, over his shoulder.

"A very good friend of mine showed me on a shoot – goes down very well after a day on the estate." Gazzer agreed and very soon a few of the others joined in, supplementing the hip flask with shots from the bar.

After the tea ceremony, most of the pilots moved back into the mess, Doogy and Koval going for Harper's offer of the caravan, rather than stay in the sergeants mess, where they would generally find themselves excluded from its social life. Becoming a sergeant was automatic on completion of flying training for a non-commissioned pilot, and the other sergeants resented it.

Once they had unpacked, the pilots reconvened at the mess bar.

"Sir, can I have a word?" asked Harper, looking over his shoulder to check that no one was within earshot.

"What is it?" replied DC.

"Well, it's just that I noticed that Johnny doesn't seem to be his usual self. Don't suppose I would be if I'd just done what he did of course. I wondered if it would be possible to put him up for the next leave."

"Very good of you to think of him Harps. On the other hand I don't really want to reward crass stupidity. Is that how the boys would see it?"

"Definitely not. You'd be seen as being kind and sympathetic."

"Not sure I want that either! They'll think me weak."

"Definitely not sir."

"Okay I'll think about it. We might be having a busy day tomorrow though. Sitskrieg to blitzkrieg - our first taste of France, according to Group. But that's classified, so you'll not blab. Let me think about it."

Thoughts of dinner and The Ship were forgotten as the Squadron moved from tea with whisky to beer, wine and whisky straight, courtesy of Harper. A game of mess rugby developed – a chair placed at each end of a room and a cushion thrown in the middle. The rules were simple: first team to win would be when one of its members sat in the opposite chair, holding the cushion. What it meant in practise was a large human pyramid, squirming and changing shape as it meandered slowly around the room, sometimes not moving at all for minutes at a time. Taking part was absolutely hilarious, apart for the ones at the bottom of the pyramid. The final score was 2-0, 3 loose fillings and a brace of broken teeth.

DC was right about French operations. At 9pm he despatched Intel to break up the party, the mess bar closed to pilots and everyone sent to bed to reconvene for 0500 at dispersal.

43

The Squadron took off at 0700 in three sections; Red and Blue together in two groups of four Spitfires, Orange as a single unit of four Hurricanes. The weather was bright and clear: the same cold air mass which had crossed the country the day before.

For the first time, Harper was Orange Leader. Tactics and navigation for the section would be his responsibility. Harper climbed to 15,000ft initially, tracking out of the airfield heading 135 degrees. The Hurricanes crossed the Thames 3 minutes later, just to the east of Tilbury. Harper tried to relax for a couple of minutes, despite the new level of responsibility. Looking down and right he could see the lines of ships crowding in Chatham dockyard, the sun reflecting in the water, highlighting the triangular wake left by a steamer heading out into the estuary. Harper pulled the chart out of his flying suit for a position check. At 6 minutes he wanted to be 1 mile south west of Sittingbourne. He was spot on, the 5 degree heading adjustment to the right for a westerly wind had been perfect. Harper put the map away and concentrated on accurate flying, and keeping a lookout. Occasionally he looked round at the other pair, off to his left and lower, and Gazzer, his wingman just off to the right - Harper stuck two fingers up at him and got a middle finger in return.

At 12 minutes Orange section crossed the coast at Folkestone, blown 5 degrees east of track by the stronger westerly winds aloft. Harper corrected with a turn 10 degrees right and then stowed the map again, concentrating even more on accurate flying, even though he could clearly see the French coast. The novelty and adventure of this first channel crossing didn't elude him. Harper noticed that now he was even more sensitive to the sound of his Merlin - engine awareness of pilot proportional to the square of dependence.

"Orange section radio check" said Harper. The pilots transmitted in succession;

"Orange 2."

"'3.''

"'4." Harper started a slow climb to 20,000 feet now, as briefed, bringing his oxygen contents and supply rate into his instrument scan. Height would improve their chances against anti-aircraft guns. Ahead he could clearly see the point of Cap Gris-Nez. The channel was alive with ships; convoys with destroyer escorts going in two directions, warships on patrol, ferries tied up together and moored out at sea because the docks were full. The scene was stunning, helped by the glorious sunlight of a cloudless day. Harper could also see a thin yellow line ahead, running just above the horizon. It looked like cloud, dirty cloud. But then Harper realised what it must have been - high altitude pollution, caused by thousands of fires across Northern Europe.

Orange section crossed the Cap after 19 minutes flight time, a mere 7 minute crossing. Now Harper's task was to proceed inland for 20 more miles and sweep the area, north to south, for enemy aircraft, duration 60 minutes. He turned the bezel of his compass to '18' and then judged a 50-degree, right turn to begin the sweep. The compass swung, settled and agreed with his judgement.

"Bandits 3 O'clock. Many planes!" said Doogy. Harper felt as if he jumped out of his skin, but quickly calmed himself and stared hard out to the right, up and down. There, at least 20 black specks, flying in the same direction as Orange section, maybe two thousand feet higher.

"Cool it, they're ours" replied Abbo. Again, Harper stared hard. He was right – they were Spitfires on the same sweep, at their start height of 22,000ft. Harper breathed a sigh of relief.

"Well done Oranges, keep scanning" But now he noticed something else: a problem. His cockpit was icing up. The water vapour in his breath, coming out of the mask outlet, was icing up the windscreen.

Harper rubbed it with his flying gloves but it iced up again within a few seconds. In the end he concentrated on two points and rubbed them almost continuously; the first above and in front of his head where the sun shone through, where the fighters would come from, and the second in the middle of the front screen. Harper wondered for a moment and then tried to open his canopy so that he could see out. He couldn't budge it – it was frozen solid.

"I don't bloody believe it!" said Harper, at once feeling claustrophobic. He wouldn't be able to bail out. Then he remembered his service revolver. In 1940 carrying one was an option – one that he had taken up. He could try and shoot his way out if he had to; aim at the lock maybe, or stitch some holes across the canopy and punch his way out. In reality it was unlikely he'd be able to, but it gave him something to pin his hopes on and he calmed down a little.

"Two bandits in the sun! COMING STRAIGHT DOWN!" said Abbo.

"Orange section Tally Ho!" replied Harper. He couldn't see them, but instinctively pulled up towards the sun to meet them head on, Gazzer following, the other pair staying low. Now he could see them: two silver '109s, guns blazing but still 2000 yards away. Harper armed his guns and put the bead of his gun sight on the closer one. He glanced back at his speed – 180mph and decelerating. He couldn't hold this climbing attitude for long before he'd stall, but the massive closing speed brought the '109 in range in a few more seconds, Harper's speed now down to 100mph. Harper opened fire, a long continuous burst, simultaneously pulling and pushing the stick gently to keep it in his sights. Now that familiar wings/nose/wings/nose flashing again. Harper had been here before. At the last moment he started a roll gently, progressively to the left so that he wouldn't clobber Gazzer's Hurricane. He continued the roll until he was on a knife-edge and falling away, the altimeter unwinding, the airspeed increasing and the wings now responding to him pulling on the stick. The aircraft turned sickly around the other way and Harper kept the dive going, scanning madly for the two fighters, rubbing looking, rubbing, looking again. They had disappeared.

"Lost them!" said Gazzer.

"Me too" replied Harper. "Orange section regroup over Cap Gris-Nez."

"Orange 2."

"'3."

But no '4.'

"Orange 4 radio check?" No answer. Harper rubbed and scanned around but he couldn't see either of them. Then, out of the corner of his eye he spotted Gazzer closing in on him from starboard, smoking tracer going past him."

"GAZZER, ON YOUR TAIL! PULL LIKE HELL!" Gazzer's Hurricane immediately pulled up and over to the right, the tracer following but hosing out beneath and behind. Harper stayed on track and waited for what seemed like for an eternity of rubbing and scanning before he saw the '109 pulling round in a steep turn behind Gazzer, airspeed higher, the turn radius much larger.

"Orange leader attacking!" said Harper as he rolled and pulled round behind him. The '109 had overcooked it: overshooting the Hurricane, breaking off the attack, descending at high speed. Harper followed him down. He didn't want to take his eyes off the target but he had to keep checking the sun every few seconds. Rub, scan, rub, scan behind, scan ahead. A quick glance at the altimeter: down to 5000ft now and unwinding like crazy. Down and down they went, all the way to the ground. Puffs of black smoke appeared out of nowhere – ack-ack. Occasionally he could here a muffled 'whump' even above the sound of the roaring Merlin. Rub, scan, rub, scan behind. Finally the '109 was levelling off, turning right, back towards Germany. Its wings rolled level, heading just north of east, Harper still descending, closing in. He knew he'd only have the speed advantage this once. Down, down.

"Don't waste it… keep calm… hold fast" Harper repeated to himself, a mantra. The '109 was flying straight and level, Harper was closing. It didn't know that he was there, couldn't do.

"Orange leader, Orange 2, you ok?"

"Standby." Harper was 200 feet above and 300 yards behind, still closing, but not so fast. 250 yards, 200 yards, rub, scan, rub, scan. 150 yards, 125 yards, 100 yards. Now their speed was equal - in a couple of seconds the '109 would be pulling away. Harper aimed more carefully than ever before. And fired. It was a perfect shot - the bullets hitting home just behind the cockpit. The '109 pitched up for a moment

200

then straightened, Harper firing all the time. Multiple hits, puffs of smoke, bright flashes, pieces flying off, an explosion at the front, the right gear leg starting to come down - the hydraulics must have been hit - the aircraft yawing in the direction of the gear leg, slowing up. Then an almighty explosion in the fuselage, the aircraft diving vertically into the ground.

"GOT HIM! GOT HIM!" shouted Harper "Sorry, Orange leader, turning for Cap Gris-Nez! Regroup!"

"WEY HAY!" shouted Gazzer.

"Well done from Orange 3!" said Abbo. "I've got '4 with me, radio failure. See you there!"

Harper couldn't believe his luck. He turned through 150 degrees and pointed towards The Cap. The frost on the screen was already melting, turning into rivulets of water which he cleared with the sleeve of his flying jacket. He tried the hood – still stuck fast. He started to realise that the gun idea was nonsense - at least it had the desired effect at the time. Harper translated into a climb to get out of the way of the flak, the speed coming back. Then he thought he smelled something – was it anything?

Or was he just being jumpy?

There, again: Glycol. He looked at the temperature gauge. It was rising.

"Fuck it!" said Harper. "This is Orange Leader, I've got a coolant problem. Keep you posted." He could clearly see the Cap ahead, the 20 nautical miles of channel beyond it and, faintly in the distance, the Dover coast. Instinctively he had pulled the nose up even more and retrimmed, to gain height and time. He checked the radiator shutters – they were wide open. Another tug of the hood: still frozen.

Harper wanted to go home. If it weren't for the hood he'd chance it. One last try: Harper yanked it back as hard as he possibly could – it slid open.

"Right, I've got my hood open. I'm going to try and get back across. Orange 3 and '4 continue patrol, Orange 2, come with me."

"Orange 2."

"'3 and '4 wilco."

Harper turned onto 310 degrees as he crossed Cap Gris-Nez and checked his watch. If he could just hold on for six or seven minutes, plus maybe another one to find a field, he could make it. His eyes were glued to the temperature gauge. It was rising slowly but steadily, the smell of glycol unmistakable and constant – he must have hit a piece of the '109's debris and holed the radiator, or damaged a pipe somewhere.

Six minutes to go. The gauge was coming up to the red line. Harper looked ahead and down - a ship was burning in the middle of the channel. An oil tanker. The flames were spreading steadily across the sea. Harper checked his altimeter: 2500 feet. If the engine quit he'd have about two minutes to bail out or ditch.

Five minutes to go. What would he do? Bail, or ditch? Harper looked at the sea surface; it seemed quite smooth, certainly not rough anyway. Temperature gauge again: the needle nearly on its stop. The engine seemed unconcerned. Harper was shaking like a leaf.

Four minutes to go. Bail or ditch? The ultimate outcome would be the same. The smell of glycol was becoming stronger, hotter. Could a smell actually get hotter? Harper thought about it. Yes it could - *this* was.

Three minutes to go. Harper looked over his shoulder. Gazzer looked back and raised two fingers - this time they were crossed. The engine was getting really hot now, the whole cockpit heating up. Harper shoved the canopy open even more.

Two minutes to go. So bloody close. But the engine note suddenly changed, running rough, a mechanical thrashing, growing louder. Gazzer was closing in, moving forward and down, looking up and over his left shoulder.

"You've got a trail of grey smoke, coming out from the bottom of the cowling."

"Its getting hot in here. Might be jumping soon." He could probably just about glide to the beach, but not over the cliffs.

One minute to go. Forced land on the beach for sure, if he had to. Suddenly a blast of intense heat, thick black smoke and oil fumes came bucketing out of the bottom of the cockpit. He couldn't breathe. He clicked open his Sutton harness, pulled the canopy all the way back and kicked the stick forward with his left foot. For Harper it felt as if he was flying in space for an instant in time, before his head was tugged back by something. His body rotated backwards in space, his legs coming up, so that he was in a sitting position but upside down and backwards. The tugging ceased as his radio lead snapped, the aircraft falling away from underneath him - away from above him. The air blast was enormous. Harper splayed his hands and feet out, slowly coming upright and stable. He reached somewhere *down*, relatively, for his D ring and pulled like hell, rolling onto his back again because of the destabilising effect of one arm in the airflow and one against his chest. Then the parachute canopy blew open with a loud 'crack' and Harper was jolted upright, swinging wildly in his harness, a wave of nausea coming and going as he stabilised.

He was already down to about 500ft. Suddenly a massive explosion made him look round. The Hurricane had crashed into the sea next to the tiny Folkestone lighthouse on the pier just ahead, sending up a huge plume of spray. Perversely, Harper wondered if he'd get into trouble for it, as if he wasn't in enough trouble already: he looked down and realised he would be landing in the sea. With no wind he'd have landed on the beach – it was nearly low tide - but instead he could see he was being carried backwards, out into the channel. Now Harper could hear an engine, he looked round to see Gazzer banking past him 1000 ft away, at low speed, waving like crazy. Harper waved back.

"Bye Gazzer" he said. He looked over his shoulder for one last time before he hit the sea, as if to check that there might be a tree or a building floating around out there. In fact there *was* something: a 36ft long fishing boat. The skipper had watched the whole scene unfold, positioning the boat in exactly the right place for when Harper hit the sea. Harper splashed down 100ft forward of the bow of the boat. He spent less than 2 minutes in the water – enough time to release the parachute harness but not enough to inflate his Mae West, before being hauled bodily out of the sea by two of the biggest men that he'd ever seen, their hands like four bunches of bananas.

44

"Hello, operator? Rainham 143 please. Yes, I can. That's right. Yes I know it's an RAF aerodrome." Harper was sitting in the coast guard's station in Folkestone, wrapped in two blankets, with the black, Bakelite phone in his right hand, a tumbler half-filled with rum in the other. His clothes were hanging out to dry on radiators, on hangers in a bathroom, and out of the window in the sunlight. His Irvine, sheep skin flying jacket had been consigned to a white canvass bag with his service revolver still in its holster, beyond hope. Over the next few days and weeks the jacket would unstitch itself, long before it had completely dried out. "Hello, its Flt Lt Harper: ops dispersal please." He had a brief tug of regret, knowing that several pilots would jump out of their skins when the phone rang. "Hello Greg, its Tom. Just to let you know I'm ok. Thanks a bunch! Newspaper ad; 'Lost: One-eared, one-eyed, three-legged dog. Answers to the name of 'Lucky'. Yes I know I am! Don't put me back on the board today – I'm having a large drink. Oh really? What did he do? Oh shit! …Ok, soon as I can. Catching a train I think, when my clothes have dried out a bit - mummy always told me about chaffing."

Intel had told him that Johnny landed with his wheels up again.

By lunchtime Harper decided that he would be dry enough to travel. The coastguard boss gave him a lift to the station, but not before he had refilled his glass and the hip flask. Harper climbed onto the train with his canvas bag over his back, went straight to 1st class, found a relatively quiet cabin, and sat down on a furry seat, opposite to a dark-haired woman in her mid twenties - the most beautiful woman he had ever seen. Harper had to tell himself not to stare, instead feigning interest in the dreary scene outside the window. The beautiful woman was reading a magazine. She looked up briefly at Harper, then down again, frowning, disturbed, just pretending to read. Harper was immediately aware of what he looked like to her, and what she was thinking. He thought about desire for a few moments, then resignation, then hope, and resignation again. Finally, he felt inside the Sou'wester he had been lent by the coast guard and pulled out his hip flask. The rum tasted slightly salty at first, but then pure. The woman hunkered down and raised her magazine higher.

As the train pulled out of the station, Harper fell asleep. It felt like forever. He had his Spitfire nightmare again in grisly detail, but this time it had a happy ending, when he dived into into a lake and put out the flames. Then another dream: driving his Alvis off a cliff, and landing softly on the back half of a blown up bridge. A big jolt. The jolt of a train carriage being butted up against by a new engine.

"I say, are you getting off?" Harper opened his eyes. The beautiful woman was standing over him. "Are you getting off?"

"Oh right… Sorry, where are we?"

"If you didn't drink in the day you'd know! We're at Maidstone – all change. London is it? Or don't you care?" The beautiful woman looked seriously pissed off with him.

"I need to get to Rainham," said Harper, still sleepy.

"Oh, Essex! That says a lot, doesn't it. You'll have to catch my bloody train to London, then the tube to Tower Hill, and another one to Hornchurch. Or change at Bromley, catch the ferry at Gravesend and a train from Grays. I don't know why I'm telling you this!"

"Christ" said Harper, holding up his ticket. The beautiful woman snatched it, read it, and then took one small step back.

"No you're booked all the way to London and back out. On 1st class too. I'm glad that somebody loves you."

"Do you work on trains?"

"No of course I don't! Do you?"

"No. I'm a fighter pilot" replied Harper.

"Oh really! I'm Churchill's private secretary."

"Are you?"

"No of course I'm not! You're drunk and I've had enough silliness! I'm calling the guard!"

"Do what you bloody like," said Harper. The beautiful woman's eyes blazed. She reached up, grabbed and pulled the emergency rope. Nothing happened for a few seconds, the beautiful woman collecting her things in an animated, dramatic fashion, opening the door of the cabin - which opened into the corridor - and starting to move outside. The guard met her trying to come out as he came in.

"Can I help you madam? Sir? Its an offence to pull the..."

"Don't call him 'sir'! He's a bum!"

"No, he is 'sir,' he's a Flight Lieutenant on an operational fighter squadron and he ditched just outside Folkestone harbour. Now what's the problem?"

"Oh no! Oh I am SO sorry! I really am! I..."

"Please. Stop it. My head hurts" replied Harper.

"But why do you... you look like you've been in a fight!" And, to the guard: a quiet "Are you *sure*?" with a pleading face.

"Yes I am sure madam. As I said, it's an offence to pull the cord. I'm afraid that I'm going to have to ask you to pay a..."

"No, please don't! Look I'll make sure that I'll get him on all the right connections. Please don't fine me. I really can't afford it."

"Subject to the regulations of the..."

"Look. I know I'm a state. It's not her fault. Either let her off or post the fine to me."

"Sir. That will be absolutely fine. And there'll be no... fine! If you'll pardon the pun."

"He who puns would pick a pocket" replied Harper, shaking the guard's hand with his own, a ten shilling note in the palm, and walking outside with his bag over his shoulder, the beautiful woman chasing after him with two small suitcases.

"Look I'm so sorry. I'm a bloody fool, far too self-important for my own good. I mean it though, really."

"Sorry?"

"I'll help you on you're way."

"You don't need to. I'm a big boy."

"It's on my way."

"Why, where are you going?"

"Well, Liverpool, but don't worry about that. I'll be your... wingman isn't it?"

"Indeed it is" replied Harper.

45

Harper reached the aerodrome just after 8pm. The beautiful woman had left him at Hornchurch station, crossed the platform and gone back to Aldgate East on the tube, en route to Liverpool. But not before she had told him that her name was Deborah, she came from Liverpool, she had been visiting her mother, she was 25, she was single and her boyfriend had been shot down and killed in a Bristol Blenheim in December 1939. Harper also knew that she was 5ft 8in tall, had long, straight, chestnut hair, green eyes, her parents were Australian and her grandparents Irish.

And Harper knew that he had fallen in love with her. He couldn't work out if it was her initial belligerence towards him - her apparent unavailability, the wicked sense of humour, the style, the smell of her, or her pure, sweet charisma. Perhaps it was all of those things. Harper had all of those things playing on his mind as he walked into the officer's mess, still wearing his Sou'wester. He didn't notice the curtains drawn to darken the room, the green baize over the wall lights casting the room into a green glow, and the fact that the pilots at the bar had bizarre apparel draped over their heads, consisting of green tissue paper and assorted shellfish carcasses.

"LOOK, IT'S NEMO!" said Gazzer. Cheers and laughter erupted and spread through the bar as Gazzer tried to bundle him - repelled - and then tried to pour a pint of beer over his head - repelled again - the contents ending up over the lower half of Gazzer instead. "Really did wonder if that was it old boy!" said Gazzer, when things had settled down a little.

"And I didn't?" replied Harper.

"Love the coat! Very authentic! Tell you what, can you imagine what the government would have put on your mess bill if you'd hit the lighthouse."

"I can see it now. Invoice for the month of May; pints of ale: 12. Shots of whisky: 20. Packets of crisps: 10. Lighthouses: 1. Grand total, 1 million pounds, 3 shillings & sixpence. Anyway, where's Johnny?"

"Ah, he's not here. Don't worry about it" Said Rhino. Harper wasn't so love sick that he didn't notice a few eyebrows lower, a few looks away. "We're assembled here this evening to toast both your victory, and survivability." The pilots raised their glasses in unison. "And here's to the end of a bloody busy day." The pilots had been called out twice more in the time that it took Harper to get back from Folkestone – a rhubarb along the Thames and then another sweep at Calais.

"I bet Hawkers are toasting me too' said Harper. 'They'll have to increase production."

"Me too" said Abbo.

"Why's that?"

"Because my one's on the bottom of the Thames estuary. Got hit by flak."

"What, theirs or ours?"

"OURS!" said a few of the boys in unison.

"But, what were they aiming at?"

"HIM!" said the boys, pointing at Abbo. Gazzer aimed the contents of another beer glass at Harper. The glass-shaped contents went through the air, keeping its form, hit his Sou'wester and splashed away onto the floor.

"You've completely lost the plot mate," said Abbo.

"But why were they aiming at you?" said Harper, as if he didn't understand what friendly fire was.

"Because they thought he was one of them!" said Gazzer. "You've got to stop. What's wrong with you man? You look like you've seen a ghost."

"A vision, for sure." Harper told them all about the girl, before Rhino told him about Johnny being suspended from ops pending interview. And that DC had flown through the 85ft high electricity cables, which ran across the fields, 1000 yards south of the airfield boundary.

"Christ, is he ok?"

"Gave him a bit of a shock!" replied Gazzer. It was impossible to get a straight answer from Gazzer.

"No, but really, he's ok?"

"Just cuts and bruises" replied Jock. "But his crate is a bit worse for wear. I was right behind him when he did it. He got too low on approach. Lost his left leg on one of the masts and it flicked him onto his back. Third in one day, hey."

"What, he lost his *leg*?" replied Harper, extremely concerned.

"NO, HIS GEAR LEG!" said Jock as, simultaneously, two pints of beer were tipped over Harper's head. The act stopped him thinking about Deborah for a couple of minutes.

At 9pm the bar was closed to the pilots again – DC had decided that it was a good system – and Harper went to bed after showering the smell of beer out of his hair. But he couldn't get the thoughts of Deborah out of his mind. He lay in bed, awake past midnight, thinking how he might be able to get to see her again. In the end he flicked his bedside lamp on and wrote a letter to Eric.

Harper T. A. Flight Lieutenant
Officers' Mess – Room 12
R.A.F. HXXXXXXXX
Essex

Hello again old son,

Hope you don't get this one before the other. Can't help but write, seeing as I ditched today –first time I've been for a proper swim since you and I in Skegness in '39... Holed my rad' shooting down another '109 (over somewhere that I can't say or the censor's 'll knock this letter about) & dropped it into the sea at Folkestone. Another very frightening day.

I'm coming to the conclusion that the hardest thing to deal with is the waiting during our days here (& nights - I find no matter how tight I get the thoughts of what I'll be doing the next day aren't far away.) I suppose its like having a case tried in court when one is not able attend – one's fate being decided in a place which isn't known, by people one doesn't know, if you get it. While I'm writing this to you some pretty fraulein might be sitting in an ammunitions factory loading the round which has my name on it, into a magazine belt, while somewhere on an air base sits a young kraut who I don't know either, & one day in the next few months he'll fire that very bullet into my left ear & it'll come out of the right one. Like my fate is in someone else's hands & there's nothing I can do about it. Chilling thought isn't it.

I think that I think too much.

We all hate the bloody telephone here – I'm one of the worst. If I get through this, when I get home I'll have Gray disconnect it. In fact I'll get some lighter fuel and give the bugger a ritual burning. By the way, just found out the number here is Rainham 143 and ask for dispersal if you need me urgently. But, if you want a chat, write - don't phone!

A good tip: exercise helps – it burns away the stress. I'm going to try and do a lap of the airfield whenever I can: either running or walking depending on what went on in the 24hrs before. We're getting a squadron dog tomorrow, no today actually, & I'll take him with me.

211

I said there's nothing I can do about my fate, but there is of course: strive to be the best bloody fighter pilot this squadron has ever seen. When I'm not practising with the Jerries I'm going to use the Boss's shotgun at the bomb dump. We've got some traps rigged. Works a treat. My aim is getting better all the time. Keeping fit, talking tactics ALL the time etc. I might be becoming a crashing bore but at least I'm still here, touch the wood.

I met a girl today, can't even begin to describe how lovely. I felt as if I had toughened up before I met her – don't chase skirt, ignore hearth and home - but now I'm getting all unnecessary again. What's to be done? I've GOT TO see her again as soon as I get some leave. Will ask my C/O if I can borrow a Hurricane and take a trip once the rest have had their go. I wonder if you'll be able to borrow a bomber once you're on ops!

All leave cancelled at the moment because of the France thing though.

Write soon – don't forget Gray & Co.

Tom XXX

Finally, past 1am, Harper drifted off to sleep. No more Spitfire nightmares - this time he dreamed about a beautiful woman with green eyes and long dark hair.

46

The pilots assembled at dispersal at 0500. Doogy and Koval were already making breakfast when the boys arrived from the mess: Harper and Gazzer in the Alvis, Jock and Rhino sitting backwards, on the boot, the rest in the ambulances. DC was in his office interviewing Johnny, and he had left the door open. The pilots couldn't help themselves but to listen in.

"...Once is circumstance, twice is happenstance and three times is an act of war. Do it again and you'll be grounded. Do I make myself clear?"

"Perfectly clear sir."

"You're one of our better pilots, but right now you're letting the side down. Dismissed!"

The 'D' word was the prompt for everyone to dive out of the way and look busy before Johnny came through the door. Gazzer and Harper went outside for a quiet chat and a cigarette.

"I think he wanted to give him the cane," said Harper, lighting up.

"If Johnny's not careful he'll get far worse than that" said Gazzer. "He'll get dismissed from the service for LMF."

"I'm sorry but I have no idea what that is."

"I'm not surprised old boy. Its lack of moral fibre and the chances are that the word will get round where he lives - the authorities have a strange knack of letting it slip out. Anyway, you know what Ginger used to say; stay away from the unlucky and the unwell."

"Yes well now Ginger's buried next to both isn't he. I feel sorry for Johnny – he's one of the good guys. He's just not coping very well. I did ask DC if he'd send him on leave. I know it's all cancelled for now but surely this is a becoming a special case."

"Don't know how it works. We're all nervous in the service. You've just got to get on with it. That's the way I see things." Rhino had been hanging back but now came out to join them.

"While you're doing the old chestnuts, have you heard this one?" said Rhino. "Fear is poison in combat."

"I suppose so" replied Harper. "Showing it around too much is, definitely. Its not the way we were brought up, is it?"

"No it isn't" said Gazzer.

"He knew what he was getting into though. In the first war nobody had a clue. The three prerequisites for joining the Royal Flying Corps were being able to ride a horse, fire a gun and sail a boat."

"Maybe our selection's a part of the problem," said Rhino. "But it's bad for morale to have him moping around. Shape up or ship out. There - that's another one."

"Well its certainly bad for Spitfires" said Harper.

After breakfast, Harper, Gazzer and Rhino decided to go for some target practise, collecting the guns and a few boxes of cartridges from DC and walking round the peri' track to the dump. Gazzer took the lead of Bentley, the new mascot – a charming black and white collie. By the time they arrived, Jones had taken up position on top of the fire engine ladder to disperse the clays, complete with lit cigarette for wind direction.

Rhino didn't miss. Every clay first shot: ten out of ten. Gazzer had a shaky start, but found his mark, missing the first three with both shots, and getting five out of the next seven with his first shot, two of the remaining three with his second. Harper was next, hitting all of his clays, most with his first shot and all of the remainder with the other.

"Nice shooting," said Rhino.

"Not as good as yours" replied Harper. "Talking of good shots, did you hear the story about the first war. There was an officer in the trenches, up a ladder, trying to improve his men's morale. He climbed to the top, stuck his head up and said; 'Don't worry lads! They couldn't hit an elephant at this dista...'" Harper performed a mime of a man falling backwards off of a ladder.

"It can't be true!" said Gazzer, bent over, laughing.

"It absolutely is" replied Harper. It was.

During the practise, Bentley had been tied up against the fire engine. When Gazzer finally straightened up again and turned round, all he could see was a lead still tied to the truck, and an empty collar.

"Bugger! Bentley's hopped it!" he said.

"I think the formal term is 'bolted'" replied Harper. "He's definitely not a gun dog is he? We're not going to be very popular if we don't find him - the chaps were looking forward to having him around." The shoot was interrupted in favour of finding the mascot. The boys started to work back round the peri' track. Halfway round, they stopped and looked over the hedge at the wreck of DC's Spitfire in an adjacent field. A lone policeman was defending it from souvenir hunters. The mast that he had hit was missing its top, the HT wires broken, a gang of workmen from the electricity board just about to start repairs.

The boys were distracted again, this time by the popping noise of a series of red flares fired from the tower, the ident' light going on at the mast on the north west side, flashing, its *dot dash dot*. Then they watched as a lone Spitfire taxied out almost to where they where standing, the pilot ignoring them, his mask already clipped on his face. He also ignored, or chose not look at the signals from the tower to 'stop-return' and opened up across the field, retracting the gear the instant the Spitfire was airborne and staying low, screaming over the dispersal hut. Then he banked steeply around the perimeter of the field and rolled out heading east. A steady red aldis was now shining from the tower - it meant the same thing as the flares and ident: 'Stop-return.'

"Bloody hell, it wasn't Johnny was it?" asked Harper.

"It bloody well was" replied Gazzer. "That was his new Spit - no tail markings."

The boys carried on walking round the peri' track at a considerably faster pace, picking up to a light jog when they saw another series of flares coming out of the tower – green this time - and increasing to a full on sprint when they heard the air raid siren.

"RED, BLUE, ORANGE SECTION! SCRAMBLE!" shouted Greg, ringing the bell as the pilots neared the dispersal area.

"What's going on?" Harper asked Greg, panting, as he got to the hut.

"Johnny's just taken off without permission, and now we've got a full on air raid to deal with."

"What in hell is he playing at?"

"I have no idea but its not going to be good news is it?" 2 minutes later, six Spitfires and two Hurricanes took off. The Hurricane pair consisted of Gazzer and Koval. DC, Harper and Abbo stayed on the ground: no aircraft to fly. The grounded pilots jogged across to the shelter with the fitters. When they got there, they found Jones with the dog, a piece of string tied round its neck.

"Well done Jonesy - where did you find him?" said Harper.

"In the back of the fucking fire engine. He's been sick in it."

"Well he's not going to like this very much is he" replied Harper, referring to the air raid. A couple of minutes of silence followed, and then, from the east, the low, unsynchronised engine sound of the German bombers. As the sound grew louder Harper could start to hear fighters attacking, their engines screaming as they dived on the bombers, their machine guns rattling. The dog seemed to sense what was going to happen next, its whole body shaking, it's tail between its legs. Harper felt like the dog. Then, a series of explosions, the ground shaking slightly - bombs, but a long way off.

"Sounds like they're dropping their sticks, " said Abbo.

"What does that mean?" replied Harper.

"You're getting lovesick mate. It means they're getting turned back. They drop their stick of bombs so that they've got more speed, more chance of evading us." Harper looked down at Bentley. The dog didn't know what to do with itself.

"I bloody hate this. It's ten times worse than simply not being able to go up and shoot at the bastards. We get bombed into the bargain."

"I know – not feeling pleased with myself."

"I'm going outside." Harper walked to the entrance and cautiously peered round the side of the blast wall covering the front. He looked up just in time to see several large fragments falling from the clouds. He instinctively knew that there was too much debris for it to have been a fighter. Two, maybe, but more like a bomber. The heavier components fell much faster than the broad, flat pieces like wing sections and control surfaces. He could make out an engine with a propeller still on it, still rotating, another engine attached to a wing stub, falling slightly slower. Harper stepped out of the shelter to watch where they fell. Strangely, the heavy parts landed noiselessly in the shallow valley to the west of the field – not the slightest bangs or thumps - the lighter parts landing a mile or so downwind.

"Well done chaps!" said Harper. The engine notes started to fade, a muted cheer coming out of the shelter. The all-clear signal sounded on the siren soon after, the pilots and fitters starting to return to the dispersal area. As they walked across the grass, one of them shouted and pointed towards the south. Everyone turned to look – the object started off as an indiscernible speck just under the clouds with a thin black curving line behind it, and manifested into a bomber being chased back in the direction of the airfield, one engine smoking, two Hurricanes on its tail, exchanging diving attacks.

"Looks like a Heinkel," said Abbo. Suddenly the aircraft exploded and dived vertically into the ground, 6 seconds before the sound of the explosion crossed the airfield.

"Well, it was" replied Intel.

"And 1 mile away" added Harper.

The squadron aircraft all came back in to land safely, everyone crowding round the ones with black streaks aft of the gun ports - because they had the tales to tell. As he taxied in, Gazzer stuck his fist in the air with forefinger extended again, pulling 'the trigger' and blowing on the end. Harper and Abbo gave him the thumbs up. He shut down and jumped down off the wing, a broad smile on his face.

"Would you like me to confirm my half?" he said, to Intel. "I'll walk over and find a bit of it if you like?"

"No need! Thanks for the show" replied Intel. Don't suppose you saw Johnny?

"Funny old thing. No. But I did hear the controller asking about a target going east along the estuary. He vectored a section to attack it, and they said it was friendly. Could have been him?"

"Yes, possibly. I'll check through with Group and see what I can find out." While the two were talking Gazzer had noticed that the left arm of Harper's flying jacket had split its seam at the shoulder. He crept round behind him when he wasn't looking, grabbed it with both hands and pulled it off cleanly in one go.

"Dah daaah!" said Gazzer.

"You're a bastard" replied Harper.

47

By late afternoon, the Squadron had claimed six Bombers and one fighter in a total of four sorties, for no losses. DC stood the squadron down early again, when bad weather blew in from the south west. Unsurprisingly the weather didn't stop the ATA with their deliveries, new Spitfires arriving throughout the afternoon and evening. By nightfall the squadron were back to ten Spitfires, two Hurricanes. No pretty *Atta girls* this time though. The Cosford ATA were doing the deliveries, the crew consisting of ex-1st World War fighter pilots, all now in their late 40s.

The stage was set for a piss up, even though the fate of Johnny was in the back of everyone's minds. The only caveat from the boss was to be tucked up in bed by 9pm.

The evening started well. The main body of pilots walked into The Ship at 6pm, accompanied by two Atta boys, cheering in unison at the sight of a complete rudder from one of the bombers that had fallen near the pub, mounted over the fireplace with a hook and chain. Next, their attention was drawn to five nurses sitting in a corner, chatting animatedly, silenced briefly by the boys' grand entrance. To a girl, they realised that they were gawping at the impressive show of blue, and made a slightly too-forced effort of re-immersion in their own conversation. Lexy launched a frontal attack to break up the formation, followed by a flanking move by Jock and Pipe.

"Looks like Pipe wants to recruit a few brides for his mobile brothel," said Rhino.

"I can't get the vision of him humping someone in a caravan out of my mind" said Harper.

"Well you need to old boy" replied Gazzer. "Does he have a nickname? We can't keep calling him Pipe."

"Its 'Chewy' but don't ask me why" replied Harper.

"Chewy Pipe. I Wonder?"

"Maybe its because he likes them to chew, you know, his pipe."

"That's made-up rubbish" replied Gazzer. Their conversation stopped as DC suddenly walked into the bar. No one knew what to expect.

"Hello chaps, nice to see you're enjoying yourselves! Just thought I'd pop in for a bit of the sauce."

"Nice to have you along sir" replied Rhino. "What are you having to drink?"

"I'll have a pint of shandy please." There were a few sniggers among the boys, Harper's shoulders doing their usual gentle rocking for a while, before DC launched his speech.

"Just a quick comment about what happened today. I am very proud of what you chaps pulled off. Very proud! The beers are on me for the rest of this evening, bearing in mind that our transport awaits at ten to nine. So you'll have to swill it. And I'm also pleased to announce that, as of half an hour ago, Tyler and Kowalski have two very nice, shiny Spitfires to fly tomorrow!" There was a roar of approval and backslapping.

"Way hey! Cheers boss!" said Gazzer, raising his glass, followed by acknowledgements from the rest of the boys.

"Thanks boss. I look after her," said Koval.

Harper and Abbo looked at each other with questioning faces.

"Don't know about you but I'm knackered" said Rhino to both of them, interrupting the silent communication.

"You're forgetting, I didn't do anything except watch you knocking yourselves out" replied Harper. "How many sorties did you do?"

"Three. One's enough!"

"I agree, actually."

"Ah there you are Tom," said DC, wandering over with his shandy. "You too Abbo. I know what you must be thinking. But you've not been singled out. Just before I came here I put your four names on the table and pulled two up. If you were a couple of rookies I'd leave you on the ground, but you're not. So I'd like you to fly as a pair for a few days until we can get the last two Spits. Shouldn't take long."

"Not a problem boss" replied Abbo.

"Me too - I'm fine about it sir" added Harper. Except that he wasn't really. "Is there any news about Johnny?"

"Intel called Group and they collected some radar traces from Chain Home. There's one going east on the river, then a gap of 20 miles or so, and another on a slightly different course, crossing the coast between Margate and Ostende. According to them if you plot a time line at the ground speed of the first trace, the second trace starts pretty much where it would do if it was the same aircraft, flying at a constant speed. Then it disappears."

"Christ" said Harper. "It sounds like a suicide mission. Belgium's crawling with Jerries."

"I really do hope you're wrong Tom, but somehow I think you're not. It makes no difference to me of course. If he comes home he'll be grounded and court-martialled. All I know is that I've lost another experienced pilot and another Spitfire. The aircraft aren't such a problem but the dilution of experienced pilots is already starting to be felt on some of the front line squadrons."

"Not just us then" said Abbo.

"No, not just us."

The interception by Lexy, Jock and Chewy proved successful and the nurses ended up in a rowdy circle of increasingly happy, drunk pilots, for the most part their tiredness forgotten. DC left at 8.30pm in his car. 8.50pm came and went, the ambulance drivers bribed with a very substantial whip round from the boys, equivalent to half a week's pay each.

"That's not a sight you see every day," said Harper to Gazzer. Bruce had fallen asleep in an armchair with his pint still in his right hand, balanced on his knee, his head back, his mouth open, snoring gently. It was too good an opportunity to pass up. The event started with the boys, and then the girls, taking turns to draw on his face with a pen. Bruce ended up looking like a glasses-wearing Guy Fawkes. Then one of the girls moved round the back of the chair, undid her shirt to reveal her bra, and squeezed her ample breasts together, just above Bruce's upturned face, the crowd turning crimson with suppressed laughter. The scene was captured by the barman - he happened to be the part-time photographer for the local newspaper. Even the flash bulb didn't wake Bruce. The final act, with, inevitably, Gazzer at the helm, was to balance various ornaments on the beer glass, until it finally toppled into Bruce's crotch. The room erupted into wild screams of laughter, people literally falling about on the floor, the barman joining in despite the regular tinkling of breaking glass adding to the stew of sounds and voices. Then Rhino noticed something – he quickly ran round the room, with his forefinger on his lips, *shushing* everyone. The laughter died almost as quickly as it erupted. Bruce had woken for a few seconds and then fallen asleep again.

Now they were on to Round Two. Gazzer made all the boys take their belts off and then linked them up, three and five at a time to make restraints. They tied Bruce to the armchair with the long belt combo around his chest and then round the back of the chair in one big loop. And another for each arm, vertical, to gently clamp them to the armrests. Next the boys picked the chair up and carried it carefully through the double doors at the back of the pub, which opened onto the garden, and round to the side of the pub, where the ambulances were parked. Gazzer had a quick word with the drivers, gave them the remainder of the contents of his wallet, then jumped up on the bonnet with Harper and Rhino. The three of them dragged, with some difficulty, the chair with Bruce in it, firstly up on top of the bonnet and then onto the roof of the ambulance, the second half of the operation easier than the first. Lastly they lashed the legs of the chair to the roof with 30ft of rope from the ambulance's equipment box.

"Right, let's go for a drive!" said Gazzer. Everyone had been crying with laughter. Now, the girls looked at each other incredulously, laughing even more deliciously when they realised that the boys meant business.

"Where!" said Harper.

"To your 'Arse End of course! See how quickly he can get round it." Everyone piled into the two ambulances, Gazzer at the helm of the first one, with Bruce on top, Harper driving the second. Most of the girls jumped into the second ambulance so that they would get a better view. The duo set off for Harper's bend, slow at first, constantly checking to see if Bruce had come loose, and progressively faster as they became more complacent, topping 45mph on the downhill section before the bend. The girls were squealing with delight. Finally they hit the bend itself, taking it in formation - a two-ambulance echelon starboard, Harper on the outside. Someone heard a faint 'aaaagh,' prompting Harper to look up and left. Bruce was awake, his hands gripping the arms of the chair, his knuckles white with exertion.

"YOU BASTARDS! YOU BLOODY BASTARDS!" shouted Bruce, unable to do anything constructive to remedy his plight. The sight of him up there, fully awake, was even funnier to the girls.

The formation returned, slower now, to The Ship for last orders, Bruce still strapped to the chair. Two pints for each man were ordered; one to drink, one for the final ceremony. Back outside again, they circled the ambulance. Bruce had got free but had yet to climb down. After a 'three, two, one go!' the boys doused him with nine pints of beer.

"I'm going to shoot the lot of you," he said, unable to suppress a laugh.

48

The pilots got to dispersal at first light. Two of them hadn't been to bed, the result of a successful night with their respective nurses. The boys loped into the hut and crashed out anywhere they could, Greg opening the windows to get rid of the growing smell of booze in the room despite the chilly morning air. Then he woke Doogy and Koval in the caravan by throwing a dustbin lid at the door. Finally he lit the fire and put the kettle on. Harper kicked Gazzer on the floor – he was already snoring.

"Wake up you bugger. Listen we can't give DC the bill for the whole evening. A. It'll tell him how much we quaffed. And, B. It's too much anyway – nearly 20 pounds for Christ's sake! That's what he earns in a month probably."

"Is it really?" replied Gazzer, yawning. "I have no idea what I'm paid old boy. I'd do it for free."

"Would you really! Absolute tosh." Harper walked to DC's office, tapping on the door as he went in. "Hello sir, hope you're well."

"Crikey Tom. You look worse than after your crack up. I trust you got to bed at a reasonable time. Was a busy day though," forgetting that Harper hadn't flown at all on the previous day.

"Oh absolutely sir" Harper calculating privately that he'd had less than 3 hours sleep. "I've got the bar bill here. I hope you don't mind but its 6 pounds and 15 shillings."

"Really? That much! That was an expensive shandy! I'm sure I can find it somewhere. Worth every penny if it cheers the chaps up. Now listen Tom, I've had a rethink overnight about this two Hurricane thing. I didn't think it through properly if I'm perfectly honest about it – not like me at all."

"You could probably do with some leave. Don't think you've taken a day off since you came here."

"You're absolutely right of course. The problem I've got is that you can't keep up with the Spitfires unless we throttle back and that's something never to be done in combat. And if we get say, a sweep over France I can't send you and Abbot over there on your own. 72 Squadron went up against over a hundred fighters a couple of days ago."

"One hundred?"

"Yes I know it's... quite impressive, shall we say. Now I do have a proposal. I can call my friend Loel – he's C/O at '601, Biggin'. Have you transferred for just a few days. As long as it takes to get two new Spits, plus any replacements of course."

"Oh."

"Not keen?"

"Well, you know. This is my Squadron sir. Wouldn't really want to leave them for any length of time. Especially now things are hotting up." The telephone started ringing. Harper stiffened up, immediately proud of himself for not jumping visibly.

"RED AND BLUE SECTIONS SCRAMBLE!" shouted Greg. There were audible groans as the pilots gathered their equipment and started to stumble across the grass, their pace picking up for the last few yards as reality hit home. DC had forgotten that Harper was still standing in his office, as he collected his flying kit.

"What about Abbo and me?"

"Hold on... what is it Greg?

"They want a patrol, south east, angels 15."

Ok, yes you too. Follow Blue, Rhino's lead. Operate independently though, as a pair. Let Abbo lead."

"Got it!" replied Harper, running out of the office to pick up his Mae West, helmet, goggles and mask. Jones was already at the Hurricane when Harper arrived, plugging in the trolley and running round the front of the aircraft. Harper strapped in by himself. DC ran up behind him.

"OK, situation's changed. Group wants all available aircraft at Beachy Head. There's a formation coming in from Abbeville. Stay on frequency, and if you get into trouble you can R.T.B. Buster all the way - we can spare the Hurrys now."

"Thank you sir" And, to Abbo, still climbing into his Hurricane: "Come on you, get your skates on!" Abbo looked back and laughed. Harper thought how brave he looked.

Three minutes later Harper and Abbo were climbing out of the airfield in a pair: Abbo was Yellow 1, Harper Yellow 2.

"I always told you we were yellow" radioed Abbo.

"Oh, tee bloody hee," replied Harper.

"All Sections! Radio silence!" said the controller. The Spitfires and Hurricanes headed 120 degrees initially, climbing to 15,000ft on request by the controller. At Ashford they climbed again, to 23,000ft, the Hurricanes lagging behind, trading speed for climb rate. Harper could hear the first rasps of communication in combat from '601's Spitfires, followed by seemingly endless silences. He checked the aircraft's 'T's and 'P's a few times elaborately, trying to curb the fear growing within him. And yet he was happy to be airborne again. A part of the Squadron again.

"Yellow section, position please" asked Rhino.

"3 miles, falling back" replied Abbo. Harper's senses were at their most acute. His eyes adjusted to infinite, scanning forward and up, left and right, thumb in the sun, then back down to the instruments.

"Red section, multiple targets! 1 O'clock, level. Tally ho!" Abbo looked over his right shoulder at Harper, raised a fist with the thumb up and then looked forward again. Harper didn't have time to acknowledge the gesture. "Red section tally! Go for the bombers!

Ignore the fighters!" Harper wondered what they had seen. He scanned ahead again. There, he could just see them: what looked like a swarm of insects – bombers – two separate swarms of smaller specks way above them. It looked like there were at least fifty bombers, maybe one hundred fighters.

"Christ al-fucking-mighty" said Harper to himself.

"Yellow section tally! Go for the bombers!" said Abbo. His nose went down slowly, Harper following, staying on his wing. The specks grew larger. Abbo was deliberately heading off to the left side so that he could pull round and attack from the rear. Harper checked with his thumb in the sun – he couldn't see them yet, but he knew they'd be there, maybe up above 30,000ft, the fighters immediately above the bombers acting as a decoy. Harper spotted a black curving line behind one of the specks, then another, then another bomber exploding – three or four men dead, just like that. With less than a mile to go to the nearest bomber, a few sporadic bursts of machine gun fire came up towards the two Hurricanes, arcing lazily beneath. A few seconds of inactivity followed, then all hell broke loose. Over one hundred machine guns opened up together - that golden bird cage effect again, tracer everywhere, and they were only the bullets he could see. Harper heard a 'thump' and 'twang!' then nothing for a few seconds, then 'THUMP!' again. There was no way to follow every source or evade. But Abbo pressed home the attack. As the bombers passed by to the right he started rolling gently towards them, to give Harper time to notice and begin adjusting, and then carried on rolling and pulling until they were behind the main formation, closing rapidly on two stragglers at the extreme right.

"Yellow section, arm and check," said Abbo - he sounded as calm as if he was ordering a beer.

"Fuck it," said Harper, seriously annoyed with himself at not already remembering to do it. Abbo was going for the left of the two: Harper instinctively went for the right. Abbo opened fire at 200 yards and so did Harper, both perfect aims, scoring immediate hits on the bombers, Abbo's bursting into flames, Harper's pushing and diving out of the way to the right. Harper followed it down, carrying on with 2-second bursts, until the right wing erupted in flames. He rolled wings level and started pulling out, checking over his shoulder, thumb in the sun, right and.... something caught his eye at extreme left. It was a fighter, rolling wildly, half of its left wing missing. Harper watched it go down, realising that the pilot would be trapped inside. It was a Hurricane. Abbo's Hurricane. Almost immediately the sky was full of '109s. 'THUMP! THUMP! BANG!' Harper didn't have time to think – he immediately rolled and pulled hard right, blacking out despite tensing his stomach and calves. He heard and felt another 'WHUMP' but couldn't see. He pulled even harder, feeling the strain of the airframe through the stick, counting 'one, two, three' and then pushing and rolling the other way. Then stick to neutral - zero gravity, why? - stick back slightly. His vision came back quickly. A yellow-nosed '109 flashed past his nose going vertically up, on flames from wingtip to wingtip. How could that be? No, not vertically up, vertically down. Because Harper was upside down.

"FUCK! FUCK! FUCK!" he said, checking the stick to neutral and then pulling again, blacking out again, shaking, sweating, knees knocking. The altimeter unwound wildly, passing 10,000ft, but enough height to recover to level flight in a half loop. He should have half rolled. No more impacts. Harper blacked out once more, and then his vision returned on the up line. His eyes darted around wildly, a thumb in the sun, a look over his shoulder, a look ahead, a look below. He was flying completely alone. It seemed preposterous but that's the way it was. Harper brought the aircraft round in a 360degree turn, but there was nothing about, the altimeter reading just under 5000ft. The controls felt strange; stiff and ineffective in roll, far too light on the pedals. There were bullet and shell holes everywhere. The aircraft was wallowing through the sky like a wounded bird. He would try to get home. At least the engine seemed to be running ok. Harper turned the aircraft back towards the north west, noticing for the first time that his flying goggles were wet on his face. He didn't feel injured, no obvious pain. He could see out of both eyes, sort of. Harper took his left hand off of the throttle, bit the fingers of his glove, pulled it off with his teeth and put his hand up to his face to check. Then he realised that it was water. The tears splashed down his cheeks.

228

49

Gazzer walked into the dispersal hut, looking for Harper.

"Anyone seen him?" he asked. No one looked up. Everyone knew. Gazzer checked in the caravan and then along the flight line to the lone Hurricane. Harper was under the wing, laying on his back, his hands behind his head, still wearing his goggles to disguise his eyes.

"You ok old boy?" said Gazzer as he sat down.

"Couldn't be better. Love getting my friends killed."

"Do you want to tell me what happened?"

"Not really."

"Think you should."

"The long version or the short version."

"Short."

"I'm a c**t."

"Oh really? How does that work?"

"I was supposed to be his wingman. And I was too busy trying to get a fucking bomber."

"It doesn't work like that old boy. You can't be a wingman all the time. You've got machine guns too – they're there for you to shoot at things as well as the other chap." Rhino wasn't far behind Gazzer, walking once round the Hurricane and then sitting next to him on the grass.

"Before you go on a guilt mission, have you had a look at your aeroplane?" said Rhino.

"No."

"It's riddled with holes, Harps! I've just counted ten. Big ones! You're rudder's hanging by a bloody hinge. What happened?"

"We went in as a pair, attacking a formation of '17s. Abb... Abbo got one and I got the one next to it. His blew up and I followed... mine down. When I looked back he was missing a wing. Couldn't get out."

"How do you know he couldn't?"

"How the fuck are you going to get out of a fighter rolling round itself three times a second."

"He might have pushed out"

"What?"

"Abbo was, I mean Abbo is an aerobatic champion from before the war. He'd know that if you push the stick forward and unloaded the G then the wing wouldn't be giving a rolling moment anymore..." Gazzer was shaking his head from side to side. "...And the roll would stop. And then he'd be able to...?" Harper wasn't listening. He said 'why, why, why' under his breath while Rhino continued to talk.

"Did you hear me?

"What?"

"I said that Doogy saw a Hurricane cracking down – not one of ours – it went down vertically and took the wing off one of a pair of Hurrys. That sound's like you." Harper sighed.

"Maybe."

"Well it's not something that happens all the time is it? *Must* have been you! Wingman or no bloody wingman, it wouldn't have made a difference. I can't see how you'd have been able to do anything."

"Thanks, but I don't think..."

230

"That's it!" said Gazzer. "Stop thinking. Let's take Bentley for a walk. Come on old boy."

Reluctantly, Harper agreed. The three of them got Bentley and his lead from the hut and started walking together round the peri' track, Gazzer and Rhino trying to force some conversation. Rhino first.

"…And there were two '109s, one behind the other. I started firing but I was pulling and turning so hard I couldn't see what I was firing at under the nose. The old Hurry's better, right Harps! Anyway I aimed for the front one and shot the rear one down!"

"Way hey" replied Gazzer. "Let's pick the pace up a bit. Come on Harps. What's that Harry Lauder song?"

"'Keep Right On 'Til The End Of the Road'" replied Rhino.

Harper groaned. He pulled his latest letter from Eric out of his pocket, reading while he walked, trying to concentrate on something.

> *L A C Harper E*
> *Room 4 Block 48*
> *R.A.F. S. Cerney*
> *Nr Cirencester*
> *Glos.*

Dear Tom,

> *If fate should ever put you in control of an Airspeed Oxford & you happen to be at 8,000ft for god's sake don't put the nose down & see how fast you can go. I did of course & had a hell of a job to pull the crate out of the dive again. Finally when I got back there was a window missing & I had to make up a story about slipping out of a steep turn.*

> *Even that was a bit tricky as I was meant to be practising R/T, air to ground. Actually I reached about 280mph, bloody fast for an Oxford. I often wondered what the labels in the planes which say "Not to be flown above 270mph" meant. Now I know it means the windows drop out. All this was yesterday*

The letter was undated.

> *Today, the clouds have been at about 500ft & we were just recovering from an R.A.F. lunch in the barrack block when a plane was heard*

*advancing on us. Someone shoved his head out of the window &
announced it was a Wellington. The "Wellington" started machine-
gunning all & sundry. Actually he got...*

There was a page missing. Gazzer and Rhino had stopped talking now,
taking turns to throw sticks for the dog. Cursing, Harper hunted for the
missing page in his pockets but he couldn't find it. In the end he
carried on reading, out of sequence.

*...c**t addressed yours to me likewise. Still it got thro' O.K but don't do
it again.*

*I've reground the valves & decoked Mary & she's now in the process of
erection again. The exhaust was getting bloody hot & she was losing a
bit of power. It'll probably be worse now but it's the principal that
counts. I finished off the valves with a little light machine oil, of course,
got quite a good finish. Actually I merely got the biggest holes out & left
it at that.*

Can't think of any more news,

Love to everyone, Eric.

Harper realised that he hadn't really been reading anymore, the
information getting somewhere into his brain, but then lost before
reason and storage, crushed by the overwhelming tide of memories of
Abbo, thoughts about what he could have done differently, grief and
guilt.

At least the guilt was receding a little, Harper starting to acknowledge
subconsciously that the collision hadn't been the result of his
inattention. Gazzer and Rhino were talking in earnest. Harper tried to
concentrate on their conversation. It was Rhino's turn again.

"…in the first war. It was really bad for morale in the trenches."

"What did they do?" asked Gazzer.

"Simple. Our boys went for their supply lines, cut off their food and
drink. You know, beer and bratwurst. Soon as we did it, German
morale went through the floor. That's what we've got to do when
we're over enemy territory. If you see a lorry with a beer logo or a
sausage on the side, make sure you shoot at it!" Gazzer and Rhino
laughed together, but Harper's mind had drifted away again.

The three completed their lap of the airfield and Harper walked back to his Hurricane, feeling only slightly better. Jones was bending down, working on the rudder.

"Hello" he said. Jones looked up quickly then back down. "How's it going?"

"You fucked it good and proper this time sir."

"What's the damage?"

"One of the shells went straight through this hinge," said Jones, pointing to the base of the rudder. "Another one's gone through the aileron assembly, starboard wing. Done all the joints and connectors. How did it fly?"

"Like a sick pigeon."

"And a shell's exploded above you're right gear leg. Don't know how you got it down."

"It was a bit slow. Can you fix it?"

"Yeah, in about two years. We'll be loading this one on a Queen Mary."

"So I'm bloody grounded." Harper wanted oh so desperately, as never before, to go up again. To shoot them all down.

"No doubt about it" said Jones, looking up. But Harper was already walking back to the dispersal hut. He walked straight past the boys, all heads still down or turned away, and into DC's office.

"Hello Tom, I heard what happened. No need to..."

"Sir. Can I have a Spitfire?"

"Yes. Yes you can. I've already earmarked it. The next one's yours."

50

The Old Rectory

Wellum Road

Liverpool

18th May1940

My Dearest 'Bum'

Hello darling, I do hope you are well. I've been thinking a great deal about you, especially whenever I see an aeroplane flying overhead, and there's been a great deal of that recently. Yesterday a German bomber came over my house and the dog jumped in the air. At least 3 feet I think!. – I've never seen it go so high! It was hilarious, for a few seconds anyway. I ran outside just in time to see another one go over. I saw the black and white crosses. I thought it looked like the scariest thing I'd ever seen. Mummy and daddy want us all to go back to Australia soon but I told them I won't go. Not for now anyway. Because things have changed.

I can't tell you how much I am missing you. I Can't wait to see you again. Do you think you'll get some days off soon? I know its hard for you. It's become a family ritual to sit round the radio in the evening, listening to the news. Except it all seems such bad tidings.. What a shenanigans it all is. I know you said that they exaggerate the combat losses but its still bad news isn't it. Holland fell they said this evening. Shocking isn't it?

I'm writing to you from my bed. I'm wearing a rather beautiful green silk night dress sent to me by my friend in Singapore. Matches my eyes darling! It took 4 months to get here but it was worth it. I'll wear it for you when I see you again.

I can't wait to meet your friends. They all seem so real to me, the way you talked about them. I would particularly love to meet Gazzer of course. And Abbo: There's a difference between a ladies'man and a man who is loved by women. He sounds like the latter to me.

Harper stopped reading for a moment, tried not to think about Abbo, and failed. He checked his watch. 4.15am. He'd have to be getting up soon.

If I did go back to Australia, you'd come out and visit wouldn't you? You'd love it there .No war, everything peaceful. You might even want to stay with me. I must go back one day. I'm more at home there than anywhere I've ever been in my life.

I know how difficult it is for you now but you must know that I care for you. Please come and see me when you get a chance.

All of my love

Debs x x x

As much Harper tried to get it behind him, he kept being reminded about losing another friend. He washed and dressed quietly, quickly, so as not to wake Gazzer. He went through the back door of the mess where his Alvis was parked, let off the parking brake and rolled her gently backwards for a few yards before climbing in and firing up. Harper drove out of the airfield and up to his Arse End. No speed trial this time, though. Harper parked quietly and watched the sky for a while, smoking a cigarette. The eastern sky was already light, still dark in the west. The border between night and day.

Harper wondered, if he survived, what he would like to do next. It would have to be flying of course. Could he live in Australia? If he married Debs, maybe he would be able to join up there. Or maybe fly in the airlines. It would be a lot to give up: England, the estate, his friends, his job. For the first time in his life, Harper felt trapped in love. He lit another cigarette with the butt of the first one and watched the sun come up. He wouldn't have had to be at dispersal at first light - no aeroplane to fly. Hopefully that would change soon. Thoughts of the Spitfire cheered him and he drove back to the airfield in a different frame of mind.

When Harper arrived at dispersal, the fitters were already servicing the Spitfires, running up the engines. Greg was making breakfast for the boys, the smell of eggs, bacon and toasting bread wafting out of the door.

"Morning Harps" said Greg. "Want some?"

"Not for now thanks. Just tea I think." Harper helped himself from the teapot.

"We think we know what happened to Johnny."

"How so?"

"I've received an intelligence report from Group. On the day he went, they recorded some 'unusual aerial activity' as they called it, over two airfields in Germany. Can't pronounce them. It seems that we had an agent at the second one. He reported a lone Spitfire making strafing attacks about the same time as Johnny left us. He damaged or destroyed twelve aircraft on the ground."

"What happened to it?"

"It was shot down by ack-ack, pilot killed."

"So he did commit suicide."

"You could put it like that."

"Another one."

"He already was, wasn't he."

"I wonder how many he got on the first one." Harper couldn't help himself but think about the kill ratio. "Its not bad odds?"

"It's not about the aeroplanes. It's the pilots we need to take down. It was one nil to them unless any of them bought it on the ground. Johnny was bloody good before he lost himself. We've got a replacement coming in this morning. F/O Wells from '72."

Harper had nothing else to say. He topped up his tea and wandered over to the main gaggle of pilots.

"Morning Harps" said Rhino. "I was just telling the chaps here about your catatonic state thing."

"Oh yes."

"Well explain it then. I can't, far too complicated."

"Bloody hell, bit early in the morning. Do I have to?" Rhino's look said 'yes'. "Anyway, you do yourself down. It was my theology teacher if you remember. He said that if you believe Darwin's theory of natural selection - which most of us do - then the catatonic state is the evidence of god."

"Bloody hell old boy" said Gazzer. "You're sounding intelligent."

"Shut up" replied Rhino. "Go on, we're all ears aren't we chaps!" Some of them didn't look like they were.

"Well, he said that when we're under extreme stress, at the point where we give up hope of survival, everything becomes calm and we feel no pain." Now Harper had the attention of the room. "That's the catatonic state. And his argument was that, seeing how the next step is usually death, there isn't any advantage to the species. The catatonic state couldn't have evolved because of natural selection."

"And?"

"And so it must be god."

"I don't get it," said Gazzer.

"I do," said Rhino. "You're very clever."

"Not me, my theology teacher." Chewy decided to say something. It didn't happen as often as with the noisy boys but when he did, it was usually worth listening to.

"There's a military expert who wrote a book about this stuff. He says that the best soldiers, so likewise the best combat pilots, are the ones who have given up hope. Because they stop worrying and can start to function without fear."

"Or mercy" added Jock. "I've read it too."

"They won't be getting any mercy from me" replied Harper. "Not now." Suddenly Harper had an overwhelming urge to go outside and be by himself for a moment, which he did. And lit a cigarette.

Harper couldn't put his finger on exactly when or why it just happened, but the gnawing rot of anxiety inside him had disappeared. Harper felt like he had just turned a corner.

51

Harper was sitting on a deck chair outside the caravan, talking to Doogy and Koval, when he heard the sound that he had been waiting for all day. The sound of an aeroplane coming from the south west. From Southampton. The Spitfire came in low and fast, circled the field as it slowed, lowered gear and flaps, and touched down perfectly on three points. Harper watched as it taxied in across the grass and shut down next to the dispersal, coincidentally and ironically to Harper, parking almost exactly where his Hurricane had been standing before its last flight. A small, slim pilot jumped down. Another girl. Harper couldn't help himself but to jog across the dispersal to the aircraft. He felt like a baby with a new toy.

"Hello, good flight?"

"Oh yes thank you. Little bit of weather on the coast but its nice inland."

"I'm Tom Harper. This one's mine!"

"Oh, lucky you. I'm Joan." She was pretty and petite and wore collar and tie with what looked like, but wasn't, an RAF uniform minus its rank, ATA wings, tan leather gloves. When she took off her helmet and goggles she revealed short, wavy, dark brown hair. Harper thought that she looked Scandinavian, Icelandic maybe. And not more than 20 years old.

"Crikey!" said Harper, under his breath.

"Sorry?"

"Sorry, you're just … so, young."

"I've been flying since I was 15 actually. Youngest girl in Britain. They only brought in the age limit in after I started."

"So you learned to fly before you learned to drive."

"Considerably before."

"Well done you. Would you like some tea?"

"Yes please, especially if you've got some bread and jam to go with it. They were mean at S'ampton and I'm famished." The girl was charming, the first time that Harper had met someone who stopped him thinking about Debs for a moment, not that it changed anything. The two chatted in the hut for 30 minutes, the boys crowding round, until the low-powered thrum of an approaching Oxford signalled the end of the conversation. Then Harper went back outside with his flying equipment and climbed into his Spitfire.

A small step up on the wing, two paces, and he sidled and climbed through the open hatch. Harper was itchy with excitement as he fumbled with the straps. He took a deep breath, told himself to get a grip, and put everything together correctly on his second go. The Sutton harness and parachute were the same as the Hurricane, as were many of the gauges and switches. The gear and flap controls were separate − a much better arrangement − the gear lever was on the outside of an aluminium barrel, marked 'chassis,' 'up,' and 'down.' The cockpit was considerably smaller than the Hurricane. Tight, even. Harper felt as if he was sitting *in* an aeroplane instead of on top of one, inside a greenhouse. He brought the little cockpit side door up (it reminded him of a Tiger Moth) and latched it into place. He felt down the right side of the seat for the battery switch, the 'ground-flight' switch, turned the fuel on (one big tank between the engine and fuselage − no room in the wings,) set the throttle half an inch open, switched on the mags, pushed the kigas primer seven times, a thumb up to Jones, a thumb back, and then pushed, simultaneously, the 'start' and 'boost' buttons at the base of the instrument panel. The Merlin fired after three blades, barking and blatting into life - it sounded the same but felt entirely different, its mechanical clashing singing through the metal, stressed skin of the fuselage. The fumes smelled the same, just more intense, because of the proximity of the exhaust stubs to the cockpit. The Spitfire felt like it was straining at the leash. Harper looked across an elliptical wing at Jones and smiled. Jones smiled back, as happy as Harper had ever seen him – he was taking a girl out on the R71 later. And then he mouthed something. Harper mouthed a 'what?' back with a puzzled expression. Jones did it again. It was 'go get the bastards.' Harper started laughing. Jones ran round to pull the cable out of the cowling and then round to leading edge of the left wing, waiting for Harper's thumb for the chocks. Harper signalled, saw them go, and held the stick hard back as he released the brakes, by pulling the brake lever on the front of it, allowing the retaining clip to fall out of *lock.* Harper squeezed the throttle open and the aircraft surged forwards, startling him for a second. It was *so much* lighter, skittish compared to the Hurricane. And that nose - it seemed to stretch ahead to infinity. He couldn't see over it or particularly round it. As Harper moved forwards he started weaving left and right so that he could check ahead, looking along the mean direction of travel. It felt exaggerated, but looked entirely normal to the boys gathered outside the hut, watching their friend. The exhaust fumes were making his eyes water – he had to pull his goggles on to protect them. Harper looked down at the coolant temperature – it was already rising fast, the right gear leg masking the radiator.

He sped up a little for the last bit of the journey to the holding point. He pulled round, into wind to do the run up, even more aware of nosing over. Brakes on, stick hard back, open up to 1200rpm, check the tail not rising, check the mags - no more than 150rpm drop on each side, no more than 50rpm difference, exercise the constant speed prop. The temperature gauge was already nudging 100 degrees. Time to go. He taxied out to the runway, lined up, ran a few feet forwards to straighten the tail wheel, paused, and then gently opened the throttle about 1/3rd forward. The aircraft galloped forwards, and left, even with 1/3rd of the power available. Harper pressed the right rudder all the way, holding the stick back hard. The aircraft was tracking straight now, just little dabs of right rudder needed to keep it there. As the ASI needle passed 40mph the stick was coming alive and Harper let it find its neutral position in the airflow. He pushed the remaining 2/3rd of the throttle forwards, counting 'one thousand, two thousand, three thousand' as he did it, right rudder all the way now. The acceleration was immense, his head shoved back against the headrest. It only felt like a second or two later that the Spitfire was ready to fly, pulling itself into the air at 80mph, the acceleration continuing. It already felt fantastic; light, lithe, harmonious, powerful. Harper squeezed the break lever, took his left hand off the throttle to hold the stick, then his right hand off the stick to raise the gear – gear lever down, pause, inwards, pause, upwards pause and release. The gear lever sprung back into position, the word 'up' now showing on the indicator. Suddenly Harper noticed that the aircraft wasn't climbing anymore. The nose was going down. Something was wrong, the ground was getting closer. The throttle was closing.

"FUCK IT!" said Harper as he changed hands quickly and pushed it open again, pushing right rudder to stop the aircraft crabbing left, simultaneously pulling the nose up, and then tightening the throttle friction nut even more than he already had. On the ground the boys were laughing as Harper porpoised away. That old chestnut – he wouldn't do it again.

"Numpty" said Harper to himself, checking the temperature gauge – if his gear leg was still hanging out the engine would have started overheating by now. The speed rose rapidly. He pulled the nose up higher to stop the Spitfire accelerating too much, to stop it *getting away* from him. He rolled into a turn – the stick felt light and responsive, the roll rate much faster than the Hurricane. The ASI was hovering at 200mph, the VSI (vertical speed indicator) showing 2500fpm. Harper pushed out on the stick at 2000ft and let the speed increase. The acceleration was astounding. His left hand went down by the left of his seat to dial in elevator and rudder trim, to let the aeroplane fly hands and feet free. But the speed carried on increasing – every few seconds he had to adjust the trim again. The ASI needle blasted past 300mph and he pulled the stick back for a loop from straight and level. It was the lightest of pulls, the aircraft soaring round the loop, Harper having to keep direction with right rudder on the way up and over the top as the speed decreased, the yawing moment increasing. He soared down the other side of the loop, the speed building rapidly - the ailerons stiffening up but still feather light in pitch - and let the aircraft descend all the way down to ground level. Soon he was over the Blackwater estuary. Harper flew past a fishing trawler and waved at its crew – they waved back frantically as he went past them at 350mph, pulling up into a victory roll. He did another one over Mersea Island.

The Spitfire felt like Harper's friend's Grand Prix-winning Auto Union D-type, compared to a 1920s Bentley. It was light, powerful, manoeuvrable and fast. It was absolutely, completely, awesomely, wonderful. He flew a short sequence of aerobatics, gaining altitude and energy with each manoeuvre. It was effortless.

Then Harper noticed a voice coming through on the radio. It was the controller - he was vectoring two sections, somewhere over the Thames Estuary. Harper couldn't hear the section leaders, only the instructions from the controller and white noise in reply.

"Red section turn right heading 120, climb angels 15." Harper turned south and started climbing. He put his oxygen mask on and set the regulator. Hold on, were his guns armed? He looked left and right at the red patches covering the gun ports. He turned the ring on the firing button and gave it a squirt. Yes he was. "Red section, fifty plus targets, 12 O'clock range 10 miles."

"12 O'clock 10 miles, Red section." Harper could hear them now – they must have climbed - better radio range. It was Rhino's voice.

Harper checked his watch: 2pm – he had been airborne for 20 minutes. He checked his fuel: 30 gallons gone, two thirds of a tank left. He checked his map: 10 miles to go. He would get there at the same time. He wouldn't interfere unless he needed to.

Rhino was flying as Red leader. Gazzer was Red 2, Doogy and Koval - Red 3 and 4 respectively. Blue section was behind them. Gazzer looked out across the estuary and then back at Rhino, holding loose formation, flying slightly higher. Gazzer took his left hand off of the throttle – it was shaking – and looked down at his knees. They were trembling slightly. Same as usual. Then he looked forward and saw the enemy for the first time: thirty Dorniers , thirty Messerschmitt 109s above them. Two other squadrons were intercepting another, larger wave of fighters and bombers 30 miles behind them.

"Red Section, arm and check" said Rhino. Gazzer checked his guns. They fired once and then jammed. He hit the button again - no response. And again - no response.

"Red 2. Stoppage! Guns jammed!" said Gazzer, punching his knee with his left hand, cursing.

"OK, shit! Standby." replied Rhino. "Red section continue. Red 2 stay on my wing."

"Wilco, Red 2." Harper had been listening in. He could see the enemy bombers now but not the fighters, and not his own Squadron. If he got there maybe he could look after Rhino. He went to buster with the throttle, pushing the lever through the inhibiting wire at the forward end of normal travel. Then Harper noticed something. He didn't have the shakes. He wasn't even sweating.

"Must be cooler in here!" he said to himself. He really had turned a corner. And he hadn't been paying attention – the altimeter was at 22,000ft and climbing. "Get a grip!" said Harper as he pushed the stick forward and started to accelerate back down to 15,000ft in a shallow descent. The speed went up to Vne, and past it. Harper waggled the ailerons to see what they would feel like. Stiff, was the answer. He pushed and pulled on the stick – light as a feather. The rudder still worked too.

"Red section, targets 12 O'clock low. Tally ho!" said Rhino.

"Blue section tally! Targets as they bear!" Jock's voice.

Harper checked the sun. Nothing for a moment, then the flash of a reflection. A fighter. Or fighters - must be.

"Come on, you bastards" said Harper. He checked his tail and then scanned round, back to the sun again. They were there all right, ready to pounce. Another scan round – another group of '109s visible now, just above the bombers. He still couldn't see his own Squadron. Harper rolled left and right to check his tail again. All clear. There! Four '109s diving straight down. Harper watched and followed their direction of travel down to... eight Spitfires.

"Red and Blue sections! Four '109s diving at you!" shouted Harper. As he said it the Spifires broke up in pairs - he couldn't know if they had seen the bandits before he called it. Harper chose the last of the four '109s and followed it down, still checking the sun, still checking his tail. He steepened his descent slightly so that their vectors would converge. It was looking good, distance closing. A little more adjustment and Harper was on his tail, closing fast.

"You... beautiful... bird..." he said as he came within killing range, opening fire at 100 yards. The tracer went above the target - no recoil.

Harper aimed lower and tried again. A direct hit! The '109 immediately burst into flames, the dive going vertical as the elevator fell away. Harper couldn't follow it – too fast now. He pulled up and zoomed skywards, trading speed for height. And what a trade. He was climbing at a crazy angle, the ASI only gently unwinding. So much energy. Now he could see another dog fight going on between two Spitfires and a '109. He would close the gap, join in if he could. He levelled off and accelerated towards them. The fight started going downhill. Now it was easy. He accelerated like crazy on the down line, let them finish their runs and came in firing from 200 yards. The '109 exploded, killing the pilot instantly. For Harper it had felt as easy as making a decent cup of tea.

Gazzer was looking after Rhino's tail. And his own. It was an exhausting job, his head constantly turning, looking for the enemy and then back to the leader to try and hold some semblance of a formation. Now Rhino was pulling round behind a bomber, closing from the rear. Gazzer looked up and over his shoulder and spotted a lone Spitfire pulling out of a steep dive, then back to Rhino – nothing on his tail – then back to the Spitfire. It was same level as him now, closing in, no tail markings, Harper's Spitfire, Harper! With a Messerschmitt 109, 100 yards behind him and closing.

"TOM! '109 ON YOUR TAIL!" screamed Gazzer. "PULL OUT HARD!!"

"All Sections! Radio silence!"

The Me 109 was immediately behind Harper. Before he had time to react it started peppering his wings and fuselage with canon shells.

"FOR CHRISSAKE!! PULL OUT!!!" shouted Gazzer. There were multiple hits and explosions, all over the aeroplane. Gazzer watched as the Spitfire gently arced upwards and rolled through the sky onto its back, trailing smoke. The roll translated into a dive, the Spitfire gently rolling as it went down vertically, leaving a perfect spiral ribbon of smoke behind it. The '109 broke away as the Spitfire accelerated downwards, and disappeared into a cloud layer far below.

Gazzer stared, his body frozen, as the Messerschmitt pulled out of its dive and turned away, descending into the same cloud layer, out of sight. Then, from somewhere deep inside him, there formed a place of tranquillity, his own calm voice telling him; that everything was okay, that it would have been a perfect way to die.

-.-

Acronyms, abbreviations and banter.

A

ace	fighter pilot with 5 confirmed kills
ack-ack	anti-aircraft fire
Admiral	RAF officer in charge of Air-Sea rescue boats
ailerons	flaps on trailing edge of wings to provide roll control
altitude	height above sea level in feet
ammo	ammunitions
angels	altitude in 1000s of feet eg angels 15 = 15000 ft
Annie	Avro Anson two-engined trainer/liaison aircraft
Apron	tarmac surrounding a hangar
ASI	Air Speed Indicator
ATA	Air Transport Auxiliary – the RAF's aircraft delivery service
Atta boy/ Atta girl	Pilots of the Air Transport Auxiliary
AWOL	Absent Without Leave

B

base	home airfield
beer goggles	the beautifying effect of drinking alcohol
bag	parachute
bakelite	thermosetting plastic used in minor aircraft castings, especially electrical equipment
balbo	large group of aircraft
bang on	very good
beat up/ beat-up	strafing run, low level flying, beers in pub
beehive	group of bombers(hive) with a top escort of fighters (bees)

beer lever	aircraft joystick
Belinda	barrage balloon
belly-landing	large attack landing with wheels up
biggy	a big something!
bind	tedious duty
bingo	30 minutes fuel remaining
blab	gossip
black/ put up a black	something bad/ something done badly
black-outs	navy blue nurse/WAAF knickers
blip	a return on a radar screen, showing a target
blitz buggy	ambulance
blood wagon	ambulance
bod	body
body-snatcher	stretcher bearer
bogey	hostile aircraft
boss	reference from junior rank to a senior rank or commanding officer
box clever	avoid an undesirable task
brains trust	Central Trades Testing Board
brassed/ browned off	depressed
bride	girlfriend
brown bread	dead
bull'	bullshit
bumf	leaflets dropped from the air
buster	fly at full throttle/maximum speed
bus-driver	bomber pilot
buttoned-up	well-prepared
buy it/ bought it	crash/ crashed
buzz	rumour

C

cabbage	bomb
camp	military station without an airfield
camp comedian	station commander
canteen cowboy	ladies'man
chain gang	aircraft general hands
chair-borne division	RAF administrative personnel
chocks	triangular rubber or wooden blocks or metal frames placed under the wheels of a parked aircraft
chute	parachute
clag	bad weather
closing	an aircraft getting closer
closing speed	the combined speed of two aircraft closing, the sum of their vectors
confetti	machine gun fire

crack down	crash/shoot down an enemy plane
crack-up	crash/ get shot down
cowls/cowl flaps	engine cooling engine
C/O	Commanding Officer
CTTB	Central trades Testing Board flaps to increase/decrease airflow through

D

daisy cutter	perfect landing
dead-stick	glide to land - without an engine
deck	ground/ airfield
DFC	Distinguished Flying Cross
dspl	dispersal
ditch	to land in the sea
duff gen	bad/false information
drink	the sea
dwang	problem/ troublesome event

E

e/a	enemy aircraft
Egg	bomb
elevator	aerodynamic flaps on trailing edge of tailplane to provide pitch control
Elsan	chemical toilet
Elsan gen	bad information
erk	mechanic
exec, or exo	executive officer

F

fan	propeller
Fg Off	Flying Officer
fire-proof	invulnerable
flannel	flatter
flak	anti aircraft fire
flap	panel on trailing edge of wing which drops to reduce stalling speed of aircraft and enable it to take off or land more slowly, or to panic
flicks	cinema
Flight'/ Flt Lt	Flight Lieutenant
F/O	Flying Officer
fold up	crash
full bore	flat out, full throttle
ft	feet

G

gen	information
gestapo	military police
glycol	additive (antifreeze) to increase boiling point of engine cooling water
gone for a Burton	dead or missing
gong	medal
Group	usually refers to 11 or 12 Group, the sub sections/ groups of squadrons in the south east, under Fighter Command
Groupy	Group Captain - not the boss of the above though
gun	accelerate, increase throttle
gussie	officer

H

He 111	Heinkel-111 twin-engine bomber
hit the deck	to land
hoosh	fast landing
hop the twig	fatal crash
hun	German/ German aircraft
Hurry	Hurricane
Hurry bomber	Hurricane with bomb racks

I

I/D	Identity
In a spot	perilous place or situation
Iron lung	Nissen hut
irons	knife, fork, spoon
Intel	Intelligence officer

J

Jam jar	armoured car
Jerry	German/ German aircraft
jink	turn quickly in the air to avoid enemy
job	aircraft
joy	satisfaction
joy-stick	flying control stick

K

kigas	fuel priming plunger to squirt petrol into fuel lines before engine start

250

kipper kites	planes ptoecting the north sea convoys and fishing fleets
kiss goodbye	bale out
kite	aircraft
knitting-piece of	girlfriend
Kt/knot	knot, nautical mile per hour, equal to 1.14 statute miles per hour

L

LAC	Leading Aircraftsman – non-commissioned rank
Ladybird	WAAF officer
Lanc	Lancaster bomber
legit'	legitimate
line-shoot	a tall story
line book	a squadron book for recording the above
loaf	intelligence
loose off	fire a weapon

M

Macaroni	Italian
Mae West	life jacket –after the big-busted Hollywood star
Marmalade	gold brade on the hat of a senior officer
Me 109	Messerschmit-109 single-engine fighter
Me 110	Messerschmitt-110 twin-engine fighter bomber
Met	Medical officer
milk round	standard patrol route
mod	modification
M/O	Medical Officer
moment of truth	shooting at someone for the first time
m/s	machine guns
muck	bad weather
muscle in	take advantage

N

NAAFI	Navy Army and Air Force Institution
niff-naff	fuss
nursemaids	fighter escorts for bombers

O

Off mess	Officer's mess
old man, the	commanding officer
oppo	friend
ops	operations, flights etc

Orkneyitis	feeling of depression after being based in the Orkneys
over the wall	gone absent without leave
Oxford	Airspeed Oxford, two-engined training and liaison aircraft

P

pack up	break, fail
pancake	fly back to base
peck	brief attack passion-killers WAAF nickers, also black-outs
pigs are up	barrage balloons flyin
pile up	crash
P/O	pilot Officer
pip squeak	aircraft radio set
plaster	bomb heavily
prang	crash
puff	ladies man
pukka gen	genuine or trustworthy info
pulveriser	Sterling bomber
put down	land
put the hooks on	charge with a crime
put up a black	do something wrong

Q

queen	especially pretty WAAF
Queen Mary	low-slung articulated lorry for transporting aircraft, some adapted as fire engines
quis	good

R

recce	reconnaissance
rev	revolution
rigid bind	a bore
rings/ringers eg 2 ringer	reference to the rank of an officer
ringmaster	a Squadron Leader who takes a squadron into the air
ring twitch	fear of combat
rocket	reprimand
roger	message understood
roll up	hand-rolled cigarette
rookette	female recruit
rookie	recruit

R/T	Radio telephone
RTB	return to base
rudder	flap on trailing edge of tail fin for directional control on ground and improved rolling/turning in the air
rudder pedals	foot pedals to operate the rudder
rhubarb	small patrol usually to find lone enemy aircraft and other targets, often in bad weather

S

sarge	sergeant
scat	take off in a hurry to go drive away the enemy
scramble	general order to depart on a mission
scrub	cancel
sex-appeal bomb	one that hits a school or a hospital
Shagbat	Walrus seaplane
shit	bad weather
skipper	captain
sky pilot	vicar
snoop	military police
soup	bad weather
special issue	special equipment and clothing issued to military personnel
Spit	Spitfire
Split-arse	tight turn
spout	gun barrel
squadron	a group of 12 or so aircraft in a unit
squeeze the teat	hit the gun button
Sqn Cdr	Squadron Commander
Sqn Ldr	Squadron Leader
standard issue	standard equipment and clothing issued to military personnel
standby	wait for further instructions
steer	magnetic compass bearing to find a target or an airfield
Stringbag	Swordfish aircraft
supercharged	drunk

T

tap in	take on
taxi	passenger 'plane
Tally / Tally Ho	Attack, enemy sighted/ go for the kill, follow me into the attack
toy	training aircraft

toffee nosed	snobbish
trim	small tab on trailing edge of flying controls to provide aerodynamic balance in flight
two six	to give a hand

U

umbrella	parachute
upstairs	airborne
U/S	unserviceable
use your loaf	think/ reason

V

vectors	usually, magnetic bearing and range in nautical miles to a target or airfield
visiting card	bomb
Vne	Velocity never to exceed
VSI	Vertical Speed Indicator
viz	visibility

W

Waaf	member of the Women's Auxiliary Air Force
Wallah	chap/ fellow
wanks	strong liquor
wear it	put up with
week-end air force	used from 1925 (inception) to describe Royal Auxiliary Air Force
went in	crashed
Wg Cdr	Wing Commander
whistled	drunk
whole 9 yards, the	Everything, the whole lot – refers to the length of the machine gun belts in a fighter's wing.
wife	girlfriend
wilco	will co operate
Wimpey	Wellington bomber
wop	wireless operator
wrap up	crash
write off	crashed plane, totally detroyed

Y

Yellow doughnut	dinghy
Yellow peril	training aircraft (painted yellow)
yob	raw recruit

-.-

Printed in the United Kingdom
by Lightning Source UK Ltd.
132342UK00002B/61-270/P

9 780954 481414